PRAISE FOR WHEREABOUTS

"Quite a ride! With clear, bright prose, and an absolutely brilliant ear for dialogue, Gould gives us a young woman's travels and her hardscrabble journey into the woman she can become. He makes me care about these people, makes me laugh and gasp, makes me think about her story long after I've put down the book. This writer is a true storyteller."

—Elizabeth Cox, author of *A Question of Mercy*

"*Whereabouts* is a love letter to the wanderers and lost souls, a tragicomic tale of yearning and adventure that reminds us there are sometimes only two directions in life, away and toward."

—J.C. Sasser, author of *Gradle Bird*

"Scott Gould has created the ideal, road-novel hero in Missy Belue, a character who strikes the balance of being self-assured, but with eyes newly open. We run away with her at full speed, and with full hearts, riding shotgun as she explores the limits of her Southern homeplace, her family, and herself. From truck bed to Cadillac, *Whereabouts* asks us to question where we come from, learn from where we wind up, and reckon with the ride in between."

—Odie Lindsey, author of *Some Go Home*

"Missy Belue is trying to find something that feels like family connection, and in this case that means taking a road trip to no place in particular. *Whereabouts* is funny, absorbing, and affecting, with the diaphanous feel of family myth, its characters so damaged and unique you can't help but think of Flannery O'Connor."

—Julia Franks, author of *Over the Plain Houses*

"Scott Gould is a well digger drilling into the South's vast, deep fictional aquifer. Turning page after page of Gould's novel *Whereabouts*, sweet water bubbles up in brilliant characters and sharp dialogue. But then sometimes, a hard sip of trouble seeps up. What else should we expect from such a masterful storyteller?"

—John Lane, author of *Whose Woods These Are*

"*Whereabouts* is one of those stories that's equal parts tender, entertaining, heartbreaking, quirky, and redemptive. And it is wholly satisfying. Scott Gould invites us into this poignant coming-of-age story full of vividly imagined characters. Protagonist Missy Belue's complicated quest is a story that has stayed with me long after the last page. Gould has given us a beautiful Southern story."

—Rebecca Bruff, author of *Trouble the Water*

"Gould masterly weaves intrigue, heartache, and bravery into a poignant tale of a young girl whose heart no longer resides at home."

—Dev Friedlander, author of *You See Me*

"*Whereabouts* follows Missy Belue from a funeral home, where the living may be as wooden as the dead, to a road trip with characters who are simultaneously absurd and believable. Scott Gould's descriptions take you to the deep South and inside every emotion. I loved this beautiful tale, told in the tradition of the finest Tom Robbins novel."

—Carol Van Den Hende, author of *Goodbye, Orchid*

Whereabouts

by Scott Gould

ISBN 978-1-64663-182-7

Published by

köehlerbooks™

3705 Shore Drive
Virginia Beach, VA 23455
800-435-4811
www.koehlerbooks.com

Whereabouts

a novel

Scott Gould

VIRGINIA BEACH
CAPE CHARLES

For Emily and Maggie
and the Wilson boys, Herb and Connor.

"The change of motion is proportional to the
motive force impressed;
and it is made in the direction of the right line in which
that force is impressed."

Sir Isaac Newton

PROLOGUE

The college kid selling encyclopedias was the only surprise in a day that was supposed to be boring and long. Missy Belue's parents had driven to Augusta for one of her mother's appointments and wouldn't be back to Kingstree until almost dark. They didn't worry. Her mother said she was old enough to stay by herself, "especially with your attitude." Her daddy smiled when he heard that. He was proud of his daughter's backbone. And he cultivated it every chance he got. He called her an old soul. "My Missy, thirteen going on twenty," he said.

Missy eyed the fellow through a crack in the curtains. His broad forehead glowed with sweat, and his white shirt was wet and wrinkled like he'd been dunked in a swimming pool. He had a heavy bag slung across one shoulder. She decided that he was harmless, that the evil people of the world did not sweat like that. Plus, he was rail thin like a prisoner of war, with glasses thick enough to start fires.

Missy tried to sound older than her years, so she lowered her voice a little and asked him through the door what he wanted. He told her he was working his way through medical school selling encyclopedias. He held up a little brochure of some kind toward the small glass pane in the door.

"What kind of doctor do you want to be?" Missy asked.

"The kind of doctor that knows a little bit about a lot of things," came a muffled reply.

She had to open the door when she heard that because Missy was a big fan, even then, of people who knew a great deal about useless topics.

"I thought you'd be older," he said when the door swung open and he got a look at the girl in the threshold.

"I thought you'd be drier," she told him back, and the salesman plucked at the front of his damp shirt. He told her he couldn't come in without an adult on the premises.

"Company rule. I think they had some trouble somewhere once upon a time."

Missy said her parents were up in the bed with smallpox and couldn't really walk what with the way the disease was taking its toll. He backed away from the door a bit and grinned. His teeth were skinny too, the size of corn kernels.

"People don't get smallpox anymore. At least not in the United States of America. You can learn things like that in the World Book Encyclopedia nineteen sixty-eight edition." He held up the brochure again. "How old are you, anyway?"

No one could ever guess Missy Belue's age. Hair that hung almost to her waist made her look like she could be as young as ten, or closer to nineteen. She was tall for her age, with long feet, too long for her legs. Her face was the problem, if looking older was a problem. Missy had eyes that were deep and brown and, like her daddy said more than once, eyes that suggested she had seen a great deal of what the world had to offer. But it was all a lie. Missy rarely stepped foot outside of Kingstree.

"I'm twenty," she said, sucking in a swallow of air.

"If you're twenty, I'm Paul Newman," the salesman said back, mopping his brow with the sleeve of his shirt. "And in case you're keeping score, I ain't no Paul Newman." His eyes lit up a little behind the Coke-bottle lenses.

Missy liked him better once he made fun of himself, but she didn't ask him to come inside, and he didn't take a step forward. Instead, he dug in the big canvas bag hanging on his skinny shoulder. Missy didn't offer him anything to drink because she thought people should have to ask for the things they needed.

"Do you like *ess*?" he said finally.

"*Ess* what?" she said.

"The letter *S*. Do you like the letter *S*?" He kept digging in the bag.

"I suppose of all the letters, it's in my top five or ten," she said.

He pulled a volume out of his bag. "Well, good then. This here is the *S* volume of the nineteen sixty-eight World Book Encyclopedia. It's the thickest letter in the set. It is packed with the most up-to-date information in the world that begins with the letter *S* that you can fit between two covers. Now, of course, we have volumes for all the letters in the alphabet, but I am going to leave this one with you overnight. I want you and your *sick* momma and daddy to take a look." He laughed. "You can even look up smallpox. I'll come back tomorrow and sign you up for the rest of the letters. Consider it a little loan on your future knowledge. We have monthly payment plans that are truly reasonable."

He took a breath like the sales pitch had worn him out. Missy thought he might pass out on the porch. She wasn't quite sure what to do if a damp encyclopedia salesman fainted on her porch with her parents miles away in Augusta.

He passed the book through the door and made his way back into the street without another word. Inside, Missy turned the radio back up. It was a Supremes song, and she started dancing her way around the room with the book out in front of her. She had, of course, come across encyclopedias before, in school when she had to work on projects. But she'd never had one of her own, even if the *S* was on loan from a skinny college-boy salesman.

Missy settled on the couch. Casper the white cat weaved around her shins while she flipped through the pages. She finally settled on an article. The salesman was right. Smallpox was all but gone. She flipped some more and read quietly while the next song from WKSP leaked out of the kitchen radio on the shelf above the toaster. This time it was Lynn Anderson. Missy read aloud to Casper that sharks have to keep moving or they would die. She turned to the listing on sex and stopped talking to the cat. At the end of the listing, it said, "For human beings sex is more than a merely physical problem. It is involved with moral teachings and with intense psychological problems. See also REPRODUCTION." All of a sudden, Missy felt every bit of thirteen.

She didn't tell her mother and daddy about the salesman and the overnight loan of the book when they walked through the door from Augusta. She didn't want to fill in all the blanks they'd have. Her momma was, as usual, worn out from a full day of making up answers to questions from the doctors and counselors. Her daddy was tired from pacing the halls of the clinic. She knew they would be mad she'd opened the door. She decided when the skinny guy showed up tomorrow with the twenty-five other volumes, she could pretend she'd never seen him. Make him sound like the crazy one.

But he never showed. There was never a knock on their door. Missy kept the *S* to herself for months, tucked under some sweaters in her closet. She read it at night before she went to bed. Her favorite section was always the one on sharks. She kept returning to it. She loved the way sharks kept moving and moving, night and day. That seemed like a good life. Finally, Missy put the encyclopedia on her bookshelf in plain sight, and her mother never noticed. That was no surprise. Her mother always had other things on her mind. After a while, Missy lost track of that book, but she never forgot about those sharks, the way they love to move, day and night.

1.

Missy Belue walked up on her daddy slumped over the hood of their old Ford Fairlane station wagon, his head inside the engine compartment like he was listening to a secret the spark plugs whispered. Later, they told her it was a *massive* heart attack, but Missy didn't really care. Whatever the size, it was big enough to take him away for good. And that made her madder than anything else. He left her at the exact wrong time.

The afternoon of the heart attack, she was forty-two days away from graduating high school and didn't have a clue what she was going to do after she walked across the stage and snatched her diploma from the principal of Kingstree Senior High. She was sure she wasn't going to college—at least not yet. There wasn't money or grades or desire for that. She didn't have a job or a husband-in-training.

Missy had planned on talking to her father about her future. One day. Someday. Then suddenly, on an afternoon without memorable weather, he was gone, his head resting on a cold radiator cap.

Her mother appointed herself in charge of family mourning. She took to her bed and broke out several bottles from their hiding places and remained pretty much toasted and teary-eyed for a couple of days while Missy fed Casper the ancient cat or went to the IGA for bread and sandwich meat and tonic mixer. As annoyed as she was with her mother, when the afternoon of the visitation at the funeral home arrived, Missy discovered somebody new to put in the crosshairs of her misplaced, post-mortem anger—Asa M. Floyd, mortician and proprietor of Floyd Funeral Home.

Missy hated him the moment he opened his mouth and began to explain to her and her mother his personal theory of grief. He paced in front of them, his chest puffed out beneath a perfectly pressed gray suit, his fingers tracing the sharp lapels like they were stitched with Braille, his voice booming like an FM deejay. Asa was not a tall man, but his syrup-smooth, bass-clef voice added inches to him.

"Grief," Asa Floyd said, "begins in the veritable seat of our emotions. And where would that be, you ask?" He paused, but no one did, indeed, ask. "In our hearts. Hasn't a thing to do with the brain. You cannot attempt to rationalize grief. You can only let it run its true and unalterable course. Trust me, ladies. Grief and I have become quite close over the years. I toil daily on the front lines in the battle against grief."

His voice poured out so thick and meaningless, Missy imagined she could grab the sounds from the air and squeeze them between her fingers like Play-Doh. Her mother sniffled into a linen hanky. Missy squeezed her elbow to remind her she wasn't going through this alone. She smelled the breath mints her mother had gobbled in the parking lot just minutes before. They sat side by side on a stiff couch in Asa's office, the walls painted the color of dusk, the room filled with thin, brittle air, the type you might breathe at the top of a mountain. Around them, Asa's credentials floated on the wall, framed shadows on the tongue-and-groove paneling.

Asa Floyd appeared nationally certified in every possible method of disposing of the dead. He embalmed. He burned. He buried. He could even legally stack the dead in cold storage in the event of natural disasters and acts of God—other than the definitive God-like act of striking one dead, of course. And he was the only person in Kingstree who could handle all aspects of departing the earth. If you died in Kingstree and you happened to be white, you were at the mercy of Asa Floyd.

"However," he continued with his presentation, "the course of grief is often a confusing treacherous path. I am, at times like these, your guide. I can help you through the twists and turns. In this hell you've been thrust, I am your . . . Virgil."

"Bless you." Missy's mother wrestled the words from her lips. "Thank you so much, Virgil."

She cut her eyes at her mother wondering if she really believed Asa had changed his name. Missy possessed a foggy, junior-English-class idea who Virgil was and what he might have to do with her father's massive heart attack. She didn't really care. She had questions to ask. What had been done to her father, and what would become of her and her mother now that he was gone? But she didn't want the answers to come through Asa Floyd's teeth, didn't want those taffy-like sounds aimed at her.

Missy's mind whirred, consumed with the thought of seeing her father one last time. What would be his final look? What look would she offer back to him? She wondered how she should act, what she would say. She was seventeen now, the age where outward appearances trumped any other brand of anxiety.

The strangest thing she did before coming to the funeral home was to stare at her reflection in the mirror, waiting for some hint of her daddy to pop out. She was so much her mother's daughter—the high cheekbones and brown eyes. She hoped, at least, what her daddy had bequeathed her still floated around inside, carried by blood or bone or spirit.

What she really wanted was the opportunity to spit directly in the eye of death—or maybe catch it napping on the face of her daddy—and smile. Her father would appreciate that kind of spunk in his girl. Missy Belue wanted to prove to everyone that bothered to look or to ask that she could take whatever life heaped out, including death, and keep rolling along, bruised at worst, but with her head up. Her daddy would like that.

She knew people would be watching her say her goodbyes. They'd be watching Mona as well. That's what funerals were for, to see how sadly the living danced when death struck close to home.

On the couch in Asa Floyd's office, Missy felt her mother tremble against her, so she gave her another quick squeeze. It was so dim in the room, she squinted, trying to focus on the walls. Her mother, in the deep-gray dress she usually kept in a plastic dry cleaner's wrapper, was perfect camouflage for the room. She all but faded away right in front of Missy's eyes.

Asa stalked laps around his desk. He hitched his pants and straightened every correctable crimp in his suit, then motioned for them to follow him out the door and down the hall. The hallway was gloomy and empty, except for the sounds that echoed on the air—air which, unlike Asa's office, carried more of a sterile, hospital odor. Mumbles and whispers. An occasional wet sob. The soft, crepe soles of Asa's shoes exhaled slightly with each of his steps. Missy's mother hurried to stay close behind Asa in the dimness. She dragged Missy by the arm. He paused at a closed door. Missy braced herself for the grand entrance, but Asa didn't go for the knob. He just motioned with a tilt of his head.

"Car incident. Young couple lost a young son. Every day is an odd adventure in my business. Always the same thing, but never the same thing twice. Death has a thousand faces." Asa walked on and made a right turn just past a water fountain. Missy saw a small group huddled around a closed doorway, like school kids waiting for the morning bell.

A few steps closer and Missy recognized some of her long-lost uncles and cousins, most of whom she'd only heard about or seen at Christmas or in boxes of photographs. They were trying their best to look unhappy. They nodded at her. One, a man wearing a shirt that didn't fit and dusty work boots, hugged Mona and patted her lightly between the shoulder blades, his hand like a bird's wing flapping against her back.

Asa waved and the crowd parted, kept their eyes down, and let the three of them—Missy, her mom and Asa—into the room they reluctantly guarded. Inside, bright brass lamps blazed on expensive-looking end tables. After her long period in the near dark of Asa's office and the dim hallway, Missy blinked a half dozen times to soften the new light. At the far end of the room, a polished casket shined like it had been rained on, its top yawning open.

Asa spoke in a whisper that couldn't disguise his chewy voice. "Formal visitation commences in just a few moments. But I always feel as though the immediate family requires a moment to pay their respects personally, without the well-meaning crush of friends and loved ones."

Asa waved them forward. Waving seemed to be his gesture of choice. Missy tugged her mother, who followed, if not willingly at least easily, like a toddler. A few steps from the casket, Missy caught sight of her dead father. An unfamiliar, puzzled expression stretched across his face, as though he were trying to remember the name of an old song or old baseball player. He appeared to be at a complete loss. Or just plain lost. Missy wondered if Asa molded that look onto her daddy's face, or if that was actually the last expression he ever possessed. As if, when he realized his body was shutting down, he lay on the engine compartment of his old Ford and tried to recall who the American League batting champ was in 1967.

A wave of anger burned across Missy's cheeks. Then, her mouth tightened into a smile. Her father was simply too comical to mourn at that moment. A streak of rouge or blush ran like a red mistake up each side of his cheekbones. His eyebrows, which had always been thick and sun-bleached and out of control, lay trimmed and combed into a sad perfection, then colored slightly to match his hair. And the hair, brushed straight back, away from his forehead with some kind of thick gel, created the illusion of a tremendously large head. His lips, pursed on the verge of a pout, were the color of the bricks of their house.

Missy's mother slumped into her, sucking breaths without releasing any air in return. Missy listened and waited for the exhale, while Asa stood away from them, his arms crossed like an usher at a movie theater. Missy led her mother to a nearby chair, sat her down, and returned to the edge of the casket. Inside the pocket of her dress, she felt for the tube of regular-flavored Chapstick. If there was anything her daddy would miss in whatever place he ended up, it would be his Chapstick. Alive, he was never without a tube. She was sure he'd developed some kind of addiction to it. The regular, bland flavor. Not any of that silly cherry or mint. She pulled the top off the Chapstick and wiped it across her lips. Asa's face was suddenly at her shoulder, his mouth near her ear. "Lifelike, isn't he," he whispered. The smell of chewed-out Dentyne gum drifted from Asa's mouth.

She turned slightly so she could keep an eye on her father and still aim her reply at Asa. "Yessir, lifelike," she said, "if you work for a goddamn circus." She thought about shutting up at that point, but reconsidered, took a breath and plowed ahead. "You've got him made up like a goddamn clown. I hope he doesn't scare somebody in heaven." Her voice was too loud. She talked too fast. What she said ricocheted off walls probably unaccustomed to that kind of volume. From behind, Missy's mom blew out a sudden gust of stored-up air. The blood raced from Asa's face. Missy could tell it was language he'd rarely heard, especially from a teenager, and never in one of his visitation rooms. But for Missy it was nothing out of the ordinary.

It had come down this: Her father was gone. Her mother was having trouble remembering how to walk without a prop from something close and at hand, and lately that *something* was shaped like a bottle. And the funeral director was making her stomach turn. Missy felt it was the perfect time to shock anybody still alive enough to listen. So she said it, and its rumble passed away quickly—about as swiftly as her father had—without so much as an echo in the room with the coffin.

Asa backed away from Missy Belue like she was infectious. While he kept his eye on her, he felt behind him for a seat, falling into one next to her mother. Missy heard her mother apologize for her daughter.

"She's upset."

"Well, just take a look at him," Missy said. "Jesus."

Her mother stared at Asa, who put his arm around her shoulders. She buried her face into the crisp folds of his suit coat. Missy saw a tear or two dot his lapel. When the two of them finally turned away from Missy, she quickly dropped the Chapstick over the lip of the casket and watched it disappear somewhere between her daddy's suit and the soft blue coffin liner.

The rest of the visitation went smoothly and quietly. Missy spent most of the day holding her mother up by her thin shoulder and smiling at people she'd never seen before. She didn't say another word to Asa Floyd, mostly because he stayed far out of her range, but she knew he was there. She could feel his eyes studying their grief.

2.

In the days after the funeral, Mona didn't demand Missy help her clear the house of her father's things. She was patient, until the morning she began to tiptoe around the subject while the two of them sipped coffee at the kitchen table. Mona said things like, "This is the first sunny day we've had since the funeral. I wonder if that means something" or "The oil in the car probably wants to be changed. Somebody *else* always took care of that." She would sigh as Missy hummed over the top of her cup without answering in actual words. What she thought about saying was "Motor oil can't actually want a thing," but she didn't.

Finally, Mona drew a deep breath and said, "You know, Missy, I was thinking we could, you know, if we felt up to it, box up your father's things and put them away somewhere. That's what I was thinking." She paused. "And I probably know what you're thinking. I'll bet you're thinking it would be good for us to do it together. It would be—Lord, what is the word I'm looking for? Healing. That's it. It would be healing."

"You aren't even close," Missy said.

"Ma'am?" Mona said. She had begun to refer to Missy as *ma'am* for some reason Missy couldn't put her finger on. It made Missy feel older than her years.

"I wasn't thinking any such thing."

Mona tried a new tack. "I'm having a little trouble being around all these things of his," she said. "I'm afraid it's going to set me off."

For Mona, being *set off* meant steering the car that supposedly needed an oil change down to Skeet's Liquors to buy a bottle of Smirnoff, then taking a quick swan dive off the wagon. Missy knew the code.

"Did you ever consider that it might be worse if all his stuff is gone?" she said to her mother. "Sadder."

"I'm not an idiot, ma'am," Mona said. "I know what's good for me."

Missy hummed into her coffee, then looked up at her mother. There was that resemblance staring back at her again. She wished more of her father was in her face. That would be a reminder of him nobody could ever box up and bury. Her mother's eyes brimmed with tears, and it wasn't an act. Mona couldn't cry on demand. This Missy knew.

"Okay, I'll help. I just don't want to make a day of it. I don't want to dwell. I can't do that. I can't dwell," Missy said.

"No dwelling. Promise," Mona said and turned quickly toward the tiny mud room just off the kitchen. Before Missy could rinse her cup in the sink, Mona returned with two good-sized cardboard liquor boxes. Missy wondered if she'd picked up something else from Skeet's when she stole boxes.

"Looks like you're all prepared," Missy said, grabbing one of them.

"I thought we'd start in the bedroom."

For days, Mona must have been planning how this would go. She had already divided up tasks. She pointed Missy toward her father's chest of drawers and suggested she work on the top row.

"I think those are all just knickknacks and such. I'm not really sure exactly."

Mona grabbed the handles on the closet doors and tugged them open. The odor of her father's clothes wafted into the room like a fog. Missy felt her breath catch in her throat.

"So many shirts," Mona said. She almost sounded happy about it.

Before she dumped the first drawer on the taut bedspread, Missy had never really considered how much people were reflected in the things they collected, the objects they surrounded themselves with. But when the contents of the drawer tumbled out, there was her father. Maybe not alive, but *there.*

A couple of pocketknives, small ones with only a single blade. A single, fuzz-less tennis ball, for some reason. An empty money clip. One shoestring. A dusty set of rattlesnake rattles. Several coins that had been flattened somehow, maybe on a railroad track. Some crumpled receipts so old the ink had faded into hieroglyphics. A collection of fountain pens still in the boxes.

"I gave pens to him every Christmas," Mona said. "I guess he didn't want much to do with them."

Missy started to remind Mona that her husband was strictly a ballpoint man, that fountain pens had ruined several shirts and a couple of pairs of his pants. She wondered if Mona would find some ink-blotted button-downs in the closet and put two and two together.

There was a bundle of some kind, a tiny one, bound with a single, thin rubber band. Missy barely fingered the old rubber band, and it broke as if it had been waiting to disintegrate. The little pieces of cardboard it held shuffled apart and confettied to the bed. Missy had to hold one of them close to her eyes to even see what it was. *A ticket stub?* Her father had saved a ticket stub from every movie he'd taken her to, most of them at the mall in Florence, a few in Charleston. There was a stub for *Mary Poppins.* A movie was their way to get free of the house when Mona was sleeping something off in the back bedroom. Missy knew when her father herded her to the car and said, "Let's go see a picture show," they were pulling off an escape—first in the front seat of the car, then in the dark quiet of a movie theater. He'd saved the evidence of their escapes. She had no idea her father was so sentimental.

"Here. Here's a trash bag. Just throw those out," and Mona reached for the pile of tickets on the bedspread.

Missy blocked her hand. "I'll take care of it," she said. "You said this is my job."

"Yes, ma'am," Mona said, smiling.

In another drawer, Missy found a collection of old wristwatches—all Timex. Her father told her once that a Timex would last forever or until you broke the crystal and bent the hands, whichever came first. For her father, it seemed the banging of the crystal always came first. The face on each watch was decorated with spiderweb cracks, the minute and hour hands frozen in time. Missy wondered why he would keep watches that no longer worked, and she decided that the times of day were important for some reason. Twelve forty-five. Two fifteen. Half past noon or midnight. Something must have happened, something important, the precise moment he banged his Timex and time stood still.

One of the Timexes appeared to be a little different, less substantial. Missy picked it up and turned the face toward her, and she saw it wasn't a watch at all. It was a compass you could wear on your wrist. The face wasn't cracked, and the red end of the little needle still spun, hunting for magnetic north. Missy had never seen this compass before. Her father had a thing for compasses.

She suddenly remembered the compass mounted on the dash of the station wagon. It floated in pale-green jelly, all of the directions drifting around and around just above the Philco radio.

"A compass," her father told Missy once, "keeps you from heading right smack into confusion. You can never be totally lost with a compass on your dashboard."

Her father would never be lost. He was a man ruled by his directions. He actually collected compasses. He was most proud of the half dozen vintage compass roses he'd found discarded in flea markets and rundown boat-repair shops. A couple times a year, he'd pull out his collection to show Missy. "A compass rose is a work of art for directions," he'd say, laying them out on his workbench. "The directions always stay the same, but the way somebody points them out, the way somebody gives them more meaning, that's where the art comes in. You know, you could spend months, maybe years designing a decent compass rose."

He also kept a road atlas tucked beneath the front seat of the station wagon. Weeks before any family trip, he'd grab the atlas, find a yellow or pink magic marker, and plan the trip on the map, marking their way with a thin ribbon of color. He knew how many miles per day they would travel, barring any unforeseen problems. He knew where they'd stop for lunch, in what town they'd find a good motel, where they would more than likely be gassing up. Before pulling out of the driveway, he knew the total number of miles they would travel, give or take side trips and such. When her daddy had a map in his hands, Missy thought he could predict the future.

When they finally set off on one of their trips, Missy's daddy kept a close eye on the compass and the map, making sure the directions matched up. "South southeast!" he might yell. "And in a minute we should be making a bend toward the east, within four or five miles." The compass rocked like a round ship in a bottle.

Missy always thought a compass was too complicated a device for such a simple matter as moving. As a kid, she assumed there were only two directions you could move: away from and toward. And, of course, you could never do both simultaneously, because the second you decided where you were headed, you couldn't be running away from anything anymore. Her daddy was always definitely going toward something. He knew where the end of the line was on the map, the one he drew with the magic marker. Her mother was an official member of the Away From Club. It didn't matter to her where they were when she woke up.

On the other side of the room, Mona stuffed shirts and pants in a larger box that had magically appeared. She walked to the bed and studied the collection of objects scattered on the spread.

"Good lord, the junk. I never knew he had all that stuff in those drawers. Why in the world would someone keep broken watches? I mean, look at those coins? Why save those? You can't spend them. And an old wallet?"

Missy had not seen the wallet. The stitching, which at one time had been blue, unraveled at the crease of leather that looked as though it might crack with only a touch. Missy made it for her father the summer she went to a Girl Scout day camp near Salters. The leaders gave the girls the choice of making something for their parents, and Missy was the only one who cut and stitched a man's wallet.

Mona turned back to the closet, and Missy carefully pried the wallet open. There, in the space where an ID would normally show up behind the plastic, was Missy's third-grade photo, her smile a picket fence of missing teeth and her bangs cut so straight over her eyes they might have been sheared using a carpenter's level. It wasn't the photo or wallet that made Missy begin to cry. It was how happy she looked in the third grade, when her father was alive and loved to get presents from her, like leather wallets with blue stitching. She sucked in her breath and felt a sob bloom in her throat. Before she let it out, the doorbell rang.

"Now, who in the world?" Mona said, her voice thick with manufactured surprise. She fast-stepped down the hall. Missy wiped her eyes with a sweater sleeve. She didn't care who was at the door. Probably another neighbor bringing a Pyrex dish filled with something they would ultimately throw out. Whoever it was, Mona would take care of it. Missy sniffed loudly a couple of times, which was probably why she didn't hear Mona return down the hall.

"Not a welcome task, but a necessary one, no doubt," someone said.

Missy didn't have to look up. She recognized that voice. In the doorway of her father's bedroom stood Asa Floyd, wearing his suit, smelling faintly of his funeral home.

"I might be able to offer some help. I have experience with this aspect of the grieving experience as well. I just don't assist the dead. I assist the living as well. That is, if you'll permit me?"

His deep radio voice lifted into a question, but before anyone answered, Asa was in the room, gathering up the things on the bedspread.

"You see," he said, the broken watches dangling from between his fingers, "these sorts of things are rarely important to those who are left behind. Their value passed away with the deceased. I always tell people to consider all of these like Band-Aids. Just rip them off quickly and the pain subsides in seconds, never to return."

Missy couldn't move, paralyzed by an affliction she couldn't name. It might have been the fact that an intruder suddenly stood in a place he shouldn't be. Or maybe that he was touching her father's things. Or perhaps it was the anger boiling up in a place where just seconds before, she had choked down a sob. Whatever it was, she couldn't move a muscle.

Asa paced around the room too quickly. "These clothes," he said, "I'll be more than happy to carry them to the poor box behind the Methodist church. They'll distribute to those who need them most. And all this stuff?" he said, waving his arm over the bed. "You may as well just throw away." He dug into one of the bigger drawers on her father's chest. "And these personal clothing items might be better served as rags now. Hello, what's this?"

Asa pulled a thick book tucked beneath the underwear and T-shirts. "The library might have some use for this. I can ask Mrs. Evans." He tossed the book on the bed, bouncing all the things that lay there.

Missy knew what it was immediately. She hadn't seen the book in years. In fact, she'd all but forgotten about it. It was a volume of the World Book Encyclopedia, the *S* from the 1968 edition.

"Why in heaven's name would someone hide a World Book encyclopedia underneath his unmentionables?" Asa said. "What do you think, Mona? Why in the world?" Mona laughed like she was unaccustomed to being the center of an adult conversation.

"You don't know anything about this, do you?" Missy said, her sharp question aimed directly at her mother. Mona's smile faded. "You don't know anything about any of this stuff, isn't that right? None of this means anything to you? Tell me."

"Now, now, she's going through a tough time," Asa said.

"You shouldn't be here," Missy said, spinning toward Asa. "You don't belong. You don't know anything about our *times*."

"Missy!" Mona snapped. "I invited him. He belongs because I asked him to help us out."

My mother asked for help. And she didn't ask me. Missy was too stunned to know where to look, so she stared at the book on the bedspread. She thought about all those nights and all those entries she'd read—on Saturn and South America, on sharks and sex. She wondered how much her father really knew about the college boy who showed up at the door selling encyclopedias. He must have known. And the timing. Missy was getting a free encyclopedia the same day her father was carrying his wife to the alcoholic clinic in Augusta. *Is that why he kept the book tucked in his drawer? Did it mark a place in time?* She wished she could ask him about it. She realized this would not be the last time she missed asking her father questions she couldn't answer on her own.

Missy glared at Asa Floyd. "You need to leave," she said. "I don't want you here. You belong around dead people. We're still alive, goddammit."

"Missy, get out of my bedroom, right this second," Mona hissed. Missy couldn't remember her mother ever barking an order like that. "You will not talk to my friend that way."

Missy grabbed the book and headed for the door. On her way, she glanced back and saw Mona beginning to cry. Asa had already plucked the handkerchief from his suit coat pocket. Mona fell softly into his shoulder, leaning like a woman who needed a new place to cry.

3.

Missy Belue could not tell you exactly when her mother began dating Asa Floyd, officially. Probably only a couple of months after her father's funeral, certainly not long after he found the encyclopedia in the drawer, but so many things happened at once. The exact numbers on the calendar collided in her brain and ended up like pick-up sticks jumbled on the floor of her memory. Asa Floyd's suits might be to blame as well. Each was identical—a charcoal-gray three-piece with the same folded handkerchief sneaking out of the front pocket. Same sharp lapels. He was always a carbon copy of himself, no matter the event, no matter the weather. It was difficult to distinguish one Asa appearance from the other when the clothes never changed.

But there had to be a first day, a first evening, a first time the doorbell rang and there was Asa Floyd, standing on the tiny porch of their house, adjusting the lapels of the suit he wore when he dated people. Or buried them.

Where they went, Missy was never sure. Her mother rarely talked about it, and Missy never asked. She and Mona had begun keeping their distances. Maybe the couple drove the forty miles to Florence for Chinese food or went to a dance at Kingstree's mediocre excuse for a country club. Wherever they went, he wore that suit. And when he brought her back, his coat was never rumpled, his tie always drawn tight into the veins of his neck.

But her mother . . . she was the one who'd experienced some sort of magic transformation. The town talked about how well she seemed to be handling the loss of a husband. The color had returned to her cheeks. Her eyes brightened. She'd changed her medium-length hair into a style that required more time in the morning, and she fussed over her makeup. When she walked, she threw her shoulders back and her feet seemed to make only occasional contact with the ground. As she floated down the street, she called to people with an all-wrist, beauty queen wave. Everyone who cared or mattered assumed she was recovering remarkably, except Missy, who decided her mother was simply in a foggy confusion, attracted to the one guy in town who knew the ins and outs of grief.

Not that Mona and Asa kept their growing romance on the sly. People saw them out, but if odds were being laid from a distance, the decent money said Asa Floyd was simply helping Mona Belue through the toughest time of her life, and doing a damn gentlemanly job of it. If there were those who thought Asa was playing on Mona's vulnerable emotional state, they never gave those thoughts a voice. Mona seemed to be having such a fine time, no one wanted to spoil it for her. As for Missy, she continued to hope the whole situation was innocent, a momentary detour her mother appeared to have taken. And she hoped her father couldn't see it.

Late one night, Missy heard a sharp bang somewhere near the front of the house. Probably Casper the cat knocking over a vase or a picture frame. The noise sat Missy straight up in bed. For a few seconds, still in the confusion of near-sleep, she wondered why she was awake. She waited for another sound. Casper's thin wail filtered up the stairwell. He might need to be let out or might be caught under a chair, so Missy climbed out of bed, wrapped herself in a robe, and headed down the hallway, her feet finding familiar steps in the dark.

She made her way toward the direction of the noise, somewhere near the front door, maybe. A dim light melted into the hallway that led to the foyer. Missy heard another sound she couldn't identify, more human than cat. She started to call Casper but stopped as she walked to the edge of the yellow glow and saw her mother and Asa slow dancing in the foyer. There was no music. He had her dipped down low, over his knee, her hair suspended in the air. When he straightened Mona up, her hands lassoed his neck, and they danced themselves into a comfortable kiss, which showed few signs of ending. Missy snuck back up the stairs as quietly as she'd come. They hadn't noticed her at all.

In her room behind the closed door, Missy dove under the covers, burrowing as far away as she could from the couple downstairs. When there was finally no sound under the layers of quilts and blankets—not even the hum of her breathing or the slightest speck of light making its way beneath her sheets—she cried hard.

Since her daddy had died, she'd choked down the ache that rose now and again like a lemon seed in her throat. This time she let it come, remembering the times she'd watched her parents kiss each other. Pecks, usually, on the way out the door or after work in the afternoons. The kiss she'd just witnessed was different. It carried meaning with it, gravity. It was the kind of kiss that signified something important, something looming in the future. Soon her pillow was wet beneath her head, but Missy didn't move away from the dampness, not even when she heard the creak of the door opening and her mother whisper, "'Night, ma'am. I'm home," into the darkness.

Floyd Funeral Home sat in the center of town, a lurking antebellum house with a wide, long porch, supported by a row of fluted columns. On this porch, the deceased's relatives could grieve and gossip before and after services. Missy had even used the porch once to catch her breath after she cussed over the coffin of her newly dead daddy. Asa kept the funeral home painted in a bright white and had the lawn—

with its rambling azalea beds and flagstone walkways—meticulously landscaped. He, of course, didn't do it himself. He just made sure it was done.

The thick tulip poplars and live oaks threw so much shade that even in the middle of the summer, the yard and the porch snagged any hint of coolness and kept it circulating under the branches. In the winter, the trees cut off most of the chillier breezes. Floyd Funeral Home was a miracle of natural insulation. Behind the garage where the hearses were washed and waxed, Asa had, years ago, installed a kidney-bean-shaped pool hidden from general view by a tall wall of hawthorn and honeysuckle. Floyd Funeral Home was chosen as the site of the wedding because no one could think of a decent reason why it shouldn't happen there.

Once, during the fast-moving planning stages to which she was invited, Missy cleared her throat, took a breath, and began to offer up the opinion that since most people went to Floyd's when they were dead, was it perhaps a bad omen to have a wedding there? But she made like she had swallowed something wrong, cleared her throat, and kept her mouth shut. In fact, Missy kept her mouth shut about a lot of things since the night she saw her mother dipped into a kiss in the foyer, like the blink of an engagement or the fact her father was still a memory that you could almost touch or the plan that they would live above the funeral home after the ceremony. Missy never liked picking fights she was destined to lose.

On the Saturday before Halloween, five of them stood on the long porch—Missy, Asa, her mother, Rev. Johns, and Austin Sellers, the best man. Below them in the brown grass, most of Kingstree that counted for anything sat in uncomfortable aluminum folding chairs, watching the ceremony. Missy could feel them without turning and counting the faces. She heard the whispers. She even heard a few cardboard fans snapping at the air. It was a warm afternoon, a last gasp of a decent Indian summer, a strange, confusing time of year in Kingstree. The colors in the trees were building toward a bright peak, but folks still wore shorts on the weekend, still watered grass that hadn't been green since mid-September.

She did her best to look happy on the porch, to wait for Rev. Johns—a man too old to worry about trying the patience of anyone, including God—to ramble through the ceremony, which included his remark that he had been to this building many times, but "this was the first time there wasn't some deadbeat lying around."

She stood as straight as she could. She wanted everyone to get a good look at her backbone, to see that she was strong enough, that this kind of thing didn't bother her—her mother remarrying so soon after burying a husband. She bit down hard on her back teeth and felt the muscles in her jaw flare in and out. Her arms were suspended like little wings to hold her flower arrangement that she'd been given as the maid of honor. She didn't dare look down to see if the petals were trembling.

Missy noticed the longer the ceremony ran, the thinner the air became, as though the people behind her were using more than their shares. Like a knob on an oven had been turned, the temperature on the porch rose suddenly. Missy couldn't sense a breeze in sight; the Spanish moss hung limp on the branches of the oaks, and when she looked up, as high as she could into the crown of the tree behind Rev. Johns, she began to spin and fall through all the colors on those branches, wondering on her way down why she didn't feel them whipping her arms and legs when she zoomed past. But she saw faces as she flew through the branches, her mother's friends on the front row, who seemed to be talking during the ceremony, gossiping probably, creating the stories they would tell later at the beauty shop or in line at the IGA. She saw relatives spinning around her, the same ones she'd seen months ago—or was it only days ago?—at her father's funeral. The last thing she remembered was the image of Rev. Johns staring down at her, the expression on his face suggesting that he might indeed have a funeral on his hands after all.

Before Missy dared open her eyes, she explored with her hands. She felt the cool, smooth steel of the narrow table, its borders so near her hips. The edge of the table curved into a thin, metal lip—sharp under her fingers, dangerous almost. One finger found something soft just under the lip, bubblegum maybe. She moved her hands to the sides of her legs, which seemed to be in the proper places. The now-familiar funeral home smell ran into her nose thickly every time she took a breath. So she held it. Then, in the quiet, she heard someone else near her, perhaps too near, suck in a deep breath.

She cracked her eyes and found herself just inches from a pair of blue eyes so clear Missy thought she could see things happening on the other side of them—people, places, maybe the future. This person, a man, was a stranger, someone she probably should fear, she realized, but his eyes were too blue, too open to suggest danger or drama. All she could do was stare up at him. And she felt as though she might fall again.

"You're missing a damn fine party," he said, blinking a couple of times.

"Are you a doctor?" she asked.

"Nope. Pretty close though. I know what to do when people pass out. I've read all sorts of things about it. Been around a fainter or two before."

The eyes pulled back, and Missy saw they were attached to a very brown, very thin face, framed by a long, gray-and-dark beard. Thick gray hair, pulled back into a ponytail, disappeared down his back. He looked like he was in his thirties, maybe forties, except for the eyes. They were bright and full, like a young man's.

"Where did the wedding go?" She looked around her quickly and hoped she wasn't sharing space with some of Asa's customers.

"Skyles Huffman. I'm your second cousin on your momma's side. Or maybe third. I seem to forget things like that."

Huffman was her mother's maiden name. And it was Missy's middle name. Melissa Huffman Belue. Missy knew there weren't that many Huffmans around since her mother was an only child and her father, Missy's grandfather, had one brother and no sisters.

"You didn't answer my question," she said.

"I don't make it to many of these sorts of events. And I haven't been to Kingstree in months it seems. When I do come, I don't stay long. I travel around a lot."

"Why am I here? What happened to me?"

"You had your knees locked all up. Probably weren't breathing too deeply. And it was hot up there on that porch. Not steaming, but hot enough. All that adds up to is fainting. Did you know that all you got to do is shut down that blood flow the least little bit and the next thing you know, you're kissing pavement? Seventy-five percent of all faintings occur at social events where people have to stand for a long time. This I know."

Skyles tapped his temple, proud of his knowledge, and Missy couldn't stop staring at those eyes.

"Want a drink?" he said and pulled a flask from his back pocket. "Prime the engine a little?"

Missy stumbled. "I don't really drink. I'm not old—" She stopped herself, thinking she was giving away too much information.

"Well, Missy Belue, just how old are you?"

"Eighteen," she lied, fudging her age a few months.

"Fine age, that is. Here's to you," he said and tipped the flask up. Missy was a little disappointed because he shut his eyes when the whiskey bit into his throat, but after a hard swallow, they were back again, flashing blue signals at her.

He slid the flask into his coat pocket and Missy sat up on one arm. The new position made her head spin suddenly, and she paused for the world to settle down.

"Where is everybody?" she asked.

"Up by the pool, dancing and visiting. I was given the duty of taking care of you until you felt up to coming to the party." He winked an eye at her, and Missy's breath caught behind her teeth. "Just between you and me, it was just a good excuse for them to keep me out of sight. I've never won the most popular relative trophy."

Missy sat up all the way and took in the room. She saw a dozen wigs hanging on a row of hooks, like the drying pelts of small animals. To her left lay a tray packed with makeup and balls of something that looked like silly putty. Low-rising, glass-fronted cabinets displayed row after row of small bottles. A stack of silver trays balanced on one of the shelves. She decided this must be the place they made the dead look not so dead. Everything was so clean and glistening. A shiver bolted the length of her spine, and for a split second, she thought she might faint again. She felt her balance return.

"I think I'm ready to head back out. Really. I need to."

"You're the patient," he said. "But first I need a little medicine myself." He pulled out the flask again and took another quick nip, wiping his lips with the back of his wrist.

"You know, there's free champagne," Missy said. She'd heard the champagne debate rage for the past couple of weeks. Asa went on and on about the difference between brut and dry, and how some vineyards were known for their sparkling wine. He seemed to have a knowledge of wine, and Mona always beamed when he talked about foreign things.

"Miss Missy, for someone like me, champagne may's well be soda. Doesn't give me anything but gas." Skyles smiled and something clicked on behind his eyes, something bright and wild and able to shoot sparks of energy. Missy felt herself launching into those blue spaces, not unlike the way she felt when she spun through the branches on the porch.

"Come on, cousin. I'll see you to the party." He held out his hand. Missy looked to see if his palm was shaking, but it was steady and rough, hardened like it had seen some decent, outdoor work at one time or another. "But first we got to do something I always wanted to do."

Missy took his wrist and used it for balance as she slid off the table and her feet hit the floor. She was a sailor on land for the first time in months. Her knees waited for the roll of the waves to stop. She didn't have to ask what he meant, because Skyles answered without being prompted.

"I wanna touch a dead body."

He took off quickly toward the door and his speed startled her. She thought she detected a bit of a limp. *Something else that doesn't go with those eyes of his,* she thought, following him out the door. *A limp.* She wondered how he got it.

In the hall, she paused, deciding which way to go. She could follow and stay quiet, or follow and try to talk him out of snooping. Or she could just go to the party on her own. She didn't realize at that moment how hard it was to *not* follow Skyles Huffman, no matter where he was headed.

Music from the party spilled faintly into the dark halls of the funeral home as Missy took off after him. Skyles was more of a shadow now, his eyes a couple of bright-blue headlights, leading the way, door to door. She didn't notice when he came to a complete stop just ahead of her, and she ran into his back, bumping him a little farther down the hall.

"Need some work on those brakes, dear," he whispered. He sounded like a bad boy about to get in new trouble.

"Why are we whispering?" Missy asked.

"Because we are in the presence of the newly departed."

Missy huffed. "How do you know what's around here?"

"I heard Floyd talking before the wedding started. Something about a head-on car accident out near Cades. Three dead. He was rubbing his hands together and trying to work up a tear, and the whole time you could see the dollar signs spinning around in his eyeballs. What a peckerhead."

Missy wondered if Skyles remembered he was talking about her brand-new stepfather, but Missy thought Asa was a peckerhead too, so she couldn't argue. She hated the fact Asa made his living off fresh tragedy. He always said somebody had to give the dead a proper journey. Missy agreed. She just wished her mother didn't marry the guy in charge of selling tickets.

Skyles sniffed in the dark, then whispered low. "I think this is the room where they do it."

"Do what?"

"Embalm 'em," he said.

Missy straightened up. "We're not supposed to be messing around in here."

"I didn't see a stack of rule books at the door, did you? You aren't curious?" he whispered.

"Not really. Dead is dead," Missy said.

"But do you *really* know that? I mean, what if we open this door real fast, and catch them, dancing around, dead as doornails, but still having a good time? Or maybe they're packing up their souls for the trip to the other side. I'd like to see that," Skyles said.

Missy heard the cap of the flask being screwed off in the dark.

"They're just lying there," she said, remembering the painted-clown expression on her dead father's face.

"Let's see." Skyles grabbed her hand, opened the door and slung her ahead of him into the room, then scurried in behind her as he slammed the door shut. Inside was chilly, like the interior of a refrigerator. The air was the same medicinal, sanitary odor she'd almost become accustomed to at Floyd's, but now it was more intense, more of a sharp surprise. And the air was black dark, not a hint of light or flicker of a reflection. Missy blinked hard to make sure her eyes were open. She had her hands out in front of her, like a sleepwalker, but didn't move a muscle.

"Lord, there must be a light switch in here somewhere. You got a match?" Skyles said.

When Skyles talked, he asked her questions usually meant for someone older. *Did she want a drink from his flask? Did she have a match?* So far, the answer had always been no. But hearing the questions made Missy feel important.

"No matches," she said into the darkness and shook her head, then laughed nervously at the fact no one in the world could see her head moving.

"Well, we're in the right place, judging from the cold. If I could only find the lights, we might catch somebody's soul rising up to heaven. That would be something. A flying soul. I'll try to find a switch," he said.

She heard Skyles shuffling slowly somewhere to her right, but she couldn't remember if he was near the door or down the wall from it. Between the fainting spell and the darkness and the smell and his blue, blue eyes, she'd lost all sense of direction. She wasn't more than a hundred yards from her mother's wedding reception, but she was as lost as an Easter egg.

"Just stay put," Skyles whispered from a point even further to her right. "I'll find something. I just don't want to bump into you." She heard him come to a stop, then the metallic scrape as he unscrewed the cap on his flask again. He grunted in the dark. "Okay," he said, "now we're ready."

It was still blind as midnight and just as quiet when Missy heard Skyles say in a normal, measured voice, "Holy Jesus Mother Mary Joseph." He didn't sound excited or scared, just startled enough to forget about whispering.

"What!" Missy hissed. "What is it?"

A few seconds of silence in the dark, then Skyles said, "I found me a real dead person."

Missy began to backpedal slowly in the dark, her arms wrenched behind her to try and feel whatever might be waiting there.

"Put my hand right on his mouth. Or her mouth. Wait a minute." Skyles yelled somewhere in the black. There was pause. "Well, it's definitely a woman, and she's buck naked." He didn't sound like himself, his voice wound tight, running at a higher speed. He sounded too young, as though he was maybe eleven or twelve. Missy heard other things as his words cut through the dark—excitement, fear, bizarre curiosity.

Missy moaned a little as she moved. A man she barely knew was feeling up a dead woman. She backed up a few quick steps, tripped over something metal that clanked and chimed as she fell to the floor, the second time today. She bounced up and kept moving to what she thought was a door, then hit a wall and decided to go left until she found the doorknob. At least that's where she thought the door was. She was quieter now, too scared to make a noise.

Skyles yelled at her. "You alright? You ain't fainted again, have you?" Then, to himself, as though she was out cold and not hearing. "Damn, I'll have to drag her outta here now."

Like magic, a doorknob floated into Missy's outstretched palm. She tried once to turn it, but her hands were sweat-slick and shaking. She wiped them both on her dress at the thighs and went at the knob again, determined to use it or rip it out of the wood. When the door finally opened, it released quickly, surprising her, and a slant of light from a hallway window cut into the room as she stumbled through the opening.

Missy glanced back on her way out, and she saw Skyles Huffman framed in the sliver of yellow light, propped against a table, at the hip of a naked, bluish woman, him sipping from the flask again and grinning over the top of it like a man who had just discovered the unknown.

4.

After the wedding, Asa liked to say that he was now the Candy Man, his life full of M&M's—Mona and Missy. "Asa and his M&M's," he'd say and pause for them to fall into laughter. Mona always did. Missy never.

Missy began to notice her mother now laughed at other strange things, events and objects which, on the surface or even just below it, were all but humorless. Mona would be doing something, anything, maybe wiping a countertop, and she'd suddenly begin to laugh so hard, tears would leave a wet trail of drops on the Formica. Asa always laughed right along with her, like they had inside information on the world's funniest punchline. Missy could never predict what would set them off—a television commercial about dish detergent, the sound of a deejay on the radio, maybe just a look that passed between them.

In the few days between the wedding and the honeymoon, the laughter continued to erupt. Missy chalked it up to excitement about their upcoming trip, a long weekend at Pawleys Island. Half the residents of Kingstree owned houses at Pawleys, it seemed, and at any given moment from Memorial Day to the end of September, a fair percentage of the town's population migrated an hour east, to the island. Pawleys was known locally as Kingstree-By-The-Sea. And it was no joke.

At some point in the past, Asa had guided one of the more prominent families in town through a sudden tragedy, and in addition to what he was paid, the grieving family offered the use of their beach house. Mona had requested to go somewhere where the water was unreal blue for their honeymoon, but Asa couldn't spare the time away from the business, so they opted for a long, free weekend at Pawleys.

"You can close your eyes and pretend it's the Caribbean, my sweet. You'll still have the Caribbean amenities—waves and sand and the sun. The only perceptible difference is that the water is a bit grayer," Asa said. "We'll make believe it's St. Croix. I'll help you."

"But we're into November, Asa," Mona whined a little.

"St. Croix with a chill then." Asa smiled.

Missy watched her mother weakening, rationalizing, and finally arriving at some sense of happiness she would be honeymooning at the chillier first cousin of the Virgin Islands.

"What about Missy?" Asa said. Mona suggested taking her along. Asa offered a plan B.

"Missy," he said, "is quite capable of taking care of herself. Lord, she'll be eighteen in a few weeks. She could stay at the funeral home. Clarence will be a mere holler away if she needs somebody. We'll leave her enough money to buy some groceries or eat at the Caboose. So, what do you think?"

Her mother began to protest, "I don't know . . ."

Missy sat in one of the ladder-back chairs in the kitchen, in the house she and her mother were vacating soon. She wished that her mother and Asa would have these decision-making discussions when she was gone, especially the ones that concerned her. She just didn't care that much, not anymore.

"She's all but grown now, Mona."

"I just don't know. What do you think, Missy?" The two of them turned slightly toward her.

"If I'm so grown up, why didn't you ask me in the first place?"

"Point taken," Asa said. "How would you like to handle this?"

"I'd like to stay here. In my own house," Missy said.

Her mother piped up. "I'm sorry, honey, but Mrs. Huggins will probably be showing the house to people that weekend. It won't be ours much longer."

Her mother's tone was usually reserved for conversations with four-year-olds about dead animals and Santa.

"It's ours until we move. Or until we *want* to move."

Missy had fantasies that their house would never sell and things would remain like they presently were—Asa at the funeral home every night, Mona and Missy together in their own house. Since the wedding, for all intents and purposes, Asa and his new bride were only married in the bright light of day. That Missy could handle.

"Personally," Asa said, "I think you're a little far from neighbors or friends out here if, God forbid, you were to need someone's help." He instantly realized the mistake he made, suggesting that tragedy might be waiting for Missy when she was alone. "Not that a mature young lady like yourself would be unable to cope with anything that reared its head." He smiled at Mona. "I'd just rest easier knowing she was at the funeral home, with Clarence nearby. I care that much about things."

He sounded like a father, and his tone chilled Missy in a flash. She couldn't decide if he was truly trying on the role for size or simply wearing a convincing mask, but she was learning something. Even though his wardrobe never changed, Asa had a hundred faces, and he could shuffle them like a sleight-of-hand artist. The secret was trying to figure out which of them was genuine.

Missy avoided the trip to Pawleys. She didn't want to be anywhere around when her mother and Asa finally acted like married people. Instead, she packed a bag on the Thursday afternoon following the wedding, and her mother drove her to the Floyd Funeral Home. During the drive over, Mona dealt little slips of paper like playing cards.

"Here's the number of the house where we'll be," she said, sliding it across the seat without taking her eyes off the road. "And here's Aunt Cindy's number." She slid another.

"I know Aunt Cindy's number."

Missy stared out at the oaks that lined the street. Their old roots had long ago pushed the sidewalk into unwalkable chunks of cement and mortar.

"In a panic situation, you're more likely to forget things like numbers and addresses. That's why you just have to dial the operator for an emergency. It's easy to remember zero, but I wrote that one down for you, too." Her mother took a breath, gave her a sideways glance, then quickly returned her concentration to the road. The chances of her hitting someone else on the near-empty streets of Kingstree were slim, but Mona had never been comfortable behind the wheel of a car.

"So," she said, "in case something happens, you call zero and get the police. Then you call your Aunt Cindy for family help, then you call us right away."

"What about Clarence?" Missy asked.

"What about him?"

Missy rolled down her window, stuck her hand out, arm wrestling with the chilly rush of wind against her flat palm. The November air was colder. It smelled different.

"Asa said that Clarence would be around if something went wrong."

"Clarence isn't but a half a step away from dead himself. Every time he washes one of the hearses, I imagine him crawling inside and passing away. He must be in his late seventies."

It was the first time Missy had heard her mother talk about the funeral home that way. The tone in her voice was that of an owner's, somebody who had a stake in the operation. Mortician by marriage.

"Momma," Missy said after a half block of silence.

"Yes, ma'am?"

"Why are you so nervous?" she said.

Missy had watched the signs for the last half mile—her mother's death grip on the steering wheel, how she forgot to press on the gas pedal when the light turned green at the intersection in front of the IGA. And Mona wasn't hearing much of anything either, like listening was one too many things to do.

"It's been a long time since I went on a honeymoon," she said finally. "Would you roll that window up? It's winter outside."

"Well, it isn't your first one. Where'd you and Daddy go?"

"Now, Missy . . ."

"I'm just curious," she said.

Mona drew a breath with the hint of a smile.

"He took me to the mountains. He planned this whole trip out. I know that doesn't surprise you, him and his planning. We went to a little town called Bat Cave. Can you imagine that? A town called Bat Cave? We stayed at an inn called the Esmerelda. If you opened the windows at night, you could hear a little creek rushing across the rocks, right outside your window. We stayed in the same exact room where this California fellow once lived for a while and wrote the script for that chariot movie. What was it? *Ben Hur*, that's it. Isn't that interesting?"

Mona stared at the street, but her eyes were somewhere else. Missy saw it. She knew her mother had started to drift, looking through the pea-soup fog of years gone by, back to a time when she was a bride comfortable enough to be lulled to sleep by the noise of whitewater through an open window.

Missy wondered how in the world her daddy had decided on some place called Bat Cave for a honeymoon. It was just like him. Drag somebody you love to a place simply because it sounded different. Mona continued, talking so low Missy had to lean toward the middle of the seat to hear her over the hum of the engine and the rush of air through the still-open window.

"The Esmerelda smelled like woodsmoke and mothballs. It was October, and believe me, it was chilly up in the mountains. But every night your father would crack the windows and take a deep breath and tell me that it was the best-tasting air he'd ever put in his mouth. I loved it when he said things like that. You know, things you didn't expect."

Mona pulled into a drive that led to the rear of the funeral home. Missy saw Asa's face framed in the window of his office, watching as they drove past. She turned back to her mother. There were those subtle hints again, signals they were related. She and her mother had the same lift to their eyebrows and lips constantly half-puckered in a near-pout. Mona had beautiful skin, and Missy was grateful she'd bequeathed it to her daughter.

"I'm nervous because I'm scared your daddy's watching me," Mona said.

Her mother suddenly appeared older and brittle. And her fear wasn't like a kid's, not the kind brought on by a nightmare or a screech in the dark, but a fear that began somewhere down deep and rode the blood to every inch of the body. It was the fear of having made a mistake that couldn't be corrected without a considerable amount of pain and grief.

"So why in the world did you—" she started, but before she could finish, Asa had his head at the driver's side window.

"Now," he said loudly through the glass, "isn't that a sweet scenario? M and M, teary-eyed from goodbyes. Parting is such sorrow and all that. It's only for a few days, ladies."

Mona rolled the window down, and Asa leaned in. His breath filled the car with the bitter scent of Listerine. He waited a second for a response, and when it didn't come, he just plodded on.

"I'm all but ready to whisk you away, my dear. Got your bags packed? Missy, do you have the things you'll need? Clarence, step around here and give us a hand with these suitcases."

Behind Asa, Clarence hung back, glancing up at the trees, then farther into the sky. Asa's words hit his ears late, like they came on the breeze from a faraway place and needed translating, but he suddenly perked up and headed for the trunk of the car. Asa was already there, taking out bags and putting them on the ground.

"Lord, Mona, what have you got in here? Cement?" He ran around to the window again and peered in at the two of them. "You know you didn't have to pack that many clothes." He winked and took off again for the back of the car.

"I can't do it," Mona whispered.

"What?" Missy leaned over in the front seat, closer to her mother.

"I can't go away with him. I like him alright when there's other people around. But if I have to be with him all alone for such a long stretch of time . . . I just don't know what I'll do." Mona reached under the seat and pulled out a small bottle of something clear. "I can't do it," she repeated. "This the cheapest fortitude I could find on short notice." Mona tucked the bottle in her pocketbook.

"You've been doing so good," Missy said. "Come on, now."

"It's momentary, Missy," Mona said.

"God, everybody I get around drinks," she said, remembering Skyles and his flask.

"What are you talking about?" Mona asked.

Asa was back again, his face in theirs. "And now the time has come, my dear, to head for the closest thing we have to the Caribbean. Your chariot awaits!" he hollered and pulled the door open.

Mona started to ease out of the car, then whispered back at Missy, "Why do you think he said *chariot*? Why now? There were so many chariots in *Ben Hur*. I haven't seen that movie in years." She tried to smile and slid toward the door, dragging her pocketbook behind her.

Missy knew from failed experiments in chemistry classes back in high school that her nose would eventually get used to the smell, the one seeping through the floorboards into her room on the second floor of the funeral home. Her nose would adapt, and soon she wouldn't even know the smell was still there—the hodgepodge of scents that people brought in with them during the day when they came to do business at Floyd's and, behind it all, the steady, sharp odor of embalming fluid.

The upper story of the home was where they would all be living soon. The second story had a separate entrance, a flight of iron steps attached to the outside wall, its own kitchen and den, plus three bedrooms and a couple of bathrooms. Unless you had funeral home affairs to tend to, there was never any reason to go downstairs. But Missy knew dead bodies and fresh grief gathered only a few feet below.

She was picking through a plate of food her mother had left in the refrigerator when she heard the iron steps clanging. The stairway was a cheap alarm. The second the slightest bit of weight touched them, they shifted against some loose lug nuts and bolts and banged against the length of the outside wall. Missy heard him coming and was already standing at the door when Clarence eased onto the landing.

His face filled the pane of glass in the door. Milky eyes set back beneath the ridge of his forehead, lines that crisscrossed his face—dirt roads in a desert. He never smiled. At least, Missy couldn't remember seeing his teeth in the dozen or so times she'd looked him in the face. He was a big man, made even bigger by his blackness. To Missy, it seemed like he continuously carried around a shadow of himself. She had seen black men like Clarence all her life, men with too much of the world strapped to their backs as they shuffled through their days.

His breath fogged the windowpane. He knocked again while she stared into the glass, then said through the door, "I was told to check on you while they were out of town."

Missy's mouth dropped open. It wasn't the kind of voice that belonged inside that body. She realized that, along with Clarence's mystery teeth, she'd never heard him talk either. And now that she had heard him, she knew he wasn't from the South Carolina Lowcountry. His words had a full, deep volume, but they were clipped sharply, like somebody reading the news on television. There was no hint of coastal Gullah. He didn't drag out his syllables or swallow half of what he was trying to say. He sounded like he was from another country where they spoke perfect English. And it was a voice too high for such a large body.

Missy opened the door wide enough to make it obvious he could enter if he liked. Clarence remained anchored on the landing.

"You have something to eat, I see. Good. I didn't know if I should plan on getting you something."

"Just leftovers. You want to come in or something?"

Clarence looked straight in her eyes. "Oh no, no thank you. I just dropped by to make sure you were settled in, see if you needed anything."

Missy shook her head. Missy wished he would talk all night. She imagined there was someone hiding in his shirt, doing the talking and moving Clarence's mouth.

"I must tell you, there's no reason to believe all the stories." He smiled, and she saw the gleam of a silver tooth.

"Stories?"

"You know, all the funeral parlor tales. About angels and souls and spirits. The best one I ever heard was how the souls of two people got mixed up when I brought their bodies inside the home, so every night these two old lost souls float around downstairs, trying to untangle and find their bodies." He laughed behind the silver tooth. "They don't have sense enough to go to the graveyard."

Clarence didn't rock on his feet or stare at his shoes. He looked straight ahead, right in her eyes, but Missy couldn't tell if he was pulling her leg.

"I've been living over the garage for twenty years now and I have never seen anything funny going on, alive or dead. So you sleep tight. Oh, and it's supposed to get cold tonight, might even freeze, but your heat is on and working okay."

Clarence turned toward the steps, then hesitated. "I met your daddy, back when you were little. I was sorry about his passing. I prepared the hole for him."

Clarence started down the stairs. It wasn't until he reached the bottom that Missy managed to thank him, and even then, she wasn't sure what for.

The next day around noon, Angela Belton pulled up behind the funeral home in her father's Country Squire station wagon and leaned on the horn. Clouds of exhaust poured from the tailpipe. It was Saturday, and it was cold, just like Clarence had predicted. But low temperatures or not, Angela's father went to the golf course every Saturday. On days when he couldn't hit the course, when it was too chilly or too wet, he played poker at the round, felt-covered table in the men's locker room. Today, Angela dropped him off and had the rest of the day to do what she wanted with his car.

Friends since the first grade, Angela Belton and Missy were more sisters than anything else, though no one would mistake them as blood relatives. Angela was smaller than Missy and darker, her brunette hair bobbed short, just below her ears. She could never sit still for long. She had energy she couldn't control, energy that constantly searched for an outlet, forcing her to tap her feet or rock on her heels or wave her arms pretty much every waking minute.

The morning they met, that first morning of the first grade, their teacher sat the students in alphabetical order. Angela and Missy were the only B-E-L's and ended up sharing one of the wide, wooden double desks in the classroom. Since then, it seemed, they did everything important together. Every birthday, every Friday football game, every heartbreak. And whether by accident or design, they both liked and disliked the same things. They hated to dance, hated boys with loud cars, hated Kingstree. They loved to talk about leaving town—when they would, how they would, and ultimately, why they would never be able to. When they reached that gray conclusion, they got to be depressed together.

Angela and Missy were tied fast, they assumed, in a murky kind of limbo. They had graduated from high school the previous spring and had yet to form any definite plans. Angela's boyfriend was off at the Citadel. He was a junior, so she was simply biding time, waiting for him to become a second lieutenant with a sociology degree, at which time, she assumed, he would join the National Guard to serve his required time and work right here, in town. Missy had thought all along she might find a way to go to college, but when her daddy died she quit making decisions, at least any that concerned the future. She told herself she could be useful at home, taking care of her mother. Of course, this was before Mona married Asa and changed the direction of everything.

This Saturday, Missy and Angela planned to do the usual. Ride around town in the oversized, wood-paneled station wagon and appear aloof and bored to the people they passed. When Missy climbed down the noisy stairs, Angela stood outside the car, laughing with Clarence. She possessed a barroom laugh too big for her body. Every time it came out of her mouth—full of spit and gravel—it sounded like she'd just heard a filthy joke and was enjoying it a little too much.

"He thought I was bringing a dead person here in Daddy's station wagon," she said to Missy. "Now that's funny, isn't it?"

"Well, that would be a problem," Clarence answered, "what with death on vacation with Mr. Floyd and your momma. You scared me with that horn blowing. It sounded fairly urgent."

"What would you do if somebody died today?" Missy wanted to know. She hadn't given it much thought. She zipped her jacket up to her neck and waited for Clarence to answer. She blew her breath and watched the cloud. A hint of frost had hardened the perfect grass in the funeral home's yard.

"If we suddenly had a customer? Well, I'd get them ready as well as I could. Then, give Mr. Floyd a call. Put them in the cooler until he got back. There's really no reason to rush, you know. Only the living want to put the dead behind them so quickly." Clarence glanced toward the garage. He'd been washing cars in the cold air and left the hose running near one of the black Cadillacs. A huge puddle formed near the garage door. "I'd best go finish with those cars. Will you be back shortly, Miss Missy?"

His question startled her and made her, for some reason, look immediately at the tops of her shoes. She hadn't been questioned about her comings and goings since her father's death. She hesitated.

"I'm not really sure where we're going. I don't really know when—"

Angela cut her off. "We're going to the Scout Cabin, probably. We'll be back in a couple of hours. Unless somebody dies." She was the only one who laughed.

Clarence waved and shuffled back to his car washing. Missy stared at him as they pulled away, wondering how he kept his hands warm while he washed cars in winter. Angela fiddled with the radio.

"I don't understand why you can't just make something up, or hell, tell the truth. You acted like you were scared to death of that old gravedigger."

"He wanted to know where I was going."

"Yeah?" Angela said, sliding the car into drive.

"I didn't know what you wanted to do."

"You need to figure out when it's just as easy to make up a lie and send somebody on their way," Angela said. "You see how happy he was to know where we were going?"

"Okay, fine. Scout Cabin." Missy really didn't care one way or the other, as long as they were moving.

Angela found WKSP on her father's radio and turned up the song. Al Green oozed out of the front speakers. She punched the cigarette lighter. In seconds, it popped out and she lit a long Virginia Slims and cracked the vent window. The smoke rushed outside. "Want one?" She pointed to the pack on the seat.

Angela passed Missy the one in her mouth and lit another for herself. "We could go to the cabin, but I doubt anyone's there, as cold as it is."

"Something to do," Missy said and looked down her nose at the white smoke trailing from her mouth. It was the only time she ever smoked, when she and Angela rode around town.

The streets on the way to the river were all but empty on a Saturday. Missy almost liked Kingstree when it was abandoned. When nobody walked the streets or waited at intersections, the town still possessed possibility.

Scout Cabin was just a few minutes' drive from the funeral home and not really a cabin at all anymore. It was just a place on a bend in the Black River where, during the summer, folks came to swim or sunbathe in the coarse, almost-white sand. The long narrow beach subdivided in the warmer months. Younger people—the high school kids and students home from college—took the section nearest the bend, where the current picked up and headed downstream into the dark tunnel-like overhang of cypress trees and vines. The other end of the beach was always occupied by families who brought their kids to swim. There, the water barely crept along. Mothers and fathers felt safe letting their children bob in inner tubes or dive along the shallow, sandy bottom. The middle section was people who didn't fit neatly into either category.

The water was always the same no matter what time of year—dark with tannins, the color of Coca Cola or old coffee. Venture knee deep and you'd lose sight of your feet, but you could feel the grit of the bottom. Cypress knees dotted the shallow edge of the far shore where, high in a tree, a rope swing had been hung years before by some of the more daring and idiotic boys, the ones you'd find at the young end of the beach.

At some point, there had actually been a cabin, but now only the crumbling brick pilings of its foundation were visible in the pines just beyond the road that led to the beach. The cabin used to serve as a place for the Boy Scouts to hold troop meetings or stay overnight during the winter when it was too cold to camp along the riverbank. Rumor was, it burned one night years ago when some Tenderfoot Scout sat on the porch, shooting fireworks across the water just to watch the reflections. A spark got loose in his box of Roman candles, and the wooden cabin went up in a matter of minutes.

Angela pulled the station wagon past the pilings and into the gravel-and-dirt parking area. The only vehicle in sight was a beat-up red pickup with a camper top, parked next to a stand of live oaks.

"Well?" Angela said, letting the engine idle in park. "We sitting or walking? I'm good either way."

"I feel like moving," Missy said.

They started for the beach, then turned along the river, walking upstream toward the family end, where the current slowed. Missy thought she smelled smoke on the breeze, a signal that fall had arrived. Somewhere someone was burning leaves or a pile of stumps. A motorcycle wailed deeply on the highway that paralleled the river a mile or so downstream. Sound carried far on the clear air.

They walked to the end of the beach, their feet sinking slightly in the damp sand, then took a narrow path leading into a set of small sand-clay hills that had always seemed out of place to Missy. Just on the other side of the hills, the river cut under the bank, creating a deep hole near the roots of a huge cypress. In spring, someone always fished there, dropping lines for redbreast and smallmouths. This time of year, though, very few people even thought about wetting a hook. The chillier weather drove the fish deeper, made them lazy and cautious.

Angela led the way. She picked a path through the clay hills and came to a quick stop on the opposite side, put her hands out to her side, signaling Missy to wait.

"Look there," she whispered.

Missy peered over her friend's shoulder. On the near bank, a man sat with the remains of his lunch spread around him—a soda can and balls of aluminum foil. He was framed in a patch of sunlight, his legs straight out and spread apart in a V. Between his ankles, a snake the size of a baby's arm writhed slow-motion in the patch of sun. The man prodded him every couple of seconds with a stick. Between pokes, he took a sip from a round canteen.

"Who is that?" Angela said, maybe too interested. Missy couldn't make out the man's face, but she didn't care. It wasn't unusual to see people wasting time by the river.

"Keep on the path," Missy told her. "We can cut behind him. Or we can go back."

"Jesus, come on," Angela said.

For a few unavoidable feet, the girls would be forced into plain sight of the man. They would have to take the path that led them into the cypress and oaks, and getting there would leave them in the open. But this guy seemed too invested with his snake to care if they walked right over the top of his head.

When they hit the clearing, they kept their faces down and their feet moving until a voice called out, "Missy Belue, how do you do?" She stopped and turned.

First, she saw the ponytail, then the face of Skyles Huffman, a huge grin spreading the width of it. He kept talking.

"Last time I saw you, you looked like you'd run into a ghost. Or at least a dead person."

"You know this guy?" Angela was in her ear, but her gravelly voice carried all the way to Skyles. Missy's father would have said Angela learned to whisper in a sawmill.

"Know me? Hell, she's kin to me. Second cousin on her momma's side or something like that. How is Mona, by the way? The blushing bride." He took a swallow.

"She's on her honeymoon," Missy said, keeping her eye on the snake. She might've imagined it, but it seemed to be wiggling faster. Skyles noticed her interest.

"Don't fret, Missy Belue. Just a little game I play with snakes," he said and took another sip on the canteen. It was an old, dented Boy Scout model. For a moment, Missy wondered if Skyles might have been the one to burn down the cabin. He was the type of person who would aim fireworks over water. He held the canteen toward them.

"No thanks," Missy said, but Angela wanted to know what was in it.

"Flavor of the day," he said, "and today's special is . . . vodka. The mother tongue of Russia. Mother of us all." He took another sip. "You see, yesterday afternoon, this snake probably thought it was still summer. But he was wrong. Sun went down, temperature went down with it, and now this is one confused cottonmouth. He doesn't know if he should settle down for a long winter's nap or get a tan on a rock. He's as groggy as a wino. But—and this is the game part—if I keep him in the sun long enough, he'll come to his senses real slow. I like to see if I can guess the exact moment when he's about to get more deadly than fun."

"Deadly?" Angela asked, her mouth open a little.

"Well, yeah, honey. I said he was a cottonmouth."

Skyles took a second stick and using both pried open the snake's mouth. Inside was the color of milk. He touched a fang with one of the sticks, and the snake wiggled into action furiously for only a second or two, then fanned the sand slowly with his tail.

"I'd say we got a few more minutes before he starts getting real pissed. Where you girls headed?" Skyles stared up at them, his eyes wandering from face to face and back again.

Angela said, "Just walking."

"Nothing special," Missy said, too quick on the heels of Angela, then added a lie. "We're meeting a bunch of people. They're on the way."

"I heard you and your momma are moving into the funeral home. That true?" Between his legs, the cottonmouth struck blindly at the warm air he was waking up to.

"That's what they tell me," Missy said. She didn't know what to watch, Skyles or the snake sidewinding in the sand.

"They're going to stay upstairs. Nobody lives downstairs," Angela added, then laughed at her joke she thought she'd created. Missy thought Angela sounded like a silly high school girl. Missy wanted to act her age in front of Skyles. Older, if possible.

"Good, good. Don't want to get the living and the dead all mixed up, eh? Remember how that can happen, Missy?" he laughed and took a sip with his eyes shut. The snake inched its way toward Skyles's crotch, a fraction of an inch with each half-wriggle. Angela wasn't watching the snake. She had her eyes trained on Skyles. Missy was the only one who noticed the snake, and she couldn't decide whether or not to open her mouth and warn him.

"Remember what, Missy? What's he talking about remembering?" Angela said.

"Nothing important," she told her.

The snake folded inside itself, gathering its energy.

"Well, I've had just about all the fun I'm allowed," Skyles said. Without wasting a motion, he reached down—moving quicker than seemed possible for someone who looked like he did—and snatched the snake by its tail. The cottonmouth twisted and curled and struck wildly at his hand and missed badly. "Fly, you son of a bitch!" Skyles hollered, twirled the snake over his head lasso-style, then flung it into the Black River. Missy was used to seeing snakes in the summertime, cutting their frantic, whiplash trail through the water. She waited for this one to pop up from his circle of ripples, but he never appeared.

"Snakes are shy," Skyles said. "You got more chance of being struck by lightning than you do getting bit by a poisonous snake."

"How would you know?" Missy asked.

"Just by keeping up, cousin. Keeping my eyes open. Reading things, too." He tapped his temple with a finger, took a sip, winced, and capped his canteen. He tapped his front jacket pocket, too, which was stuffed with bits of paper. "I'm going to the abbey. You two wanna come along?" He asked both of them, but he stared straight at Missy. Angela answered for the both of them.

"Why not?" she said, then turned to Missy. "It'll be something different."

Missy wanted to protest about having to be home, about being expected at a certain time, but she remembered that Clarence was the only one in charge of worrying about her today.

"C'mon," Skyles said, picking up his used tin foil and empty pork rind bags. "Let's go watch those monks."

The two girls followed him in Angela's station wagon. Skyles steered the faded red pickup slowly down the dirt road back to the highway. Instead of turning right toward town, he hung a left and paralleled the swamp for a couple of miles. The road was more like a levee, a raised, asphalt hump through the soggy lowland. Black-water potholes cropped up on both sides of the road every hundred yards or so, along with cement bridges that seemed to span nothing but muddy, weedy low spots. This was the fall, and a dry one, so even the potholes were only about half full. But the swamp never went completely dry, even in the worst of droughts or the dead of winter. It just sank a little and then stank more.

Skyles eased off the gas on all of the bridges. He would stick his arm out and point at something over the side and holler back at the girls through his open window. Missy and Angela could never make out what he was saying or notice anything unusual on the roadside. From where they followed, they saw him tipping the canteen to his mouth, then wiping with the cuff of his jacket. The fallen leaves from the hardwoods blew up in the exhaust as they drove by.

When they reached the point where the swamp bordered the tobacco fields, Skyles made a right turn down a road no wider than a driveway. The asphalt gave way to gravel, then gravel to a couple of sandy ruts accordioned with sharp bumps. The pines grew thick, but in perfect, planted rows, just wide enough to accommodate Skyles's truck. He turned down one of the natural alleys between the pines and stopped.

"Leave your car here," he yelled back at them. "We'll take the truck." Angela nodded, and Missy grabbed her arm and snatched her toward the middle of the seat.

"This is stupid," she said.

"It's not stupid, it's just different."

"We shouldn't be here," Missy whispered.

"Well, tell me, where should we be?" Angela knew it was a decent question that probably had no answer. She slid across the seat and out the door, then reached back in for the keys. "Suit yourself," she said, but Missy was already going for the handle.

For a couple hundred yards they bounced along, packed together inside the cab of Skyles's truck and hemmed in from the outside world by the walls of pines. The land did a gentle rise, then leveled off. Ahead, Missy saw the border where the pines stopped. Skyles saw it, too. He whipped the truck into an opening in the trees, slammed it in reverse, and backed to the edge of the clearing, still beneath the thick canopy of the timber.

The three of them sat on the tailgate, Angela in the middle. From their elevated perch, they stared down into Springbank Abbey, a group of one-story, tin-roofed buildings that rose low in the floodplain of the river a few hundred yards below them. The buildings were each painted white, a color almost too bright for the grays and browns of the November woods. Avenues of grass, somehow still green this far into fall, divided the buildings. No trees grew in and among the buildings, but the grass lawns ran right to the edge of the woods that separated the abbey from the river itself.

From where they sat, the abbey looked to be floating on the green, as if it were not permanent, only at anchor. *If the river ever floods bad enough,* Missy thought, *this place will drift away like a lost fishing boat.*

The lowest, longest buildings were the chicken houses. That's what the brothers did. They raised chickens. They sold the eggs and manure. During the summer, when the weather turned hot and the humidity was up, clouds of manure stench floated through town, buoyed by the river flow. At this time of year, though, the cold knocked down the smell.

No one really knew how many brothers lived at Springbank or how long they stayed. There were rumors the abbey was a monk jail of some kind, a place where out-of-favor brothers were exiled to get back on the correct tack of their moral compass. Some said it was a monk training camp, where brand-new brothers were sent to learn their religious ropes. Mostly, people in Kingstree kept their mouths shut and bought eggs year-round and pickup-loads of manure in the spring. And every once in a while a school group would tour the abbey and watch the brothers go through their chants and quiet prayers.

The three of them sat at the edge of the pines, dangling their legs off the truck's tailgate, watching the lights in the windows and the couple of funnels of smoke that wound up from the larger buildings and flattened into wispy, gray clouds in the trees above the abbey. Skyles offered his canteen. Missy refused, but Angela traded sips with him, just like she'd been doing in the cab of the pickup. In the shade of the pines, it was much colder. Missy could see her breath. They sat in silence for a while, Angela and Skyles passing the canteen between them.

"Why are we here?" Missy said finally. She felt Angela startle beside her. Skyles didn't have to think to answer.

"We are here to spy on the holiest men in Williamsburg County. You realize what these guys do? They get up every morning at five o'clock, and they pray. Then they eat and they work their chickens and they pray. They sleep and they do it all over again, every day the same. Those boys got focus."

Missy tried to put an edge on her voice. "And that makes them holy, I guess?"

"Yes, ma'am. They got no distractions."

"So?" Missy said.

"You find a way to keep all the distractions of the world away, you're either holy or dead, one or the other. I'm hoping I got a while before I'm dead, so I'd like to find a way to stay undistracted." Skyles took a long drink. "A shrink would probably say that's why I drink. To keep the distractions at bay. But I don't need anybody to tell me that's the reason I'm always traveling. I travel so the distractions don't catch up with me."

Missy turned and looked beyond Angela toward Skyles. He was already staring at her, his blue eyes a little watery in the cold air.

"I feel sorry for you," he said. "I got to tell you, Missy Belue, I've felt sorry for you since the day of the wedding."

"I don't need you feeling any damn thing about me."

"What are y'all talking about? I'm lost," Angela said, the edges of her words slurring away.

Skyles didn't answer Angela. Instead, he said, "You got some shit heading your way, Missy Belue. Lots of distractions, lots of shit. You better learn to drink or become a monk . . . a nun, I mean."

The moment Skyles finished his sentence, one of the brothers stepped out of the largest building and made his way across the grass. He moved slowly, shuffling under his burlap-colored robes almost the same way Clarence walked around the funeral home. Missy could tell, even from this distance, that he was overweight. Halfway to the chicken house, he stopped and turned in their direction. His hood was pulled over his head. Missy thought he looked like the Angel of Death with a few extra pounds. She tried to push herself back farther into the bed of the pickup. "Damn, he sees us!" she hissed.

Skyles reached across Angela and touched Missy on the leg. "Watch," he said. She held her breath and glanced at Angela. Her head was cocked to the side, a thin snore whistling through her lips. *Too many sips,* Missy thought. "Watch now," Skyles repeated.

The brother raised up his arm and the hood fell away from his face. He looked up the rise at their hiding place in the pines and gave them a long wave. Then, he turned, put his hood back on and disappeared slowly into the chicken house. Skyles reached across and squeezed Missy's knee.

"Every time he does that, I feel like I been blessed all over again."

5.

Asa Floyd plotted death on the calendar.

Once the short winter finally arrived in Kingstree, he knew he would have a long list of customers—those who didn't slow down for the unfamiliar patch of black, frozen glare and ended up wrapped around a pine tree or submerged in the black water under a bridge. He watched the TV weathercast every night, quietly begging the weatherman for a cold front to barrel out of the northwest, pushing a bulge of ice and snow that might accidently dip as far south as the Lowcountry of South Carolina. Snow and ice were rare, which made them all the more deadly. Nobody in Kingstree knew how to act in a real winter.

The holidays were always his busiest time. Beginning with Thanksgiving and through New Year's, he could expect a steady attendance of drunk drivers and the people who couldn't dodge them fast enough. There was always a kid who shot himself with a new, unfamiliar Christmas rifle or a man who got lost hunting wild hogs in the swamp and froze to death before he found his way back to the logging road. Someone would grab the wrong wire stringing Christmas lights and shock himself into the next life. Asa never seemed to sleep during the holidays. He was constantly downstairs, preparing someone—overjoyed.

And now Mona was a partner in his happiness. She had become the official makeup person. "Your job," Asa told her, "is to create the illusion of complete contentment and total relaxation in the face of death." So she worked on the expressions. She noticed how some colors were naturally more alive than others. She learned to fix lips in the vaguest echo of a smile. She discovered the secret of hair and how the simple lilt of a curl on the forehead could suggest death wasn't worth the time of day. She even learned how to add synthetic hair to those who needed a patch here or there.

From her bedroom window or from behind curtains downstairs or through a narrow slit in an open door, she watched Floyd and her mother sleepwalk through December and January. Christmas became a lost holiday. Missy spent the day with Angela, while Asa and Mona prepared an elderly man who had died of a heart attack in front of his Christmas tree.

Sometimes, with her ear pressed to a door, she heard Asa speak about death like it was a blue-chip stock, with a value that rose and fell with the mercury in the thermometer. She never heard her mother answer, and that wasn't unusual. Her mother had pretty much given up on small talk. It wasn't that Mona was conducting a silent protest. She never snarled or changed her expression. She just refused to waste energy talking. If she carried on any conversations, they were with herself. The tired, bored look in her eyes suggested that the actual effort of opening her mouth and setting her vocal cords into vibration would exhaust her.

Missy noticed her mother's new brand of silence began just after the honeymoon. When they returned from the beach, Missy prepared herself for the worst, prepared for her mother to be magically younger and more alive than ever. She braced herself for Mona to be outrageously happy with her new husband. But Missy was wrong.

Mona returned from the honeymoon numb. Not long after they climbed the iron steps, Missy asked her how it went. Mona smiled thinly and nodded. "Fine, dear. Just fine." But that was the extent of the details. Asa was still as jumpy and philosophical as ever. He hadn't changed a bit. Mona wasn't happy. But she wasn't unhappy. She just wasn't herself. Missy should have been content that her mother was finding this new chapter of marriage unspeakable; it perhaps suggested a quick, painless ending. But while Mona wasn't speaking, she was doing something in her silence—drinking like the world had run out of water and the only liquid in ready supply was vodka.

Missy tried to speak to her about it, tried to make an attempt to find out why her mother was pickling herself. On more than a few occasions, she steered her mother to a chair in the funeral home and questioned her face-to-face. Her mother never blinked and always answered the same. "Fortitude. That's all it is, a steady dose of fortitude."

Missy found bottles in the usual hiding places—cabinets and drawers, behind books on the shelf. When she emptied them in the sink, her mother became more ingenious. She hid vodka inside several of the worst-selling caskets and in the pantry, inside bottles labeled *vinegar* or *distilled water*. Missy found those, too, but soon she couldn't keep up with either the supply or demand, so she quit following her mother around. The only time she saw her mother somewhat sober was when the time came to add some color or define the eyebrows for the deceased. Mona never handled the dead drunk.

For months, it appeared Cousin Skyles's prediction that something dark and disastrous was angling its way toward Missy was wrong. Once Missy gave up trying to find her mother a seat on the sober wagon, nothingness stretched out in front of her. Life for Missy slowed to a bland, monotonous crawl, and the only bursts of excitement occurred when someone died and arrived at the funeral home so their passing could receive Asa's stamp of approval. For Missy, there was no school, and with no one nagging her to find a job, she spent her days reading books, watching through her window, or winding through the streets with Angela at the wheel of the Country Squire. Mostly there was the simple, numbing act of waiting for something interesting to happen.

During the slowness, she had plenty of time to wonder about Skyles and his theories. She kept seeing that snake fighting the heat of the sun. She couldn't decide if the cottonmouth was a distraction or not. She picked apart that afternoon in the woods above the abbey minute by minute, breaking it down so she could study it like the pieces of a watch, trying to understand how all the tiny gears meshed with one another. She finally decided that the reason she thought so much about her older cousin was because she had nothing better to do.

One afternoon in early February, Asa was all but ecstatic about an accident at a crossroads near Greeleyville. In some strange algorithm of fate and physics, the pair of cars blew through the lonely country intersection at cross purposes at the same instant long after midnight, running two sides of the four-way stop. Five girls riding in one of the cars were killed. What was left of their Chevy Caprice was on display in front of the Esso station. The dead girls who still had faces were receiving makeup from Missy's mom.

"Natural," Missy overheard him remind Mona. "The job here is to make them look natural, make them have the color of a healthy person with a bad cold. Make their cheeks shine like a Christmas doll's." Her mom nodded and left down a hallway. Asa walked quickly in the opposite direction to talk with family members about the details of death. Missy took the back door outside.

For as long as she could remember, February had never been a clear month. Every day brought the same set of low-hugging, lead-gray clouds and a wind that cut through layers of sweaters. Anything exposed to the air looked naked. The poplars and oaks, the outbuildings behind the funeral home, even the set of black Cadillac hearses parked under the green carport looked barren and chilled. Spring was too far off to hope for, the past summer too far gone to be a decent memory anymore.

Clarence rubbed the back of one of the hearses with a chamois. The fender shined under his hand. He kept the cars washed and waxed, even in the winter.

"You better get ready," Missy called as she walked up.

"Those poor girls," he said. "I'm going to have my cars full of crying mommas and daddies. I hate it when young folks pass. It's so much different when somebody old dies, and it isn't such a surprise."

"They are my age," Missy said. "Were, I mean." She leaned a hip against the clean Caddy. Clarence cocked an eyebrow at her and she moved away quickly.

"But you don't go speeding through intersections with your eyes closed. Bunch of girls. Every one with her eyes closed. Never saw it coming. I heard they found beer cans. They were tempting death. Fellow in the other car walked away, I hear. God is a funny man."

Clarence rubbed harder. Missy could see the outlines of fast-moving clouds reflected on the fender.

"I don't speed. I don't go much of anywhere lately," Missy said.

"Where's that girl you run with? What's her name?" Clarence straightened up and put his hand to the small of his back, kneading an ache behind a hip.

"Angela."

"That's right, Angela. I haven't seen her around lately."

"She spends a lot of time going back and forth to Charleston to see her boyfriend." Missy wanted to change the subject. Talking about Angela and what she had in Charleston made Missy think she was missing out on something. "You know Skyles Huffman, don't you?" she asked.

Clarence cocked the eyebrow again. "Everybody knows Skyles, more or less. Known him for years."

"Have you seen him around lately?"

"Oh no, Skyles is off again on one of his trips. He's in that pickup somewhere soaking up some local color in another town.

Missy moved closer, dropped her voice though no one was around. "Where does he go when he goes away?" she asked.

Clarence smiled. "That's the funny thing. When he leaves, he has no idea where he'll end up. Just points that truck in one direction or the other and drives until he gets tired of moving. Eventually, he works his way back here. He'll pull in and ask me to help him wash the truck. He calls it cleaning the road off." Clarence's grin expanded into a chuckle. "He's an odd man. Smart too. Nobody knows much about him. The only things folks know are rumors. They say he was in Vietnam, so that's why he limps. They say he has Army money coming in every month. Some folks believe he's got family money from somewhere. The only thing for sure is he keeps traveling."

"So he just moves?"

"That's the truth." Clarence turned his head into the breeze a second before Missy heard the sound of wheels on the gravel drive. "Isn't there a name for when you talk about somebody and damned if they don't show up?"

Missy spun around, expecting to see Skyles bouncing in the truck cab. Instead, Angela wheeled her father's station wagon too fast in front of the carport, throwing dust and some gravel dangerously close to Clarence's cars. She jumped out and didn't wait for them to say hello, shotgunning sentences at the two of them through the cold air.

"Missy, damn, Missy. I have *got* to talk to you right now . . . oh, hey, Clarence. I need to talk. Can we go somewhere? Now?"

Clarence cleared his throat. "I need to ride out to the cemetery. Don't want to dig a hole in the wrong spot. Good day, ladies." He snapped some moisture off the chamois and stuffed it in his pocket.

Angela bounced on her toes like she needed a bathroom. "Missy, I got news, news you won't believe." Angela looked like a kid at a birthday party. She sucked air around her teeth, then glanced in a couple of directions to see if someone might be eavesdropping.

"Missy," she said, "I'm getting married." Angela looked as though she'd planned to announce it a different way, with a little more style, instead of just blurting it out.

"C'mon, don't play around," Missy said. "Craig can't marry you until he graduates or quits. Isn't that against the rules?"

"We can't wait on the damn Citadel. We're doing it in secret. He's here in town, right now. We're going to Manning to do it. Craig says they have a justice of the peace there who will marry anybody who can breathe and count out their money."

"You're pregnant!" Missy whispered.

"Oh, hell no. I'm just ready. We're just ready, I mean."

Missy knew she should hug Angela or say something that was right and proper. But she just stared. Angela didn't have a coat on. She shivered in the chill, her nose turning red. The station wagon's engine cooled, knocking and clanging as the parts settled down. Angela's lips quivered and her eyes watered. Her short hair blew into an unfamiliar part. She looked too fragile to be married. Missy thought, *If I hug her, I just might crush her.*

"Get in the car," she told Angela as she walked to the passenger's side.

Inside, with the engine on and the heater warming their feet, Angela told her more. The night before, Craig left school long after midnight, drove the couple of hours in the dark, and just like some lonely boy in a bad movie, climbed through her window before the sun came up. Angela said he smelled like the beach, and he took her clothes off while she was half asleep.

"I mean, it wasn't like I didn't know who he was. I'm not that crazy. I just didn't know what he was doing there."

Angela told Missy how the two of them whispered mouth-to-ear so Angela's parents would stay asleep. Craig said he wanted to marry her right away, the next day. They'd just keep it a secret from almost everyone until he graduated. He got down on his knees at the foot of her bed, held her hand, whispered up to her.

"I just had one question for him then. 'Why?' That seemed like the right thing to ask, don't you think? I mean, it was the one thing that popped into my head," Angela said, drumming her fingers on the steering wheel and pumping the accelerator on the Country Squire to keep the idling engine revved. "Know what his answer was?"

"I can't imagine," Missy said.

"He said, 'Love don't like to wait.' Isn't that something like a poem? Or a movie? 'Love don't like to wait.' When he said that, I all but melted into a puddle, Missy. I've never had anyone say anything like that to me, you know, something that sounds like it came from another world. I mean, boys will say things they don't mean, but I swear to God, there were tears in his eyes. I could see them in the dark."

Angela's voice broke down to a soft hum. Recalling the night before had warmed her as much as the heater.

"I'm happy for you," Missy said after a pause. "Really happy."

"I never felt like this, Miss."

"So, you're going today?" When the question hit Angela, her eyes popped open like she'd been pinched.

"Lord, I almost forgot. That's why I came by here. I want you to go with me to Manning. Be my maid of honor. I want you to stand up with me at the judge's. Craig's brother is going to be best man. I need somebody on my side. And I think y'all have to be witnesses or something. I'm not sure. I never did this before."

Missy's mouth went dry. She was glad for Angela, but she wasn't sure she wanted to be part of the whole affair. Hearing about it was as close as she needed to be. Angela reached across the seat and took her hand. "It'd mean a lot to us."

Angela and Craig were suddenly an *us*. A couple. A pair. Angela leaned in even closer. Missy swore the smell of the coast was still on her friend, drifting out of her hair or off her skin. She would say yes to Angela, she knew, and the second she did, she would feel completely alone.

Missy told most of the truth to Asa. She was going to Manning with Angela. He wanted to know why. "To see somebody," she said.

"I think it's a sad commentary when you have to go to a godforsaken place like Manning on a social call. Take care at those intersections," he said, nodding down the hallway where all the young girls lay dead. Missy couldn't tell if he was trying to be funny or fatherly.

"Would you let Momma know?" she called over her shoulder. "I'll be back later on tonight, probably real late."

Craig and Angela picked her up in front of the funeral home, and the three of them packed into the front seat of Craig's tiny Ford. Angela and Craig cuddled through downtown, past the high school and across the small bridge that signaled the beginning of the end of town and the start of the swamp. Missy leaned in the other direction, against the door, and watched them.

Angela and Craig were travelers from another country now, speaking another tongue, the way people in love do. Runaways in love. Missy closed her eyes as the car vibrated under her on bad tires and old shocks. Angela sang to the radio. The sounds got closer together, the rumble under her more intense. It was like a movie in fast motion, a record at the wrong speed. Missy felt sick for a minute, then the flips in her stomach quit. She shut her eyes to try and find some control. She needed control. She wasn't driving. She wasn't cuddling with anyone. She didn't feel like singing or listening to someone sing. She just didn't like being at the mercy of everything that hit her senses—the bumps and the stale smell of the beach and the warm air from the heater. Finally, it was too much to think about. Missy didn't turn to anyone in particular when she asked them to pull over and let her out.

Angela stopped her song. "What, Miss?"

"Let me out. I can't do it." Craig didn't pull his foot off the gas. If anything, he gave the car a little more juice.

"I mean it, let me out. I can't do it."

"What?" Angela's mouth was open. "I don't understand. You don't have to *do* anything. We're the only ones doing something."

"I don't know. I just can't. Nothing against you two. I just don't want to be part of this. Of anything." Missy saw they were approaching the turnoff to the abbey.

"You got to have a reason. You just don't do something without a reason," Craig said, looking away from the road for a second. "You got to have motivation."

Missy started to say something smart alecky about the military and motivation and drill sergeants, but she couldn't complete her thought.

She just said, "I just don't want to, that's all." She couldn't look at Angela. There was a second of silence as Craig took his foot off the gas.

"Just let her out then. I don't give a shit. We don't need her. We can find somebody else." Angela snuggled up to Craig and pointed straight ahead with her chin. "You're going to feel stupid about this later on," she said.

The car rolled to a stop on the weedy shoulder of the road. Missy started to say something as she stepped out of the car, but the door behind her closed quickly, slamming on the words still in her mouth. She watched them drive away, watched Craig flip her the bird from his open window. In seconds, they were out of sight. As far as Missy could tell, Angela never looked back.

Missy turned down three offers for rides—all from men she didn't recognize—on her way back to town and ended up walking the few miles to the funeral home. She had to admit, it was a relief to see the big house looming in the sunset, the outline of the trees and the roof crisp and defined in the chilly air. There were no lights on, either in the house or in Clarence's little apartment. Even the glow that perennially bloomed from the work area in the back had disappeared. *Everyone is taking a break from the dead,* Missy thought. She climbed the iron steps and noticed they weren't clanging any more. *Clarence must have finally tightened up the bolts,* she thought and smiled.

Inside the door, the air was still and cold, as if someone had turned the heat down. Missy inched along the back hall, feeling for the lights, bumping a still-unfamiliar table slightly as she moved through the darkness. Finally, she fingered the switch and flooded the hallway with light. She thought she heard a thump from somewhere, followed by a mumble.

Her own stomach growled, and she immediately assumed everybody else must be hungry, that her mother and Asa were probably getting ready to go out for dinner. *That must have been the noise.* She took a few steps down the hall, toward her mother's bedroom. The dull light from the opening flickered. Missy thought the light was the wrong color. She was about to stick her head in the open door to tell them she was home when she saw her mother pass, nude and slump-shouldered, in front of a small bank of candles on her dressing table.

Though she was still in the hall where her mother couldn't possibly see her, Missy backed into the shadows, her ear turned toward the open door. She heard Asa's voice.

"No," he said, "not enough. Go back again. Go on, now."

The clipped and harsh tone of Asa's baritone cut through the quiet. Once again, the light was broken by her mother passing from the bedroom into the adjoining bathroom. The shower came on and Missy heard her mother gasp for breath. Asa crossed in front of the candles and called into the bathroom, "And don't rub when you dry off. Just pat yourself down."

Over the sound of the shower running, Missy heard her mother catching and losing her breath. The water turned off, and in only a couple of seconds, her mother retraced her damp steps to the bedroom. Missy eased close enough to look at her. Mona was a long-waisted woman, still possessing a figure that sloped and curved at her hips. Her breasts drooped and waved slowly when she walked, in rhythm with her hair, which was dry and combed down in a much younger-looking fashion than she normally wore.

Missy stepped back into the darkness separating her from the candlelight. From where she hid, she could see the bed. Asa stood fully dressed, a shirt and tie, pants. Only the perfectly pressed suit coat was missing. The candles flickered from some slight, invisible breeze, and Asa glanced quickly toward the door, in the direction of the shadows. Missy froze, hoping she was deep enough in the darkness to remain unseen. He turned his attention back to Mona, satisfied they were still the only living souls in the funeral home.

Missy knew this was the second she should leave and retreat toward the front, then maybe make some awkward, intentional noise to let them know she was home. She suddenly thought of Angela and wondered if she was married by now, if she was on some sort of quick honeymoon. She shook that thought away. She kept her eyes open.

Mona lay on the bed, on top of the covers. Even from where she stood, Missy saw her mother shivering, her teeth clenched in an attempt to keep still. She lay flat. Asa stood over her, then adjusted her hands at her side. He brushed her bangs from her forehead, but it wasn't a compassionate gesture. It was clinical, practiced. Missy could tell it was something he did without thinking too much. But maybe she was wrong. Maybe it was as gentle and thoughtful as he got.

"Perfect," Asa said, putting his hand on her thigh. Mona shivered again.

Missy had already bypassed her chances to leave. She was too far into the story now, far enough that she wanted to see how it ended. She wondered if she should burst in, but she had no idea what was happening. When she was a kid, she had never seen her mother and father in bed, other than for sleeping. A few times, she'd heard bumps in the night that she chalked up to limbs in the wind or a bored cat. Never anything more. But this, this was about to be more, but it wasn't her mother, really. It was someone who refused to talk, someone who sipped vodka and took showers cold enough to steal breath.

"Don't you move," Asa said. "Don't you dare move a muscle." He took down his suit pants and his underwear, then spread Mona's stiff legs. She turned her head slightly to the side, but he snatched it back straight with one hand. "I said don't move. You're dead, remember?" he hissed. "You are dead."

With his shirt and tie still tight around his neck, Asa entered Mona with a quick shudder and began to move too fast, too soon. Mona stared white-eyed and unblinking above his shoulder, toward the shadows waving on the ceiling, while he groaned into her cold shoulder. Missy watched until it was safe to walk away, her empty stomach lurching. She snuck back the way she'd come, back down the now-quiet iron stairs, then ran behind one of the clean Cadillacs under the carport. She squinted her eyes shut and dry heaved onto the cement behind the rear fenders until she almost passed out. When she opened her eyes, she could see the candles still flickering in a couple of the windows above the funeral home.

The next morning, the morning after Missy retched over the cement drive, the same two faces sat across from her, as always, eating their breakfast. There was small talk from Asa. He wanted to know about Manning and what time had Missy gotten in the night before. Her mother looked across the top of her orange juice, which was no doubt fortified with a splash of vodka. Mona's empty, gray expression caught none of the bright, early-morning light that slanted through the blinds in the tiny breakfast nook.

When she let Asa's questions pass overhead without an answer, Missy suddenly understood why her mother had ceased simple conversation since her honeymoon. *It is so damn easy to be quiet.* It took so little energy and only a small degree of willpower. She understood. At that point, talk was trivial, a waste of good air. Missy looked at her mother and tried to make her own eyes go blank, the same way her mother's had. Only when she heard the tires on gravel outside did she glance away, in time to see the cab of Skyles's dirty pickup roll by on its way to the carport. The rumble from his exhaust shook the windows where they ate and stared at each other without talking, the only sound the heat turning on and lukewarm air beginning its rush through the vents.

6.

The trips with Skyles began early that same morning. From where they ate their silent breakfast, they heard the gravel crunching beneath his tires as he wheeled the pickup down the drive. Missy went to the side window to spy. Through the glass she heard the muffled dialogue between Clarence and Skyles.

"The prodigal man. You have returned one more time," Clarence said.

Missy watched Skyles slide awkwardly out of the truck. "Got to wash some of the road off, Clarence. Got a hose?"

"Oh, you know what I have. All I do here is wash cars and dig holes."

In a few minutes, Clarence and Skyles were soaping the fenders of the red pickup and wire-brushing the tires until they shone a dull black again. The runoff of suds and water cut a wandering path down the drive toward the walkway that led to the swimming pool. Missy no longer heard them, their voices no more than mumbles on the air, but she could tell from the sounds that they were happy, and after the previous night, she longed for happy.

She walked to the carport, dragging her feet in the gravel to make a little extra noise, trying to appear as though she weren't sneaking. They caught sight of her in the middle of a good laugh. Clarence quieted immediately and turned his attention to the lathered rear quarter panel. Skyles kept on giggling until he stopped to take a breath.

"Well hello, Miss Missy Belue," he said. "Grab a rag and get busy."

"You're doing just fine," Missy said. "Except right there. You missed a spot, Clarence." Clarence's brow furrowed, and he cocked his head at the paint job. Skyles smiled at Missy.

"I've been in Florida. It's still warm there. Bugs all over my grill. You know, they got more bugs per square mile in Florida than any other place in the lower forty-eight states. Now, Alaska, they give Florida a run for their bug money. Alaska mosquitoes are the size of butterflies."

"Really?" Missy said.

"I wouldn't lie. I came home to wash the bugs off and mellow out for a while. You and your friend been back to the abbey?" Skyles looked her in the eyes. She wasn't used to being watched while she tried to think up answers to questions.

"I've been by the turnoff. No closer than that though."

"Man, I should've told you to go out there. Somebody's got to keep those brothers in line. You don't keep an eye on them, they start sucking eggs and try to convert all the chickens into Christians. Ain't that right, Brother Clarence?"

"God loves the chicken, too." Clarence dropped his rag in the pail of dingy water and reached for the hose. Skyles and Missy stepped back while he thumbed the end of the hose and rinsed the truck.

"Ain't a trace of Florida left on her," Skyles said. "You want to help me dry her off?" he asked Missy. She glanced around for some towels but didn't see any.

"Sure. Hand me a towel."

"Towel?" he said. "Just hop in."

Missy didn't understand. She wasn't sure how to dry the truck from the inside. She slid into the passenger's seat. The cab of the pickup smelled like the inside of a refrigerator after a long vacation. The odors hovered somewhere between rancid and exotic, and only a brave, determined nose could tell which. She thought she caught a hint of perfume and whiskey, mixed somewhere with a top note of old sweat. There was a cooked hot-grease odor, carrying the memory of onion rings or fries, and the smell of damp wool hung heavy in the air. Though it wasn't cluttered with objects, Missy imagined a good deal of the known world was floating around in Skyles's truck.

Clarence was already wringing out the wet rags as they drove by. Skyles cranked his window down and called out, "Thanks, now. I'll see you in a day or so. I'm staying around a while, I believe."

"You'll be gone soon enough," Clarence said, flashing a smile at them, his silver tooth catching some random light.

A quarter mile outside of town, Skyles said, "This is how I dry her off," and punched the accelerator. They'd left town, crossed the river onto a rough two-lane, where the speed limits rose and the houses disappeared. The truck lurched and tried to keep up with the thin whine of the engine. In a few seconds, they bounced down the swamp highway, somewhere in the neighborhood of sixty. The seat under Missy vibrated as though it had shaken loose from its bolts. "Look there," Skyles said above the sound of the engine. He pointed at the hood.

The round beads of water danced up the faded paint, pushed by the wall of air, shimmering with the rumble of the tires. Then the droplets splayed away into nothing when they got close to the windshield. In four or five miles, the hood shone dull red, and there wasn't a drop of water left on the truck.

Skyles slowed to the speed limit. "Beats having to rub her down with one of those chamois cloths. Clarence can't understand why I waste gas just to dry her off. Seems to me, spending all that energy rubbing is the waste. You will burn up a helluva lot more calories with a chamois. I wonder how many you burn washing a car?" He rubbed his beard and swung the truck onto the road that led to the abbey.

"Got time for a little monk watching?

"Not really."

Time was, of course, the one thing Missy had a surplus of. Skyles knew she was lying.

"Just where do you have to be?"

"Home," she said.

"Distractions, girl. I told you they were coming. You need to learn how to escape."

"Look, I don't know you all that well, but you seem to make everything into some kind of earth-shaking event. You got some kind of weird philosophy about every little thing. Some people call distractions *life*, you know. Just getting by. Going to the store, arguments, fixing meals. I don't call those distractions. It's just the way it is. You and your snake and your monks and your truck. What are those? Seems to me, you're about the most distracted person in the world. You just don't sit still long enough to realize it."

Missy stopped for a breath and Skyles grinned at her. It was the most she'd said at one time in months. He reached under the seat and pulled out his canteen. He took a long sip from the tiny spout.

"You always talk in chunks like that? Lord, you do have some energy running around inside there, I'll give you that." He chuckled into the canteen and took the two-rut into the woods toward the abbey.

The rides became ritual.

Every couple of days, Skyles rolled into the funeral home and washed his truck—with Clarence's help—then he and Missy dried it off in the wind, always ending up in the woods above the abbey. Asa never seemed to mind that Skyles showed up and used his water and soap, and Missy never asked if his appearances were something new or a long-standing tradition. She simply didn't care to find out, especially if it meant having to talk to Asa.

When they were together, they had conversations while Skyles sipped on his canteen. Missy never saw him drunk or out of control, just more thoughtful, it appeared, with the whiskey. Fueled with alcohol, his philosophies expanded, became more universal. Most of them were based on the places he'd been and the people he'd known or the things he'd read in magazines and newspapers, usually local papers from the towns he passed through. Missy loved the talk. The sound of his voice and the tales of his travels hypnotized her, let her drift a little.

One afternoon, he tried to hold her hand, and she pulled it away. He smiled and winked, and five minutes later, he tried again. This time she slapped his wrist like a grade-school teacher. He winked again. The third time, she gave up and let him stroke her palm with fingers that felt slick like the surface of a magnolia leaf, and he told her half a story about driving on the beach at Daytona. The story didn't really have an ending.

They both lived with that for a time, hand-holding and the steady beat of stories stroked away on her palm. It was safe enough, she convinced herself. When he slid over in the seat one afternoon to kiss her, she didn't move, didn't respond, only shut her eyes and breathed in the new, sharp smells clinging to his beard, the ones she'd never been close enough to detect. She tasted the sharp bite of the whiskey in his mouth. She thought, *I am moving fast toward someplace I have never been.*

Other than that early slap on the wrist, Missy never said no to Skyles. He told her that he was just one of her distractions, and she was born to have them. "It's the most down-to-earth fate you can find," he whispered. "I can stop this anytime I want, you know."

"No, you can't," she said, taking his hand and linking her fingers between his. That was the moment the two of them moved from the tailgate to a sleeping bag beneath the camper top. Missy let her cousin, two or three times removed, take her away for a few, rushed minutes.

While he was inside her, she did not think about his age or hers. She imagined she was in another country, where the weather was different and the language was so fast and foreign, she couldn't follow conversations. There were no monks nearby in her daydreams, no chickens, no ice-cold women lying still for their husbands. There were instead places where she was a stranger that everybody liked.

It didn't hurt her. It didn't bore her. She knew there were things in life more terrible she could fall victim to. The rides with Skyles were the only times when she didn't have to think about the next day or the next week, and she only had to think about those other countries, those imaginary places. And that made Missy Belue happy for a few minutes.

Missy's excursions with Skyles snapped her mother to attention, even in the midst of her boozy state of mind. Mona and Asa had probably guessed what Missy was doing when she drove away with Skyles a couple of times a week, but they never came straight out and named it.

"I'm all for families maintaining a closeness," Asa said, "but Skyles Huffman does have a reputation as somewhat of a rounder, you know." Missy had never heard anyone use the word *rounder*. Asa sounded like an actor in an old black-and-white movie.

Her mother was more direct. "He's your cousin, for goodness sake, Missy, and he's probably old enough to be your father. Think about how that looks for us around town."

She knew Asa and her mother were fishing for answers, for better information, poking around with stick-sharp assumptions, hoping to jab a hot, raw nerve somewhere. Her mother had done this before, probed into secret places about boys—always boys, never men—and what her daughter did with them. And to her credit, Missy hadn't done much. She was certainly not unfamiliar with what could happen in the back of a car or on a den sofa when the parents went to bed, but she had never been serious with any of the boys at her tiny high school. She found them boring. Most of them had never been anywhere or seen anything. They were more interested in deer season than the future.

When Asa and Mona tried to shake information out of her, Missy didn't flinch. She said she and Skyles were only riding around, wasting time. If they persisted, she told them she was nearly eighteen, and she could do what she wanted, and if they didn't like it, she could always move out. Asa did most of the talking now that her mother was limiting her daily word count.

"Perhaps you could concoct some useful things to do, instead of moping around your room or doing God knows what with that Huffman fellow. You could go to tech school in Florence or help out around here. I think we've been more than understanding since your father died—sorry to bring that up, Mona. But that's all past now. There are plenty of options for a girl like you."

A girl like me, Missy thought. *A girl like me.* A girl who closed her eyes tight and tried to squeeze a picture of the future into her mind's eye, even as she smelled the funeral home stench seep through the floorboards, and the only things she saw were images from the past skittering behind her eyes. Scenes from when she was little. Like the Christmas she caught her father playing Santa, putting together her new bicycle. The time at the beach when they fell asleep on a float and the lifeguards had to rescue them. Always her and always her daddy, always years ago. She couldn't remember what her mother looked like before the funeral, could barely remember what her father looked like after it. Missy Belue was losing things without even trying.

A girl like me is lost, Missy thought. *That's what I'm like now.*

"I'm feeling a little overwhelmed to do anything important," she said. Asa and her mother sighed and let her be. Missy discovered she enjoyed frustrating them, enjoyed being cryptic and vague.

Every trip down the street with Skyles in the pickup, every time out the swamp road and through the woods to the rise above the abbey, Missy learned more about him. He was, *indeed,* her third cousin, the product of some marriage on the skinny, outer branches of the family tree. She discovered how restless he was, how the only time he was happy and not moving was when he watched the brothers come and go on the grass strips between the giant chicken houses at the abbey.

They spied on the monks gathering eggs or cleaning coops. In the trees, Skyles told her the stories about the trips he'd taken. Actually, they were half-stories, unfinished snippets. For instance, he'd say, "One time I parked on the side of the road in Montana to catch a few winks, and when I woke up, the truck was covered by a snow drift a half story high."

And that would be the end of it. No details concerning how he dug himself out or who rescued him. He gave up only selected bits and pieces of his past, never a complete picture. Nothing about how he always had money to fill his gas tank. Nothing about the limp. He painted incomplete canvases. And it bothered her at first, but with each trip to the abbey and each half-story, the bother faded away. Missy Belue began to enjoy filling in the gaps for herself. Mystery wasn't necessarily a bad thing.

One afternoon under the pines above the abbey, Skyles told Missy he was leaving—not permanently—just for a few days, maybe weeks, depending on which way he headed.

"Need to put some foreign dirt on the truck," he said.

She didn't hesitate. "Let me go with you." Skyles stared out the bed of the pickup, toward the tops of the trees.

"It's traveling around, Miss. It's just going and going. You'd get bored of it." He reached around for his canteen.

"More boring than living in a funeral home?"

Skyles had not bothered to get to know her at all. If he'd poked around, if he'd asked, he would have discovered that moving was Missy's passion. Ever since she was a child and her father took the family on those summer trips in the station wagon, she'd longed for a time when she could put her own miles behind her.

But Kingstree was one of those small, motherly Southern towns that didn't give up its young easily. She and Angela and all their friends had geography and tradition working against them. Very few escaped. Like most people who lived in Kingstree, Missy knew there existed a kind of community incest tiny Southern towns practiced— intermarriage inside the city limits between the hometown boys and girls.

Oh sure, there were some escape routes. College. Or out-and-out bravery. But for most, for those worn down by years of tradition, especially the girls in town, the situation was repeated over and over.

Find a boy in high school, get married and pregnant—or vice versa—soon after graduation, and spend most of your days wondering how life might have turned out somewhere else, with somebody else. But still, leaving was all she and her friends talked about since they were old enough to gossip.

They would sit parked in a car somewhere and smoke the few cigarettes they'd stolen and imagine the trips they would take and the towns they would turn upside down. They talked about the men they would discover who would call them secret names and whisper to them from across a room. It didn't matter how many school field trips they went on or how many family vacations in the station wagon Missy took. Those didn't count. The idea was to get away all alone and stay away long enough to become mysterious or legendary.

Then, like strange magic, at some point they just stopped talking about leaving Kingstree. They realized that most of the dreams they'd dreamed would never be worth much more than the value of lost memories, not unlike old high school yearbooks. No matter how often they left, they always came back to a house they inherited or to the only man they slept with in high school or to a family that wouldn't let them go. Angela was a perfect example. She ran away to get married. And came back to Kingstree the same night.

"I promise you, I won't get tired of getting away from here," Missy told Skyles. She hated the way he sometimes treated her like an elementary school kid.

"Let me ask you something else," he said. "You really think you can come back here again, if you were to run off in this truck?"

"Maybe I don't want to come back."

"Well, hell, I do! I always come back. I take you with me, I'm liable to be hung when I show up again."

Missy grinned. "If they haven't hung you by now, you're pretty safe, I'd say. Nobody'd bat an eye. Nobody'll miss either one of us. Except Momma, and she doesn't talk anymore. Asa doesn't give a flip. It won't cut into his business any, and that's all he cares about."

Skyles stared down toward the buildings, watching one of the brothers carry a chicken under his arm. "You reckon he's gonna wring that chicken's neck? I've never seen anybody do that," he said. Missy knew he was stalling, gathering his thoughts. But instead of a long speech, he came out with one question.

"Why in the world should I take you on the road with me?" He paused and waited for the answer. Missy thought for a moment, then crept to the verge of telling him everything. About Angela and her secret marriage, about seeing her mother and Asa in bed. About how the smell of the funeral home got in her hair, and she had to wash it out every night. About the tackle box full of makeup her mother used for the dead faces. All of the reasons why staying was more unbearable than running away. Instead, she just said, "Because you couldn't stand to leave me behind," and the second she said it, she knew it was the kind of thing a woman would say to get a man to do whatever she wanted. She felt grown up, instantly.

Down in the abbey yard, the same brother crossed to the chicken house, the bird pecking lightly at the robe covering his arm.

A few days later, Skyles rested his hand heavily between Missy's thighs, but she kept her mind off the fingers by watching the beads of water shimmy up the hood. By now, she knew just how fast and how far they would have to drive before the truck was blown completely dry.

"Your momma is gonna be one pissed white woman," Skyles said to her, but he didn't sound afraid. She kept her eyes on the road.

"She won't worry for long," Missy said. "I'll call her in a couple days. Tell her what's going on." *I'll call from somewhere*, she thought. *Wherever.* Because she had no idea where she was headed with Skyles. There was no map, no magic marker, no compass. Missy only knew she was finally making new tracks.

She and Skyles reached the edge of the swamp. His fingers crawled around between her legs. The cypress trees and their collection of knobby, brown cypress knees stood in the cola-colored water just off the shoulder of the road. She felt a finger work to the top of her jeans, then slide inside just a bit. The gray Spanish moss hung off the branches like old faded curtains drying on a line. Skyles gave the truck a little gas, and they hit a couple of dips in the road, then passed over the bridge that spanned a boggy pothole of black water. The men fishing from the bridge waved without looking up.

Soon after the bridge, they came to the turnoff for the abbey. Skyles slowed to a roll, and the last few beads of water shimmered in place on the hood.

"Last chance. You want out here, somebody'll be along soon enough," he said. "This is as far as we ever gone, you know. Me and you. On this road."

She opened her knees a little, sucked in her stomach, and Skyles slipped a few extra fingers inside the new space that opened up. He just left them there. "We got an agreement. I'm ready," she said. Skyles eased the truck up to speed, nursing the engine to an even whine.

Missy Belue didn't know how to act at that moment. She could've cried or laughed or yelled out the window or something, anything. In two weeks, she'd be eighteen. She wanted to tell Skyles, tell anybody for that matter. She had a bizarre hope that her mother had foreseen this whole escape and had gotten a message to Skyles. *Be nice to my girl and don't forget her birthday.* Eighteen was important, but only to her. To Skyles, it was all relative—miles, years, distractions. All relative. She decided to forget how old she really was.

Missy watched the last drops of water make their way up the hood. By the time they hit the turnoff to the interstate, Skyles's truck was showroom dry and shining. She closed her eyes and felt the road rumble beneath her.

7.

Skyles was never reluctant to let Missy take over the wheel, and that surprised her. She hadn't imagined him giving up control so easily. The day after they pulled away from Kingstree and headed west, Skyles rolled to a wide spot on the road's shoulder and lurched the pickup into park.

"Your shift," he said, motioning for her to take his place behind the wheel. He never asked if she actually knew how to drive. "This is different for me. I get to sleep while I move."

Missy had never driven long distances. Her longest trip behind the wheel was to the beach, maybe fifty or sixty miles, tops. Now, she was expected to handle the driving for hours at a time, she assumed, until the gas tank hit empty or the time came to stop for the night.

She always guessed she would enjoy driving for miles and miles on end, settling into the rhythms of the road, the way the front of the truck seemed to suck up the dotted lines in the middle of the asphalt, the way the hum of the tires created their own song. What she didn't predict was the hypnotic quality of the ride, how the steering wheel floated back and forth of its own accord, and the way Skyles's snoring on the other side of the cab sounded like it was magically in the same key as the rumble of the tires on the pavement, the two sounds blending into one continuous drone.

Skyles never turned on the dashboard radio when he drove. Rather than listen to music, he'd show off the latest tidbit of information he'd gleaned from some newspaper or magazine. But when she had the wheel, Skyles turned his chatter off. After several long pulls on his dented Boy Scout canteen, he fell quickly into a rattling sleep, his breath catching and gargling in his throat with every inhale and exhale. Missy was left with nothing to do but drift as the miles rolled by under her.

She wondered what her mother must be thinking. Mona would, of course, blame Skyles for everything. She might even toss out the word *kidnap*. She wouldn't give her daughter credit for the spunk required to leave town.

Other than the few times Mona and Asa interrogated Missy about her trips in the red pickup, she wasn't sure what, exactly, her mother *thought* about Skyles. He was family, but that didn't guarantee respect or love or allegiance. Yet, she couldn't remember her mother saying anything negative about him. However, Missy recalled, she wasn't saying much about anything lately. *Would Momma blame Skyles?* More likely, she would simply stay quiet and drink and bring the dead back to life a bit with her makeup kit.

If she or Asa bothered to investigate, Missy knew they'd be able to see that she'd left in a hurry. She stole Asa's GI duffel from the hall closet and ransacked her room, shoving everything she imagined she might need deep into the bag. The things she considered but ultimately rejected taking, she tossed over her shoulder, toward the center of the room. When she finished, the floor resembled the latter stages of a yard sale. She didn't pause to clean up, and now, safely on the road, behind the wheel, Missy wondered if the mess on the floor was an odd sort of goodbye note. Perhaps they could figure out how quickly and desperately she'd wanted to leave. She'd left a footprint—a carpet-framed collage of socks and panties and empty nail polish bottles and too-small belts and a tennis shoe missing its match.

While Mona would never blame her own daughter, Asa would have no trouble pointing a long, well-groomed finger in any direction he could think of. Missy imagined he would find fault with them all—Skyles, Missy and Mona. Ultimately, though, he would treat Mona not unlike one of his customers, someone who had just experienced the loss and sudden disappearance of someone close. Missy would be, in Asa's way of thinking, dead. And Mona needed to grieve a little. Missy hoped he would allow her mother that privilege.

The first time Missy daydreamed behind the wheel, a scene flickered in her head. And from that moment on, she could never completely flush it from her mind. She imagined:

Momma sitting on the couch, facing the window, staring at the gravel driveway leading away from the funeral home, the street leading into town. Momma sips her drink. Probably two sips.

"She won't be back," Momma tells Asa. He paces, blocking her view of the drive.

"They always come back," he says. "How can you be so sure she won't?"

"Mother's intuition." Momma fishes for a piece of ice with her fingers, peering through the window, sure her daughter is gone for good.

Missy was hungry, so she pulled into a Shoney's. They had been on the road for more than a week, and this particular day Missy had been behind the wheel since mid-afternoon while Skyles stretched out in the bed of the pickup among all of his camping gear. Through the screen partition, she heard him snoring away a canteen full of something clear and powerful. He tossed and turned, ignoring the occasional bumps or swerves in traffic, but woke up when the truck came to a halt.

A decent-sized crowd filled the Shoney's with its dull roar. Sour-faced waitresses balancing trays scurried around each other like ice skaters on the blade-edge of a disaster. Skyles bought a couple of newspapers from the row of machines near the double glass doors. While Missy scanned the menu or watched other people eat, Skyles poured over the articles, his pocketknife open and ready in his hand. A waitress approached the table, but Missy smiled her away.

"What is it exactly you're looking for?" she said when they had gone a good ten minutes without talking. She'd been curious about his newspaper habits, but never asked.

"Won't know until I come across one," he said without looking up.

"One what?" When he didn't answer, she decided not to press. Instead, Missy studied the crowd. The Shoney's hummed with restaurant sounds—clanking plates, silverware scrapes, mumbles. The loneliest customers sat on the isolated counter stools, the people who lingered over their meals and needed the waitress to talk to. Families were drawn to the shiny booths—mothers and fathers refereeing arguments between their kids as they tried to sneak in bites of food. A couple of kids appeared to be doing unsupervised laps around the restaurant, not a parent in sight. There were very few couples like themselves. That struck Missy as odd. *Only loners or families.* The people who occupied the space in between must have somewhere else to go for supper.

One of the kids running around loose, a blond boy with bone-white skin who looked to be no more than four or five years old, stopped suddenly at their table. He stared at Skyles's long beard, a salt-and-pepper gray, a different color than any other hair on his body. The boy turned to Missy.

"He ain't Santa Claus, is he?" he said. His voice had no fear in it. He wasn't old enough yet to know the trouble strangers could cause. Skyles paid him no attention.

"Yes," Missy said.

"No, he ain't," the boy came back quickly. "He ain't fat enough. He don't look jolly at all. And he's got hisself a ponytail." His eyes went back to the beard. Skyles raised his face from the paper and smiled at the boy.

"Nossir, my little man," he whispered. "I'm not Santa, but I'll tell you some special news." Skyles leaned in toward the kid. "I killed Santa and stole his beard. Santa's up in heaven now and all the reindeer are dead as doornails too." Then Skyles hissed snake-like into the boy's face.

The little boy cracked. The innocent confidence and the blood rushed away, leaving him even paler. He lost control of his legs and fell onto the stained, red Shoney's carpet, where he howled like a new puppy, a high-pitched siren sound that brought both a mother and father dashing from their hiding place behind the salad bar. They saw their son, collapsed in a weepy pile at the feet of a bearded man and his youngish girl companion.

Missy watched the parents approach. The mother was already reaching for her son. Missy shot a look at Skyles. "Why'd you tell him that?" she said.

"I can't stand the way children act," he said in a low voice. Then he got louder as he spun in his seat toward the parents. "Now, don't worry, folks. This little fella wiped out like Richard Petty on an oil slick. I think he's okay. Just a little embarrassed."

"Fell down?" the father asked. Missy knew his kind immediately. He would believe whatever seemed easiest. All Skyles had to do was give him a quick explanation he could chew on.

"Blew a tire, I'd say," Skyles said, smiling at the man, then calling to the boy. "Take care there, buddy." The mother pulled her son up by the arm and steered him away from the table.

Dad grinned right back at Skyles. "We're sorry he bothered you. He ain't caught up with his legs yet. He trips a lot when he ain't watching. Sorry. Didn't mean to disturb you two or anything."

Missy shook her head, and Skyles started to rise out of his chair. "Hey, we're not the kind to get disturbed easy. Y'all keep a good eye on him." The father was already making his way through the tables when he waved back over his shoulder. Skyles eased down in his chair and returned to his paper.

"You hate kids. And you lie to grown-ups." They had been on the road long enough now that Missy could accuse him of things.

"Parents are the dumbest breed of people alive," Skyles said. "Why would anybody want a child? Why would anybody want to change their life that much that quick? Now, back in the day, parents were smart about it—when they really needed kids, when there were beasts to fend off and crops to get in. Back when there was strength in numbers, parents were smart. Kids were labor. Parents turned dumb when they started having kids for no good reason at all. Kids are what's wrong with this country. You hear people say that kids are the future? That makes my stomach roll over. Goddamn nightmare's what it is. Kids are going to be the ruin of us all."

Missy had never heard Skyles talk about kids, one way or the other. And she'd never heard him go on about the state of the country. As far as she could tell, Skyles thought the country was simply a place to put roads, and as long as there were roads, he was a happy man. Missy had already learned that Skyles never hedged an opinion, surprising or not. And he didn't mind adding to it, embellishing his thoughts whenever he had the opportunity.

"It'd be best for the human race if we all just woke up on a rock one day and *was*. If we could begin life when we were twenty-four, the world would be a better place. Skip all that high school nonsense and puberty and what have you. Just start life with a full set of teeth and a full head of steam."

The waitress walked up to the table. She flipped back some used pages from her pad and waited, a good bit of her weight cocked to one hip.

Skyles smiled at her. When she returned it, he said, "Do you have any kids?"

She was expecting a food order, not a question. "Well, yeah," she answered. "Three. Oldest one is four, youngest eight months."

"Goddamn," Skyles said. "Give me a steak and baked potato. And burn the steak good." As she walked away, he spit like he had a fleck of something on his tongue. "Goddamn parents everywhere you look," he said.

This was how meals went on the road. When they sat down to eat, he would digest the fine print in the newspapers while she waited. She discovered soon enough what he looked for. It was information. Not news, necessarily, but facts that were absolutely unimportant yet completely memorable, at least the way his memory worked. Skyles

Huffman was self-taught at acting like he was borderline genius. Every day, he would plow through papers and magazines, clipping out the trivial fillers that lay between the columns of news and tragedy. The more useless the information, the better. That's what he trimmed out with his pocket knife.

He stuffed his shirt pocket with tiny scraps of paper that told him the number of tires Americans dispose of each year or the number of times a human heart beats in an average lifetime. He knew how often humans shed their mucus membranes and how quickly the enamel on teeth thinned and how flying insects were able to dodge raindrops during a rainstorm.

On the rare, rare occasions when they stayed in a motel instead of the truck bed, he watched game shows like Jeopardy and wrote down the interesting facts in a tiny notebook that he also kept in his shirt pocket. And he would commit them all to memory, eventually. Missy imagined the inside of his head resembled a cluttered but well-stocked file cabinet. He gathered bits of information like some people collected pieces of string or bottle caps. He held on to things most folks would cast away, stuck them up in his brain, and pulled one out when he needed it. That's why he devoured newspapers.

To a lot of people, he probably appeared too smart or too mysterious to be dumb. With the beard and the way he walked stooped over like a man with some heavy years on his back, he might have been some sort of a vagabond prophet.

Missy had grown used to the stares when they traveled where people could see them. Skyles, because of his beard and his gait, and her because of her flat feet and height—*willowy*, her mother had called her when she went through her growing spurts. She tended to forget she was a female until Skyles reminded her with a hand between her legs in the middle of the night or nature reminded her in the middle of nowhere, miles from a tampon.

But they were on the road, and that's what she wanted. So she washed when she remembered to, shaved her legs when she could, and the rest of the time, she just tied back her hair and let people whisper. Missy thought she was too young to waste time worrying about men and women she'd never see again.

Skyles always told her, "The world ain't but one out-of-whack circle. People will show up a second time. Somewhere. What you leave behind will always circle back and bite you in the ass eventually." She told him she only had the time and energy to worry about the people she was absolutely sure she'd look at more than once, and she hadn't met many of them.

He began to share his trivia with her. "Here you go," he would say. "Here's an AP story outta North Carolina. *Cat Survives 37 Days in a Vending Machine.* Of course, they don't tell you how the cat got in the machine or why he didn't come rolling out when somebody bought a Diet Pepsi. Doesn't matter. What matters is that a cat can live on nothing but air for over a month. That is something to note."

He would never consult a tabloid. No trash reading for Skyles. Only real newspapers would do. *New York Times. The Washington Post.* And local papers. The more trivial the fact, the better—the ones printed in the leftover spaces. "Uh-huh, here we are," he'd say. "Did you know that ninety-five percent of all household dust is in fact human epidermis? Flaky skin floating around a house. Now, who would've thought that?"

Once, when they were camped at a state park somewhere in Florida, Missy took the truck into the nearest town while Skyles was in the shower. She occasionally made runs to the drugstore or to the grocery store, always alone and always while Skyles was occupied with something else. She loved being the stranger in strange place, a walking mystery, especially to people sitting in front of barbershops or on front porches, folks who prided themselves on knowing every living soul in the county.

Even when she wasn't with Skyles, her height and butt-length hair were usually enough to stop people in their tracks. And while it had normally been long and straight, her hair took on a new texture on the road because it was so often windblown through the open windows of the truck. Plus, she washed it a lot less frequently now. Missy loved to watch herself walk by store windows. She thought she looked years older than she really was. She knew she'd regret that feeling one day. But for the moment, having the illusion of age was worth enjoying.

One day in a small town, she stopped at a bookstore. Not one of the chains, but an independent seller. The uneven, wooden floors squeaked when Missy walked in. She disturbed a cat sleeping on the stacks, and it jumped down to purr to her shins. Between the displays of Bibles and Stephen King in the window, Missy found a thin book on sale called *10,000 Facts You'll Forget To Remember.* When she plucked the book off the shelf and got it in her hands, Missy spent about a half second deciding it was the perfect gift for Skyles and about another twenty minutes reading the small entries on the pages. It was knowledge compiled with Skyles Huffman in mind.

While the orange cat whorled between her legs, Missy learned the body temperature of a hummingbird. How fast toenails grew. Why some rivers flowed backwards. There was even a section discussing the average duration of sexual intercourse and the average cost of a prostitute in several different countries.

Missy knew she wouldn't recall an eighth of what she'd just read. She could never retain facts like that. But this was the type of information that cost Skyles the price of a few newspapers each day. And here it was, in one place. With the money she was supposed to use for soap and razor blades, Missy bought the book, and even read some of it while she waited at stoplights on her way out of town.

That night, after they ate a couple of hot dogs from a little rotisserie inside the KOA campground store, she presented Skyles his book. No fanfare or anything. She just handed it to him. On the inside cover, she'd written in careful, blocked printing, *The number of minutes a honeybee sleeps every day is on p. 67. xxoo, Missy.*

Later, they sat in the folding chairs near the fender of the truck. Skyles studied the book under the dim mechanic's light that ran off the cigarette lighter. He didn't say a word. The milky glow cut into the lines on his face, brought the years to the surface. He looked from the book to Missy and back again. He thumbed the pages before he settled on one section and read for a couple of minutes, leaving them both in silence.

Missy couldn't tell if he was touched or happy or confused, and when he finally said, "Interesting. Uh-huh," she was even less sure how he liked the gift. He cleared his throat and stretched. "I'm going to be up a while, you know?" He patted the cover of the book and smiled at Missy.

Before she fell asleep, she peeked through the window of the camper top. There was Skyles at the picnic table, his hair pulled into a ponytail, scanning back and forth across the pages like he was watching a slow tennis match. He was busy with something she had done for him, and it was the happiest she had felt since they'd pulled away from Kingstree.

Early the next morning, Missy woke up cold and alone in the pickup bed. Skyles wasn't beside her, and he wasn't outside checking the oil or the pressure in the tires. She grabbed the cleanest-looking towel she could put her hand on and a sliver of soap and headed for the bathhouse, a drab, cement building in the center of the KOA property. It was a very democratic placement of the facilities, and it was one thing you could count on at a KOA. Everybody had to walk the same distance to relieve themselves.

Very few people had ventured out early for their morning constitutionals. It was still chilly for the time of year. When she passed the screen door on the men's side of the building, Missy heard the shower running just on the other side of the block wall. It was unusual for Skyles to be up before the night completely burned away, and even more unusual for him to shower so early in the week, but Missy felt sure it must be him in there, under the hot water. While she listened, she slowed her pace a bit, her head cocked toward the sound. She bumped into the tall, wire-mesh trash can just outside the door, took a quick, awkward sidestep, and reached with the closest hand to keep the can upright. She didn't want noise or a mess in the early-morning quiet.

There, tucked under a few dirty paper plates and some crushed soda cans, was *10,000 Facts You'll Forget To Remember*. The book had been thrown away, and someone had made a half-hearted attempt to hide it, burying it under whatever was handy in the trash can. Missy stared for a few seconds, thinking how strange it was that someone else in this KOA campground in Florida happened to have the exact same volume of trivial information. *Must be a real popular title in that little bookstore,* she thought.

The water turned off on the other side of the wall, and the sudden lack of noise snapped Missy back to the moment, back to the truth. Skyles had trashed the book, tossed it away like one of those paper plates or an old hot dog wrapper. She reached down, fished through the rubbish and grabbed the book, hurrying before Skyles walked out of the shower. A huge, still-moist mustard stain smeared across the front of the book, camouflaging a portion of the title. A few zeros were covered by the yellow. Now, it seemed there were only *10 Facts You'll Forget To Remember.*

On a rough wooden bench in her side of the bathhouse, Missy opened the book and could see where Skyles had cut out several random facts inside the pages. He'd removed a few dozen entries. The rest were either uninteresting or old news to him. And it didn't matter to Missy that he'd kept some of the information. In the end, he'd trashed the book, chucked the gift she'd given him. She couldn't recall the last time she'd given a gift to someone who wasn't in her family. Then, she remembered. Skyles was family.

Missy took a quick shower and tucked the book into the waist of her pants. Skyles never brought the book up in conversation and neither did she. She hid the book deep inside her duffel bag. Every once in a while, when she got the chance—when he was passed out or when the light in a campground bathhouse was strong enough—she secretly read a dozen or so facts, as though she were loading up ammunition for a battle she sensed she would have to fight one day. He never saw her reading, and he never knew she was stockpiling trivial information. He simply went back to his newspapers at every truck stop and diner they landed in, and she watched him carefully, wondering what he really thought of her.

8.

On the front side, a bright color photograph of a man wearing a white lab coat, waving a double-handful of wriggling rattlesnakes. Behind him, a gaggle of wide-eyed children three or four deep watching, their hands over their open mouths. A couple of kids running for their parents. And way, way in the background, out of focus, parents pushing their kids to the edge of the snake handler's pit.

Scrolled across the top left corner of the postcard in yellow type was the phrase, *FLORIDA . . . REPTILE HEAVEN*. The man holding the snakes looked like the Laurel half of Laurel & Hardy. On the backside of the card, Missy wrote small, neat letters, small enough to fit a lot into the blank space.

Momma,

We're far enough away, you can go ahead and forgive me for what happened. You may have even stopped thinking about me, but I think about you all the time. There's things I don't miss all that much, but I miss you every time I wake up. Don't waste energy on blame. I am well and will probably want to come home one day, but that day is still a ways off. I'll call you when I can. We're leaving Florida soon. I hope you are happy.

Love Missy.

When Missy read the message to herself, it sounded so empty and hollow she thought it would make an echo when someone finally said the words out loud. She actually tried that, too, and she thought some of it sounded snippy. She hadn't meant that at all. She just wanted Mona to know that she was alive, that Skyles wasn't a crazy ax murderer that would leave her in pieces on the roadside. Missy had learned he was fairly harmless, and she wanted to give her mother some vague notion of her whereabouts. That instinct was her dad's fault, him and his thing about maps and compasses and geography.

Skyles handed her money when she needed it. She still didn't know where or how he obtained the cash or when, if ever, it would run out. But when they needed food, he sent her into a town in the red truck with enough to cover the costs. And when she wanted a couple of stamps or some personal items, he never refused her.

Missy always enjoyed those excursions into a town. She opened the windows on the truck, turned up the radio and pretended she had a full tank of gas and somewhere to go. At the stoplights, people gave her quick stares, trying to decide what kind of girl would tool around in a big, red pickup. The young boys in their loud cars seemed to be the most interested in her, cigarettes balanced on the edges of their smiles.

Skyles made solo trips too. He'd leave Missy at the campground with a lawn chair and a magazine, and he'd take off for a few hours at a time. He always returned before sunset with his canteen full and a blank look on his face, as though he'd done something quick and painless that wiped his memory clean.

Once, when Skyles pulled in from one of his trips, Missy asked him where he'd been before the engine had a chance to cool. He said, "It's nothing worth mentioning."

"I'm curious. You can't really blame me. I'd like to know why you left me alone for so long."

"Wasn't that long really." Skyles still sat behind the wheel. He reached down and turned the key to *accessory* and the radio came on. It was a country station. That seemed weird to Missy. He never listened to the radio when the two of them traveled.

"You don't have to be scared to tell me." The second she let the words out, she knew he would turn on her with those eyes that could flash anger in an instant. Instead, he surprised her. He smiled so broadly his beard moved.

"Fear has nothing to do with it, honey. I'm just off making some secrets. You and me are together almost every minute of the day. If I didn't have some secrets of my own, you and I wouldn't have a thing left to do but turn the truck back toward South Carolina and head for your momma's. Secrets grease the wheels so they keep spinning, dear."

Missy watched him while he talked, listening to the music fill the cab of the truck. His smile lingered. There was nothing false about it. He was telling her the absolute truth as he knew it. He was out doing something he wanted to keep from her, something that dangled just out of her reach.

"So, if you aren't scared, maybe you're embarrassed," she said.

"Lord, girl, you just don't get it, do you?" Skyles reached across the seat for the canteen and took a drink. He tipped it toward her, offering her a sip, which she refused, like always. The deejay started to give the forecast for the next day, so Skyles stopped what he was saying. He was fascinated by weather. They were calling for clear skies, milder temperatures.

"Get what?" she said.

"Get that you sure think you are something, traveling around with me and doing whatnot. But you know, you aren't everything. If you were everything to me, you'd be dangerous." Skyles smiled and took another sip, then turned off the radio. "We'd have trouble then. But there ain't no forecast for trouble on my horizon. I can tell you that for sure." It was getting late, and inside the gathering darkness of the cab, Missy couldn't tell if Skyles was still smiling.

Later that night, after they had eaten cold sandwiches and some grapes that were beginning to get too soft, they lay on the sleeping bags inside the bed of the truck. Outside Missy heard a couple of people crunching down the gravel road toward the bathhouse or back to their camper trailers. A frog somewhere near the tree line bellowed in the dark, and the rest of the frogs, most with higher-pitched croaks, would join in for two or three minutes. Missy wished she could see some of the stars.

Skyles's breathing was so measured and slow she thought he was already asleep. Suddenly, he rustled and slipped his hand over her breast. She blocked it with her elbow. It was the first time in four months on the road that she refused him anything.

His other hand inched between her legs, so she turned slightly, making the angle impossible for his fingers to make any sort of progress. Skyles snorted, then said, "Something wrong." It was not a question.

"Not really." She imagined their voices floating in the thick air under the camper top. She wondered if the frogs could hear them. He tried again for the breast. She blocked again.

"I'm too old to play games, Missy Belue."

"Well, I'm just learning about a few games. You got some secrets. I've got a few things I'm going to keep to myself, too."

Missy wished she could see her own face as she talked. She liked the sound of her words and thought that she probably looked older saying them. It wasn't the kind of lines that her friends used.

"Suit yourself," Skyles said and turned toward the sidewall.

"Suits me just fine." Missy wanted the last word, and that night Skyles let her have it.

They left Florida. Skyles told her he needed a changing of the seasons, so he had Missy turn the truck north for a couple of hours, then west through the Panhandle, followed by another turn north into Alabama. He said they would keep driving until they got to mountains with blooming dogwoods. Two days later, they found some, in the northwest corner of the state, near the Tennessee border.

"In Florida, the damn place is so flat, they put up towns anywhere they want to," Skyles said as she picked her way along county roads eroding and cracking on the shoulders. "In this kind of country though, the only smart place to build towns was in the valleys, mostly at one end or the other. That's where all the good stuff is, at the ends."

"You've been here before." Missy said.

"Not this particular place, but one just like it. It isn't easy living on the side of a hill. You got to come off the hill sometime. These people have energy." He nodded as if to say he'd just given the final word on the subject. "You see a place to eat, pull us over, okay?"

Missy nodded, but doubted they'd find anything soon. It didn't feel like the road they were traveling could support a restaurant. She'd seen only a couple of cars and an empty logging truck since they'd been on this highway that skirted the side of the mountain. Missy's head was beginning to feel light, and a shiver went through her bones, carrying a chill with it. She wondered if she had aspirin in her duffel.

A yellow sign warned them of a crossroads ahead. Around the next curve, they both saw the cement-block DeSoto Truck Stop and Cafe, where according to a hand-lettered sign, you could find a *hot bathroom & clean coffee . . . ha ha.*

Skyles pointed without saying a word, and Missy swung the truck into the dirt lot. Two other cars were parked in front of the DeSoto, a Camaro built for speed and some kind of jacked-up mountain Jeep with no doors and a thick coating of mud that looked to be permanent.

"I don't know," she said, leaving the truck running. "It doesn't seem to be too popular."

"Less people. Faster service. Hotter food," he said. He shook his near-empty canteen. "And I'll bet if I hold my mouth right, they'll sell me a little something special. Besides, it's early yet. Things might pick up."

Inside the DeSoto, four tables surrounded a jukebox that glowed beneath a healthy layer of dust. A few steps to the left was a bar made from more cement blocks and a slick, shellacked piece of plywood. The DeSoto was brighter inside than Missy thought it would be. Two long fluorescent tubes buzzed like beehives over their heads and turned the walls a sickly off-white. The smell of mothballs and kerosene hung in the air. Behind the bar, an older, slick-headed man sat gazing at a black-and-white TV perched high in a corner above a large refrigerator. His arms were thick and hard, stretching the sleeves of his T-shirt, but the rest of him had long given up, turned to fat from too many hours on the stool staring at the TV screen. He was watching a news show, and only when the reporter finished his story and broke for a commercial did he turn toward Missy and Skyles.

"Stay on number fourteen, and you'll hit town in a half dozen miles." He grabbed a towel from somewhere beneath the bar and began wiping the plywood.

"What's that?" Skyles nodded toward the television.

"Mentone is probably what you're looking for. The town. Mentone." The man's voice was thin and nasal, coming from somewhere between his eyes. He bent his words like they were pieces of warm plastic.

"Actually, we're looking for some food," Skyles said.

The bartender had his eyes on Missy. He wasn't ogling, just taking her in completely, so he could tell his friends later on about this hippie with the beard and his good-looking girlfriend with legs up to her armpits.

"Food?" Skyles repeated.

"Oh, we got a few things. People mostly drink here. I got fried baloney sandwiches, chips and some green tomato pickles I canned myself last year. Two fifty for all of it. Drinks is extra. I got beer, Dr. Pepper and Collins mixer with some fizz left to it."

He turned back to the TV. "That woman," he said, pointing at the anchorperson on the screen, "has got the shiniest lips I ever seen. You forget what she's talking about just watching them lips rolling around." He reached up and turned the dial until a weather map appeared. A brunette stood in front of the United States and pointed out where the good and bad days would be.

"Now that one," he said, "she has got her act down, but her hair is too thin. Look at that. I'm afraid she'll be bald by summer. She don't have network potential. You folks want a couple of fried baloney sandwiches?" Skyles and Missy nodded. "Well, go ahead and grab yourself a seat and I'll get them going." He walked to the opposite end of the bar and through a doorway.

"How thick or thin your hair is doesn't have a thing to do with losing it. I know that because I read it. Losing hair is all genetic," Skyles said, tapping his temple.

They sat at a table streaked from its last wiping. The table wobbled on a short leg when they leaned their elbows on it. At its center, there was an ashtray filled with sugar packs stolen from McDonald's and a shaker with more rice kernels than salt.

"How does he get all those stations?" Missy asked after they'd settled in.

"Got me a big dish out back." The bartender's face just over her shoulder startled her. He had come through yet another door, and approached from the back without a sound, which Missy thought was impossible for a man that large. "One of the first ones in the county. I can pick up anything from dirty Mexican soap operas to Australian-rules football."

He laid two paper plates in front of them. Skyles smiled. He knew he'd found a kindred soul of sorts, someone who also collected things that were ultimately useless. In this case, TV channels. On each of their plates sat a sandwich—a couple of pieces of baloney, fried until the edges were curled and black, stuck between slices of spongy white bread. The heavy doses of ketchup had begun to leak through the bread. The juice from the green tomato pickles puddled among the chips, giving them the consistency of wet cardboard.

"Can you pick up any of those channels out of New York, like those transvestite shows? I read about them, but I've never really seen one."

Skyles dug into his meal, feeling confident that a man who could access dozens of television channels could undoubtedly fix a decent sandwich. Missy wasn't so sure, but she figured the lightheadedness and the chills were from lack of food, and this was her only option. The plate in front of her was taking on a Christmas look, with the ketchup and the green runoff of the tomatoes. She closed her eyes and pretended she was starving and blind and that food was nothing more than smells you could chew. And this didn't smell all that bad if you didn't look at it.

The man, whose name was either Kal or Lester—he left the choice entirely to them, saying he would answer to either just as fast—joined them at the table. He and Skyles fell into a conversation that halted only when the two of them cocked their heads toward the television like a couple of dogs that had just picked up a train whistle. By the time they had eaten the last of the baloney, the afternoon had gone black, the moon was already up, and Skyles announced they would spend the night in the parking lot of the DeSoto. He moved to the bar, where the two of them began to play around-the-world with the satellite dish. They watched a beauty contest from a country where all the women were dark and wide-hipped. Then a cricket match from India. Next a fishing show in Spanish. From inside the DeSoto, they combed the sky, snatching signals from the air, looking for that transvestite cable show out of New York City.

Missy wandered back to the truck. Her stomach tumbled, making angry, unsettled noises, and she felt a fever coming on. She tried lying in the front seat, hugging her knees, hoping she wouldn't throw up. She hated throwing up. She would rather cut off a finger.

There was pain, as though something molten she swallowed had settled and grown hard in the pit of her belly. Each time she felt it begin to rise toward her throat, she clutched her knees together and whispered over and over, "Christmas morning, Christmas morning, Christmas morning . . ." It was the happiest thing she could think of, the only distraction she could summon. The mantra didn't work. Her stomach churned.

She'd been this sick once before, when she was nine, the time she was convinced she saw God. It was during a bad fever in the middle of August. Mona took her outside to sit in the sun for a few minutes, to get some color back in her face. As she sat squinting from the brightness, she could have sworn God was swinging in the hammock slung between a couple of pines near the edge of the backyard. He was fast asleep, snoring like a steam engine. Nobody stood beside him, pushing the hammock, but it moved steadily back and forth on its own.

Missy told her mother that she saw God sleeping in their hammock, and Mona popped her quick on the top of the head with her fingernails. "Just for that he'll probably strike you with a fever so high your brain boils away." She went on to say Missy was seeing things because her brain was already so heated up and that she wouldn't remember any of this tomorrow.

"So don't worry about it," Mona said, but Missy wasn't given a chance to forget. A couple of days after the fever broke, Mona took Missy down to the little county newspaper office in town and had Missy explain to a tall man in a starched, white shirt what she had seen. In a square, brown room that smelled like the inside of an ink bottle, the man wrote down everything she had said. Every time she answered a question, he raised one of his eyebrows. The better the answer, the higher the eyebrow went.

"What did God look like?" he asked, his eyes glued on a yellow pad of paper.

Missy couldn't remember details, only the fact that it was God was rocking in the hammock. So she lied. "A little like Santa Claus. But skinnier. Like Abraham Lincoln maybe." The newspaperman cocked his eyebrow.

"Was there any other person or god-like being there with Him?" he asked.

"Jesus," Missy said. "He was there. He walked up later and helped push the hammock." The eyebrow all but jumped off his face.

"You never mentioned Jesus," Mona said.

"You never asked. You never asked me any questions at all. Jesus came later."

"Which side of the hammock was Jesus on?" the man said.

"The left, if you were standing in front of it."

"So," the man said, "on God's right?"

Jump went the eyebrow. Before long Missy had all twelve disciples taking turns pushing God in the hammock. She had prophets showing up and the Virgin Mary and animals two by two. She threw in a couple of wise men because it was starting to sound like Christmas around the hammock.

"I told you. This child has seen a glimpse of Heaven," Momma said. "Her story needs to be in the paper. People need to hear about her."

"Could be," said the man. "We don't get God sightings every day," and he led them to the door.

This time, however, Missy's momma was nowhere in sight. Neither was the man with the eyebrow. She was all alone and needed to get out of Skyles's pickup. With one hand on the door handle and the other on her mouth, she spent the next hour heaving onto the parking lot. A couple of cars bathed her with their lights as they arrived. One honked. She probably looked like just another DeSoto patron who ventured a few beers too far and was trying to save face beside the fender of a truck.

Three different times, she rode out the knee-buckling waves that shivered the length of her body and tried to walk to the DeSoto's entrance so she could ask Skyles for help. But her breath hit the chilly spring air and formed sick-smelling clouds that settled around her head and blocked her way, confusing her. Sweat ran into her eyes, and she imagined she was running a long race in the summer. She heard giant gnats buzzing in her ears. She turned for the safety of the truck, but the night had somehow eaten it and thrown it back up as a shadow at the edge of the parking lot.

Think, girl, she told herself. *You are in a valley. Everything good is at the end of the valley. Skyles said so. He knows. Everything you need is at the end of the valley.*

Missy felt the dirt turn to asphalt under her feet. "Downhill. The end of the valley," she whispered and began to stumble down the slope, unaware that the glow of the DeSoto faded with each step she took. She kept sucking in air. *Air will keep the baloney down,* she thought. *Will keep those sour green tomatoes down.*

Only once did the air fail her, so she took a few quick, blind steps off the road to puke and felt the ground disappear in front of her. She grabbed at a tree. Below, far down the slope of the mountain, the tiny star lights of houses and streetlamps dimpled the black. She threw up into open space, hoped the people below were sleeping heavy and deep and wouldn't hear what was coming their way.

Away from the shoulder and back to the road, the slope was gone. Missy turned lazy circles on the centerline of the highway, trying to decide the direction of town. The metallic taste in her mouth ran into her head, stopping there to pound behind her eyes. She shut them, then remembered to worry about headlights and the heavy, fast machines they were usually attached to, so she shifted to the edge of the road and decided to walk until she found the grade of the hill again.

In minutes, she rounded a curve and saw lights behind the trees. She walked faster, her steps beating out a rhythm with the clanging in her head. She no longer felt nauseated. That was over. Next came the emptiness, the sensation that she had been wrung out like a washcloth. Her mouth, dry as an oven, tasted like dirty socks. The trees broke, and in front of her, she saw the pickup and the roofline of the DeSoto Truck Stop and Cafe. She fast-walked the next fifty yards and saw Skyles, leaning against the back of his truck, lifting the canteen in a kind of drunkard's greeting.

All that work trying to get to the end of the valley, all that work and I went in a circle and I didn't go anywhere.

She plopped down in the middle of the highway, the dotted yellow line splitting her in two. She sat Indian style and began to cry. Tears ran into her dry mouth. The salt burned her tongue. Only when a tear dripped on her foot did she notice that she hadn't been wearing shoes. She'd left them in the truck, which was somewhere over there, near the lights she couldn't quite bring into focus.

Skyles gathered her off the asphalt and helped her to the truck like she was an invalid aunt. He spread out the sleeping bags and lay her down.

"Jesus, Missy, you look for shit. Have you been doing drugs or something?" He didn't wait for an answer. "Didn't your daddy tell you not to play in the traffic? I come outside for a breath of air, and you've gone and run off like some kind of house pet."

He closed the tailgate and talked through the screened window. "I'm going to lock this up. You want to tell me what's going on?" She didn't say a word. "Suit yourself. I'll be out in a bit to see about you. Me and Kal are watching a soap opera from Italy. The women all kind of look the same. You want something else to eat?" She heard the latch on the tailgate click. "Suit yourself."

Missy shut her eyes. Her head had settled and so had her stomach. But there was an electric buzzing in her ears. The last thing she remembered before falling asleep was a wave of chills flowing over her, and an image flashing across her mind's eye, a picture of a dog locked in a car in a hot grocery store parking lot, yapping at all of the people. She thought it would be funny to bark at Skyles when he came back. By morning, when she finally woke up, she'd forgotten all the plans she'd made the night before, sick and feverish in the dark.

9.

One chilly morning later that spring, Missy watched as the film of dew on the camper window dried in the sun. She could see where someone—probably some young, droop-eyed boy—wiped a love letter in the dampness the night before. Smeared across the window. *I love louise so,* it said.

So what? Missy wondered.

So, Louise has a lover boy, she thought, *and he wrote messages above our feet while we slept.* She had discovered that sleeping in the bed of a pickup, even with a camper top over their heads, opened them up to the worst of the night, perhaps to the lonely, lovesick boys and wet air that settled on the windows. She shivered in her seat when she pictured someone that close to them in the dark.

"Possum running across your grave, girl?" Skyles asked, watching her shimmy as he wheeled the truck into a parking space on the street.

Already, even by that time of the morning, he twisted and fidgeted behind the steering wheel, trying to find a comfortable position for his legs. A couple of times a week, he complained about his legs, that they were in a sad condition, that he couldn't keep the right amount of circulation pumping through them.

"It's a vascular curse," he said.

Because of his legs, they had fallen into a new and regular pattern. When they were on the road after breakfast, he would drive for only an hour or so before asking her to take the wheel. And he didn't even bother trying to sit in the passenger seat. Rather, he crawled into the back and stretched out, so his heart could have a straight shot at his feet.

Since the night of the DeSoto, Missy had wondered a great deal about the state of Skyles's heart, even more when he complained of his legs. It didn't strike Missy at first that shutting her up in the pickup like a misbehaving animal was borderline sin. She'd been too sick and fuzzy headed to consider it. But with some days and miles between then and now, she began to see it was something worth thinking about. *How well does his heart beat? Is it darker than I suspected?*

"Possum on your grave?" Skyles asked again.

"It's the damp," Missy answered, shivering again. "It gets in and I can't shake it."

"Turn on the heater and beam that vent on your feet. You lose some of your warmth through the feet, you know. Something like sixty percent. I read that somewhere." He reached instinctively for his front shirt pocket.

Missy stopped writing postcards home. She began calling from the road. The first time she called was the hardest. Missy had waited a few seconds before dialing the last digit. When her mother recognized her voice, Missy heard the breath catch in Mona's throat. Missy took that as a good sign, that she was missed and maybe forgiven. And Mona tried to be nice, but soon she lost control and spit out the words "embarrassment" and "sin" in the same sentence. That first call, Missy heard Asa's thick voice in the background.

"I told you this would happen. Just hang up," and the phone clicked to silence.

During the calls after that, Mona didn't disconnect, and Missy gave her momma plenty of chances to ask about Skyles and the truck, but Mona never took them. Instead, she treated her daughter like a neighbor on the phone. She gossiped about births and deaths, then found a reason to end the conversation. They never said anything important.

Missy called home again when they stopped for breakfast that chilly morning. Breakfasts were timed according to the condition of Skyles's legs. If they were bothering him, he liked to prepare them for the long ride in the truck with a big breakfast. But if there was no discomfort, just juice and coffee, maybe a piece of toast, then back on the road as quickly as possible.

It was Sunday. Missy knew her momma would be getting ready for church. Mona's mind would already be focused on sin. On the other hand, Sunday morning was usually a sober period for her because she had to confront God and the congregation at the same time. Missy knew her momma liked to put her best face on when meeting important people. This Sunday, the phone was busy over and over.

Outside, after they finished breakfast, Skyles shook a bottle of soda he had plugged with his thumb. After a couple of good jolts, he aimed the bottle at the rear window of the camper. "Carbonation's supposed to cut road film. Don't know how it'll do with this window writing. I used to get whipped for this when I was a kid, drawing faces and such on the glass. Somebody ought to be whipped." He talked too fast and laughed a high-pitched giggle. "Somebody," he repeated.

"Why not leave it?" Missy said quickly, trying to catch him before he let go with his thumb, trying to avoid seeming anxious.

"I can't see out the back with all this."

"You never look out the back anyway. I'll be driving in a while, so leave it. It doesn't bother me at all. Leave Louise up where I can see her."

He stuck the opening of the bottle in his mouth, his thumb still stopping the hole, then let the soda explode. His eyes watered as he swallowed hard to keep up with the foam.

"I don't know why you got to be so strange," he said. "'Leave this,' you say, but you can't say why. This might've been good, you know, to see if soda cuts through window scribbling. One idea like that and next thing, bam! For all you know, spraying soda on the back window of a truck could've been the thing to make me a million. Damn if I'll let a woman and her strangeness get between me and a million dollars."

He slammed the door on his side and cranked the truck, then called to her from inside while the engine idled loudly. "You drive. I'm upset now," he said, reopening the door. Skyles climbed over the tailgate into the bed. From inside one of the rucksacks stashed against a wheel well, he pulled out his canteen.

He'll rest until lunch, Missy knew, then he'd refill the canteen at some roadside store and spend the afternoon the way he spent the morning. Lying down was good for the circulation problem, but it bothered Missy that someone so committed to the road slept away so many of its miles.

Skyles was one of the few people she'd ever met who could sleep when they were mad, and after a dozen or so restless miles, Missy heard him snoring in the back. She passed time with the highway markers, counted roadkill for a couple of hours—ripe skunks and curious dogs that wandered onto the pavement. Skyles woke up when she stopped for gas, and he drank the last of the canteen before he could focus his eyes.

"Where are we?" he asked, clearing his throat.

"Halfway," she told him, which meant absolutely nothing since they never really knew where they were headed.

The gas station shared a wall and an entrance with a liquor store, and Skyles tried to talk the man behind the counter into unlocking the red dot and selling him a bottle of something. Missy imagined the man lecturing Skyles about it being Sunday, how in this state, it was against God's law and everybody else's to sell liquor or beer or wine on Sunday, and how a drunk was easy prey for the Devil.

When she walked by on her way to the pay phone, Skyles was telling the man in a calm, measured tone that without the proper liquids he could very well die. He pulled a crinkled newspaper column from the shirt pocket collection. The article said that just a touch of alcohol per day may actually prolong life. He quoted from the article like it was scripture.

"Here's a Russian man who drank a pint of vodka a day until he died . . ." He paused for effect. ". . . at a hundred and five."

The man ignored the fact that Skyles wanted to add years to his life. "How long it take you to grow that beard?" he asked.

Missy tried her mother again on the pay phone outside the station. The nagging thought that she *had* to talk to Mona buzzed through her head like a mad bee. The phone rang over and over at her mother's until Missy finally hung up and tried again to make sure she didn't dial the wrong number the first time. *At this time of day, she might be outside,* Missy decided.

"I take it you know where we're headed today, huh?" Skyles asked when she returned to the truck. He sat on the tailgate, pouring whiskey from a bottle into his Scout canteen like a careful chemistry student. He wasn't upset anymore, even pleased he'd convinced a complete stranger to choke down his Sunday ethics and unlock the liquor store. "I mean, I'm giving you the out-and-out deed to the road today."

He crawled back inside with his full canteen, and Missy sealed up the truck and the camper top. On the window, *louise* had turned a chalky brown, brown enough to make her think Louise's lover boy must be a tall man with an angry, heavy hand.

Early that morning, she had pictured him as thin and quiet, a boy who snuck around with his feelings leaking through the tip of his finger like blood through a pinprick. Scribbles were the wrong way to find out what someone else thought. She was betting Louise never knew somebody loved her enough to write notes on the windows of strangers.

She heard Skyles banging through the boxes in the cab behind her, looking for something to eat. He knocked on the window of the cab and held up a wedge of orange stuck on the blade of his pocketknife. He knew she hated oranges and had a fear of open knives, and the whole of it made him grin as he slid the blade between his lips.

Missy said a little prayer for a good, surprising bump as he picked his teeth with the knife point, his face pressed close to the cab window.

After he ate, he stuck his face back in the rear window and let Missy watch as he rewarded himself with several long pulls from the canteen. Then he settled in for the rest of the afternoon. He didn't even wake up when she stopped for gas again. Around six, just as the sun dipped below the tree line, Missy found her way back to the same little campground from the previous night, the one just a few miles off the interstate. Skyles didn't stir when she parked the truck. The same fat man with the tuft of red hair perched behind the same counter in the tiny store. He owned the campground, which was actually a dozen dirt plots bordered with rotting, creosote railroad ties. A gravel two-rut ran down the middle of the campsites. She already knew the prices, so she had the money ready.

"Hold on," he said from behind the racks of beef jerky and cheese nabs. "Second night in a row ain't but five bucks, you know. I thought you was gone."

Missy thanked him, and with the change, she bought a large packet of instant soup and a couple of pieces of soft bubblegum. They were about out of groceries, and Skyles would need something with a lot of quick sugar when he woke up that evening.

When she rolled down the gravel, she tried to remember the campers from the day before. It looked like most folks were still there. She was able to find the same site they'd used the previous night, and she opened up the tailgate. Skyles moved a bit, but only to shift to the other side of the pickup bed. Missy shook the canteen. It was almost empty. He probably wouldn't eat the rest of the night and would only get up to weave into the trees and pee.

Missy had driven in a circle for a reason. She wanted to find out about Louise's man. She hoped Louise's man had more modern toilet habits than Skyles, because Missy spent the next couple of hours hanging around the entrances to the dull, cement block building that served as the campground bathhouse. She was back to see what a man alone and in pain looked like. She was back to get a look at Louise's lover.

The bathhouse was a sensible place to start. That is, if Louise's lover had stayed an extra night, too. It was a gamble. She watched fathers holding their sons' hands as they carried towels into the shower. And uncomfortable women with nylon bags of makeup and shampoo. She never saw a man who looked like he had been hurt enough to write on a strange truck window. As it grew late, when the people stopped coming to the bathroom, she snuck into the men's side, just to see if Louise's name was popular in places other than wet pickup windows.

She studied the graffiti on the bathroom wall until she heard the door at the entrance throw out a squeak. Missy had just enough time to latch herself into the last stall in the row and sit like normal. A man banged through the swinging door next to her and groaned as he lowered himself. She felt safe because she was wearing shorts and, from the knees down, she could pass for a skinny man squatting and doing his business. She hadn't shaved her legs in weeks.

She ducked down far enough to watch the space between them. That's when she saw Skyles's silver, hand-tooled belt buckle clank on the floor beneath the partition. Her heart thumped. She wanted to let him know she was there, wanted to ask him why he used up all the effort to make it to the bathhouse, why he didn't hug the trunk of a tree like he usually did. But she kept her mouth shut. He sat for a long time, long enough to make her think he'd brought one of his newspapers. *Maybe he passed out*, she thought.

But she couldn't figure the noises she heard coming from his stall. Not body sounds or the whisk of clothes drawing up a bare leg. It was a scratching, the kind of noise that came from a kitchen at night when mice were out. She put an ear to the plywood partition, and the scratching turned to a harsh raking under her ear. When she pulled back a bit and glanced toward Skyles's feet, she saw tiny shavings and flecks of wood the same dull-green color as the rest of the bathroom.

Skyles continued to scratch until suddenly the belt buckle rose, and he called out over the top of the stall. "Okay, neighbor, you win. I can't waste all night in here." He washed his hands in front of the mirror, and through the space at the doorjamb, she watched him shuffle out.

Inside Skyles's stall, the seat was still warm on the back of her thighs. To the left, in the plywood, she saw the fresh carving: *louise hurt me good*

Only when she finished a fast shower next door in the women's side did she realize she didn't have a towel, so she dried off with handfuls of tiny, rough paper napkins stacked on the sink. She left a mess on the counter for someone else to clean up when the daylight rolled around again.

Back at the campsite, the soup she'd bought was thin, but enough to feed them both. After they ate, she lay staring, listening to the sounds in the campground, until Skyles woke up and rolled into her half of the sleeping bag. She thought about stopping him, about Louise, then decided it wasn't worth the effort. All she thought of was his clean hands. She was thankful he'd washed them. Those hands pinned her down, then worked their way under her hips, and she still listened for anything outside, in the trees or on the highway. Trucks, maybe, that couldn't afford to stop for the night, or the red-haired man, double-checking the lock on his little store. On the breeze, she smelled the creosote from the railroad ties even though Skyles's beard dangled in her face. He only lasted a couple of furious minutes, ending with a final tired push, and he rolled off almost immediately, groaning as he went down. She heard him rustle for his canteen.

"Where are we anyway? It looks familiar," he said, and when she didn't answer, he flopped over to his side of the truck.

The next morning, for breakfast, they ate at the same diner as the day before, and the waitress treated Skyles like a regular. Her friendliness and familiarity confused him, and the look on his face suggested he hadn't been let in on a decent joke. He just smiled. He was too foggy to realize they'd driven in a huge circle yesterday.

Missy tried to call home from the phone in the back of the diner, beside the door to the kitchen. Through the porthole window, she watched the cook on the morning shift sample something with two fingers—grits or cream of wheat. The back door of the kitchen was open, and from where she stood next to the phone, she could see two dogs, brown and rheumy-eyed, belly down in the dirt, waiting for the cook's mistakes to sail in their direction. The kitchen was already hot early in the day, and she felt a thin rush of warm air escaping through the space between the swinging doors.

The phone rang busy this time. The steady clip of the signal reminded her of the sound of tires over the grooves in the concrete interstate, the way she could beat out a rhythm depending on the truck's speed.

She imagined herself on the highway alone. Thumb and chin both out. She saw the greasy-breathed trucker who would pick her up and ferry her from stop to stop. Or a college boy looking for an experience with a long-haired hitchhiker. A girl might stop for her and wonder why she smelled like she did and why she traveled alone. She might pull her hair under a hat and grab her crotch and pretend to be a man from a distance. Missy could see herself now, and she was doing more than driving in circles with her third cousin.

The door swung open, and the waitress gave her a nod toward the tray she balanced. The sight of the eggs and the biscuits with gravy turned Missy's stomach. Skyles whistled at her, pointed to the food the waitress set on the table, and waved to Missy with the other hand.

This will be easier because I have been able to imagine myself alone. She'd seen the picture in her mind, so it could become real now. Missy walked up and stood while Skyles took a sip of his water. He jabbed his finger at the newspaper.

"Will you look at that? One aspirin a day can keep you from having a heart attack. What do you know?"

Still standing, she said. "I know all about that. I read it in a book I gave you. What do you think about the name Louise? I think Louise is a fine name, don't you?"

He waited for a minute, cracked a sick smile and turned his face back into the newspaper. *Another joke he didn't quite get,* Missy thought.

He hid his eyes and pretended to read. Missy left his smile dangling and walked through the kitchen door, past the cook, who sat in front of the walk-in cooler, still sweating in the flow of air. After Missy walked by, one of the dogs rose and followed her, thinking she had something for him, until Missy chased him away with a rock and a glare.

10.

The things that happen.

Quick, strange, unpredictable things, like trains hitting people, people who glanced at the oncoming bright light and never had a second's time to wonder which way to run. Or the boy Missy actually knew who lost his hand to a piece of loud farm machinery. He told her it happened so fast, his brain couldn't keep up with the pain. He said it didn't even hurt when he looked down and saw that all he had left was empty space where his palm used to be. Surprises sometimes carried bad endings.

Missy didn't want surprises. Didn't want any trains fighting her for space on the tracks. Didn't want to look down and find missing body parts. That's why she left Skyles. Things were beginning to surprise her. Like Louise. Whoever she was. The feel of Skyles's tires on the road had begun to lose their comfortable hum. She remembered the click of the latch on the tailgate at the DeSoto the night she was sick, how he locked her in.

Ahead of her were four lanes with faded lines down the middle. This was no interstate. It was an old state highway that ten years earlier would have been packed with cars, most of them loaded with families or teenagers heading toward or leaving the beach. Every thirty miles or so stood a lonely motel, a low, single-story building with empty rooms that opened to a weedy parking lot, all surrounding an empty, algae-stained swimming pool. In the good days, the motels were full of people from other states, heading north or south. Plenty of places to eat along this highway, too. Some regular sit-down, mom-and-pop restaurants that served a meat and three vegetables. And burger joints that appeared overnight. Breakfast places, too—small, square restaurants. Ten booths and a grill.

Back then, when the highway was full, everybody who lived or worked on it was happy, getting rich or fat or both. A nonstop stream of cars headed toward the coast, even in the winter, when the golfers flooded the courses near the ocean, the fairways green and open year-round. Then, one day they—whoever they were—announced plans for the interstate that paralleled the highway, running the same north–south route. What seemed like only a couple years after that, the state highway became a ghost town. Missy seemed to remember something Skyles had recited to her about the interstate system, that it had been built originally for defense purposes back in the '50s and '60s—a way for thousands to flee all at once in case the Russians sent a bomb our way.

Once the interstates opened, the only cars on the small, forgotten roads were folks who were lost or in no hurry. Most businesses died a very sudden death, closing after months of no customers and loneliness. Others hung on, though they knew they were terminal. The worst thing was, from the empty state highway you could hear the traffic rumbling on the interstate, only a couple of miles in the distance. It was a constant reminder that when something changed, something else was usually left wriggling in the dust.

When Missy left Skyles in the restaurant, she didn't backtrack toward the exit and onto the interstate. Instead, she snuck around to the truck, grabbed her duffel bag, and set a course down the highway that ran behind the diner. At first, she thought she might be performing some kind of illegal act, walking down a road in the narrow emergency lane that was cracked and overgrown with chickweed and dandelions popping up in stubborn clumps through the asphalt. But they called it an emergency lane for a reason, and Missy was beginning to feel as though she had every right to be there, that particular moment of her life being the closest thing to an emergency she'd seen in months. A highway patrolman rolled by her once, gave her a quick look in his mirror and disappeared over the hill without so much as a tap on his brakes. She probably looked in complete control or completely hopeless, and he was headed for the interstate where things moved faster and caused more trouble.

In her emergency lane, the occasional semi steamed by, dodging a weigh station, leaving behind clouds of diesel fumes that settled on Missy's tongue. Dead things pointed stiff in the heat. Chunks of old truck tires lay in the grass like black fossils. And two military types, traditional buzz-cut variety, one black and one white, kept roaring by her in a dusty, green Bel Air, grinning and rubbernecking to see if Missy noticed them. They would drive out of sight, then circle back, trying to work up their nerve to stop. Missy didn't think they had much of a plan.

It was broad daylight, which made Missy feel somewhat safe. Under normal circumstances, she'd never take a ride from military men out of their uniforms. Angela told her once that was when soldiers were the craziest. Or at least that's what her new husband said. Missy knew she had no power on that highway, no protection, no gun to shoot at them, no place to run—though she'd never been much of a runner for long distances. Nothing to protect her except the look in her eye, which by now must have been a tired sort of wandering gaze.

If she'd thought more about it—about walking away from that restaurant on her own—she would have concocted a better strategy. *I'm no better off than those Army boys,* she thought. *Should have eaten breakfast with Skyles, should have never hit the road on an empty stomach.* That was stupid. What she should have done was take the truck, just steal it. That way she could keep some air moving in the rising heat.

But that very second, dodging the roadkill and diesel fumes, she began to understand something about the decisions people made.

The hardest choices required speed. They must come the quickest. Sometimes people didn't have time to think about what could go wrong. And that, she realized, was why she walked away from Skyles without a plan. She didn't have time to waste.

All the exits and crossroads she passed were marked with faded signs pointing toward little towns that oddly possessed the names of women. It made her think that she was even safer, watched over by a sisterhood of the highway. She could have followed some of the signs and gone east or west toward Jalapa, Joanna or Pauline or Ora.

She imagined they were all famous, these women. She imagined they were like her at some point in their lives, walking down the emergency lane, dragging their belongings, feeling the uneven pieces of gravel through the bottoms of their tennis shoes. They probably got to the point they were too hungry to walk any farther, left the road and started their own town. They were strong and quiet and thin women because, Missy fantasized, thin women always appeared more hungry, more desperate. She wouldn't know where to begin if she had a notion to start her own town. *Maybe you began with babies,* she thought.

"SWEETHEART, YOU LOST OR STUPID, ONE OR THE OTHER."

The yell blasted behind her, and she considered diving into the weedy ditch. For a split second she thought it might be Skyles, come to pick her up, but realized it was too early for him. He hadn't had time enough to figure out which direction she went. He was probably still enjoying breakfast.

She hadn't heard the car rolling through the gravel in the emergency lane, the Bel Air with its windows down. She was close enough to see the red carpet inside the car. On the tops of the seats, in the back window, around the mirrors. The carpet made the car resemble the inside of an expensive pillow. One of the military boys hung outside of the passenger window, grinning. The car swung back into the highway lane and pulled up beside her. It labored, moving at a walking pace. She could hear pieces of metal knocking against one another under the hood.

"SHE COULD BE BOTH, LES. IF SHE'S STUPID, SHE'S FOR SURE LOST. AND IF SHE'S STILL LOST THIS TIME OF DAY, SHE MUST BE DUMB AS SHIT."

This was the driver, yelling and watching the mirror for cars behind him. In a split second, Missy knew she was safe from him. He thought about things too much and said too much. She would be able to talk him out of anything.

"Shut the fuck up, Oscar," Les said over his shoulder. That scared her. That word. This guy wasn't worried about using it in front of a total stranger.

If she let them see she was scared, she was finished. If she ran, she'd be caught. What would Jalapa do? Or Ora? Any woman who could start her own town would know how to handle this kind of situation.

So Missy Belue looked Les right in the eye and said, "Who's Carol?" His arm was pressed against the side of the car just outside the window, making his bicep appear bigger than it really was. Stretched across that muscle was a green heart tattoo and the name *Carol.* An arrow pierced the heart and the *C* on Carol.

Talk about another woman. Throw him off, Missy thought.

"She's the one that give me this tattoo," he said, tracing the shape on his skin. "She likes to put her name on everything she does."

"We Marines," Oscar said. "Ooo-rah."

"For fucking sure," added Les. "The new kind of Marines. We're nice to women. Used to be, Marines was killing and fucking machines. Now we don't do nothing but kill. Fucking's more dangerous than war." He pulled his arm inside the window and reached over the seat into the rear of the Bel Air. He popped the back door open.

Missy knew climbing into an overly carpeted Bel Air was dumb, but she was hungry and hadn't used the bathroom since leaving the campground that morning. Plus, she was not particularly lucky with the men she chose for traveling anyway, so what did it matter? Maybe her luck was due to change.

The thought of making a trade crossed her mind. *What've I got and what's it worth?* When Missy was younger, she could trade for anything because she always had stuff other people wanted. Not expensive things, just merchandise that magically became desirable because she made it seem that way. She and Skyles traded off for many a mile, but what Skyles had taken so easily wasn't presently up for barter. She wasn't *that* hungry.

"All I want is to get a little further down the road. I have three dollars in my pocket. I don't want any trouble," she told the Marines.

"Sweetheart, long as you ain't Communist or a Navy dyke, you are safe with a Marine," Les the jarhead said, flexing Carol a little.

They drove east, Missy inside a Bel Air with a pair of Marines too stupid to be evil. Les and Oscar acted like third-graders. They kept stealing glances at her and giggling. One of them would pass gas and point at the other one, then giggle some more. The car smelled bad enough as it was, even without the military farts. The air smelled like fast-food grease and men's bodies, but it was an upgrade from the diesel fumes and dead skunks in the emergency lane.

"We heading back to the island," Oscar said. "We been on leave for a couple of days."

"All we done is drive," Les said. "We put a thousand miles on this car in two days."

Oscar and Les began to discuss all they had seen in their thousand miles. How many honest-to-God wrecks they drove by and how many people they guessed died in them. The desperate highway patrolman they saw, his cruiser sunk to the axles in a ditch, and they almost wrecked their own car from laughing so hard. There was a bus that rolled past them, carrying some rock-and-roll band she'd never heard of. When they saw her puzzled look, they sang one of the band's songs while they acted like they were playing all of the instruments.

Just when she was about to ask them to stop the car and let her get on her way, a dirty, faded sign appeared like a sunrise over the next hill. *Li'l Pancake House.* Her mouth watered with the thought of butter and syrup sliding off a stack of flapjacks. Plus, she was about to pee on the red carpet and she knew she could take care of both problems at a pancake house.

Oscar and Les didn't mind stopping for a break. Oscar whipped the Bel Air into the nearly empty parking lot and turned off the engine, which chugged and jerked even after they got out. A few clouds of thick smoke puffed from the tailpipe.

"Damn," Les said, "the Bel Air is so excited, she just wants to keep on moving. What a goddamn gorgeous machine. I'll tell you what." He kicked the tire, patted the hood, and headed into the restaurant.

"Heck yeah," Oscar answered, following on his heels like a puppy. They didn't seem to remember she was even around, which was fine. They didn't hold the door for her, not that she expected it, but when it shut in her face, she was nose-to-paper with a sign taped to the glass. *AND JOIN A WINNING TEAM!!! CAREER OPPORTUNITIES WITH MUCH BENEFITS!!!!*

Missy headed for the bathroom and sat longer than she really needed to, staring at the floor, thinking what it might be like to work at the Li'l Pancake House. The bathroom appeared relatively clean, but it was still a bathroom. Missy was not interested in bathroom work, no matter how good the benefits. Not that she was above it or anything, but Missy couldn't imagine flipping pancakes after scrubbing a commode.

Take a look at this face, she told herself in front of the mirror. If she was in charge, she wasn't sure she would hire herself to work at a Li'l Pancake House. She looked like she still belonged on the road. Her hair was so long and dirty, it spiraled into three or four different shades on its way down her back. Teeth were okay.

Smile when you ask about the winning team, she told herself, *because your teeth are one of your good features*. She didn't have any extra hair on her face. No second chin. She had good hands, a genetic gift from her grandmother's side of the family. Her grandma had expensive-looking hands until the day she was buried. Long fingers, perfect nails and never a liver spot.

Just another tradeoff, she thought. *You still got things to trade for this job.* She dried her hands under the hot air blower, trying to rub away any sign of the bathroom.

Les was strangely upset by Missy's quick decision. Oscar was a little more understanding. Les thought Missy ought to be satisfied walking down the emergency lane the rest of her life, taking rides from strangers and going where the good Samaritans took her.

"I need a job," she told him. "You have a job, don't you?"

"Well, yeah, but the Marines ain't your regular kind of job," he said. "Plus, you ain't even *got* the job yet."

"You want something regular. I can see that. Regular's good," Oscar said, but Oscar was wrong. Missy didn't want regular. She just needed to light in one place for a short while, a stopgap that would give her time to think.

Oscar filled up every tiny square on his waffle with soft butter. Twice, he asked the girl behind the counter for extra. She snarled when she brought a handful of foil pats, and Missy could see the waitress had chipped one of her front teeth. Missy wondered if the snaggle-toothed waitress was being kicked off the winning team to make a new slot.

Les stabbed at his yolks with a wedge of white toast while Missy worked on a stack of pancakes. She didn't know why they all decided to eat breakfast at this time of the afternoon. Probably because it was the first meal of the day for each of them.

Les sounded hurt, like someone had taken away his recess. "I just figured you'd want to hang with a couple a Marines for a few miles. We going back toward the coast. You could see the ocean. That's where we were headed." Les ran out of toast before he cleaned his plate, so he bothered the girl behind the counter again. Missy reminded herself to look at the waitress's hands, to see how they compared with hers.

"She ain't interested in seeing the ocean. She's interested in something regular, like I said. Anyone can see that."

"Tell me something more regular than the ocean, shithead," Les said, giving Oscar a glare. "Anyway, you know what you're going to need? You'll need money. I got a deal for you. I'll give you ten dollars if you'll do something for me." He pulled a bill from his pocket and laid it next to the napkin holder. The girl behind the counter looked over like she'd sensed the presence of new cash fluttering in the air.

Missy pushed herself back in the booth. "Whoa," she said, "I don't do that kind of thing." An image of Skyles flickered across her brain.

"Do what?" Les said; then it hit him. "Naw, I don't ever pay for that. What I mean is, you can write, right?" Oscar laughed at the sounds of the words repeating themselves.

"Yes, I can write," Missy said.

"Well, I'll give you ten bucks to write a few letters to me," Les said, relieved he was no longer confusing himself or anyone else at the table.

"We do love a piece of mail," Oscar said. "I might kick in a few bucks for a postcard every now and then. Five's all I can go."

Les borrowed a pen from the waitress and wrote their names and addresses on a napkin.

Fifteen dollars. Missy could maybe buy shampoo somewhere and wash her hair in the bathroom sink. She wasn't sure she had any in her duffel. The waitress reached over the counter toward the table and grabbed for the bills. "Want me to ring you up?" she asked.

"Yeah," Les said, "but that money there ain't for you, sweet cheeks. It's for our pen pal." He handed the waitress a ten and said, "Keep what's left over for the effort."

"You're coming up short a couple of bucks, sport. The bill's almost twelve-fifty," the waitress said. Oscar giggled with his mouth full of buttery waffle, and Les kicked him under the table.

Missy looked through the window. Fifty yards across the parking lot from the Li'l Pancake House was a brick motel called the Thoroughbred Motor Inn. At one time, it had been white with green trim around each of the doors and windows, but now the painted bricks had turned yellow-brown, the color of newspaper left out in the sun too long. Missy had some cash, a stake. She also had a couple of jarhead addresses from Parris Island, South Carolina, which she intended to use, because next to true grief, she knew debt was the heaviest feeling in the world. She had no plans to be in anyone's debt.

A foreign man ran the front desk at the motel, dark-skinned and dark-haired. Over his shirt pocket he wore a stick-on name tag. *Hello! My name is Hassan!*

Hassan charged Missy eleven fifty for the night, which was more than she expected to pay for a motel faded that badly. Her room had a bed, of course, and a small table decorated with a lopsided Olympic symbol of rings made by dozens of nights of wet glasses and sweating beer bottles. Not a lamp in sight. The bathroom was the size of a mediocre closet, and the tub had gone orange with rust stains. The water ran out the same dingy color as the tub for a minute or so, turned light brown, then finally cleared. A little sample bottle of shampoo and a tiny bar of soap sat on the lip of the tub.

For the first few seconds of her shower, Missy smelled Skyles in the steam. The surface of her skin grew hotter and hotter, and she remained under the stream of near-scalding water, letting him seep through like bad sweat. And that was when she began to cry. She sat in the orange tub while the water pelted her head, and she sobbed like a child left on the side of the road. She wasn't sad. She simply had no idea where in the world she was.

An hour later, Missy retraced her steps and walked into the Li'l Pancake House, clean and smiling. "I'm here about the winning team," she told the waitress when she glanced up. Chipped Tooth snorted, "What?"

"I'm here about the job. The sign on the door?" Missy pointed behind her.

"You got to talk with the owner when he comes in. I'm fixing to get off for the night. He's relieving me." She turned to take care of the only customer in the place.

The Li'l Pancake House looked different at night. Missy had watched it across the motel parking lot from her room as the sun went down. It pulsed with a soft, safe glow. She sensed if she could spend her nights here, take some time to figure things out, she would be all right, protected in the glow. She sat in an orange booth near the register so she could talk to the girl when she rang up a ticket.

"How you like working at a Li'l Pancake House?"

Chipped Tooth took a breath before she answered. "This isn't a Li'l Pancake House."

"But the sign . . ." Missy trailed off.

"It used to be a Li'l Pancake House. Then the tourists stopped coming, they just sort of forgot about it. I know, I know, the sign still says Li'l Pancake House, but nobody ever came to take the sign down. Now it's just a place, I suppose. One day we got a letter that we were supposed to take the sign down ourselves," she said. "Fat chance of that."

"What kind of hours do they want the new person to work?" Missy asked.

"Graveyard," she answered. "Something like nine at night to six or so in the morning. I work noon to nine. The owner, he comes on in between. Right now, he's been having to go all night since Norris quit. Norris caught something that makes him double over when he doesn't expect it. Norris, that is, not the owner. It's hard to work when you're doubled over."

She wandered down the counter and began to pull off her apron. Missy heard the door open behind her.

"Girl here about Norris's job," Chipped Tooth said toward the door while she checked her makeup in a small compact.

"And good, good," Missy heard from behind. It was Hassan, motel desk clerk. He was Hassan, Li'l Pancake House owner, too. He slid onto the stool beside Missy, still wearing his name tag. "Ah," Hassan said, "Miss Room Number 107, cash money! And you are looking for work?"

"Yes. I had no idea you were . . ." She let the sentence hang. She didn't know if this was an official job interview or not.

"And you have been employed elsewhere in similar pancake places? Do you have experiences with the griddle?"

She had to decide how much of her story to tell. She had grown up in a part of the world where life stories were normal fodder for conversation. Should she tell him that she picked peaches for her mother's uncle Billy one July, but quit when his son tried to kiss her in the back of a flatbed? There were a couple of months when she helped another cousin with his paper route, and she cleaned house for allowance until she was fourteen. And Skyles. If that wasn't work, driving him all over, she would like to know what was. She'd never really thought about all the things she'd done.

So she simply said, "Yes, I've had some other jobs." But before she could launch into her very short resume, he held his hand up, signaling that he'd heard enough. He didn't seem to want specifics.

"And you will be able to start tonight? Let's say midnight?" he asked her. Everything he said began with the word *and.* Missy felt she was missing the first part of every sentence he uttered, like she was constantly entering in the middle of a conversation. When she'd checked into the motel, he didn't so much as say two words. Just sort of grunted at her when he gave her a room key. Now, he was a different person, alive and talking and beginning everything with *and.*

"Sure. I suppose."

"And we will get you a uniform and you will stay here right now for a few moments and learn to run a cash box," he told her. "Welcome to my place."

They shook on it. Her hand was much larger than his. His fingers were delicate. She could wrap around his hand and crush his tiny fingers like soda crackers.

"You didn't even ask me my name, though," she said, pulling her hand out of his.

"Ah, and you remember signing the register at my motel? Missy Belue you are. No address. You left that blank." He grinned at her, reached across and pumped her hand again. "And now you have an address. Room 107, Thoroughbred Motor Inn."

"If you two are all through shaking, I'll be leaving," the other waitress said.

Hassan smiled at her too. "And good night to you, Wanda."

Good, Missy thought, *now I know everyone's name.*

Missy didn't realize that she would have to cook, as well as take orders and ferry food to customers. Hassan couldn't afford to pay two people on a single shift, so his waitresses were cooks and vice versa. She discovered quickly that handling both jobs wasn't such a stress. There were never more than four or five people in the Li'l Pancake House, even at its busiest times.

After she'd donned a washed-out brown-and-yellow uniform, Hassan showed her everything she needed to know to survive. "And this," he said, "is the volume control for the jukebox. Loud music is a curse. Jukeboxes should be bright-shining and musical. Not loud. Loud music is bad for appetites."

He scurried off toward the booths. He moved like a nervous animal, bouncing from hiding place to hiding place.

"And you can see that this was a Li'l Pancake House. *Was,* I say. Not now. But it still looks like one. They were all alike across the country. Hatched from the same egg." He laughed. "Shaped like an *L.* Bathrooms at this end. The men's bathroom is my office now. All of us use one." They approached the doors and Missy remembered the hand-lettered sign duct-taped over *WOMEN* that said *TOILET.*

"And the place that used to be an office is for storage, behind the spying window," Hassan said, gesturing at the two-way mirror at the end of the counter. "And our cash register is here. We will get to that later. And here . . ." He paused, collecting a breath of air. "And here is the grill."

His eyes glazed over, like he remembered something that pleased him. He patted the heat-control knobs on the metal facing of the grill. "And this is why I own this used-to-be Li'l Pancake House."

Missy was trying to be a good employee. Staying focused and excited. But Hassan confused her. "What?"

"This grill. She is a living dream." He talked as he pulled a package of bacon and a bowl of eggs from a cooler beside the grill. He flicked on the heat and dribbled some thin, clear oil onto the pitted surface of the grill with a ladle.

"And when I was a boy, I dreamed of being a short order cook. To have the hands to do a day's worth of tasks in a quarter hour. Hands each with their own minds. I longed for that. To have the patience to wait until a hamburger is truly done. To have instincts in the blood and head to make sure all the parts of the meal are hot at the same time. To be able to crack an egg with one hand." Hassan looked heavenward and closed his eyes in prayer. "The God of the Baptists smiled on me for all this to happen. And it helped, of course, that my uncle Abid died and left me money. I purchased the ancient Lil Pancake House with this grill mere seconds before its final breath, and I have kept her alive. My dream has come true. I could hardly want for more under this particular sun."

Hassan plucked an egg from the carton and rolled it between his fingers. With a quick, deft motion, he cracked it on the raised lip of the grill. With the fingers of one hand, he separated the shells and dropped the egg into the hot oil. Immediately, it began to whiten and fry.

The door jingled. Missy turned to see a customer, a young man in a too-tight T-shirt and cutoff jeans all but running to a seat at the counter.

"And crispy pig with a double shot over light!" Hassan suddenly yelled over Missy's shoulder. The noise startled her.

"You got that right, H."

Hassan gave Missy a shove. "Leaded." Missy shot him a puzzled look. "Black coffee," he whispered.

"You new?" the man asked Missy when she set the mug in front of him. Missy nodded without saying a word. She was too afraid she might say the wrong thing.

"And she is a gift from the heaven of the Baptists. To replace Norris."

The man turned his attention to Missy. "I'm by here 'bout this time every Thursday night. I drive a chicken truck." He jerked his thumb toward the window. Missy saw a long semi stacked high with feathery crates. A confused, renegade hen had somehow escaped and now strutted across the top of the load, contemplating a leap to the ground. Missy thought she heard the engine idling. "H. knows what I like, and he knows I ain't got much time to throw it down my throat."

Hassan scooted a plate in front of the man. Three bacon strips cooked just this side of charred. Two eggs overlapped into a pile of stiff grits that dripped butter. "And there you have it. With time to spare, I feel I must add." Hassan smiled broadly.

The chicken trucker ate like he was condemned, mopping up every last bit of yolk and grits with a triangle of toast. By then, he was on a second cup of coffee. Hassan rang him out while Missy watched, trying to pick up the basics of the cash register. The trucker folded the change from his ten into his pocket and tossed the coins on the counter.

"See you next Thursday," he said to Missy, then to Hassan, "Later, H."

"And you drive safe."

"I drive fast, H. I let them other bastards drive safe. Sorry, ma'am."

"No problem." Missy smiled. "I've heard it before."

When he put the truck in gear and pulled away from the light, the loose chicken was nowhere to be seen.

"What's his name?" Missy asked.

"And I haven't the slightest idea on earth," Hassan said. "He is here every Thursday. He is a regular. I love regulars. And he knows my name." He tapped his name tag.

Hassan gave Missy a crash course on the menu. How most things were prepared. How to serve them. She learned how to change the soda canisters, how to scrape the grill and empty the grease catch. Where the coffee filters were stored. How to restock the pie display and wipe down the orange booths. He went over restaurant terms, reciting them in a flat, emotionless monotone like a bored schoolteacher.

"And if something is eighty-sixed, we are out. If you are in the weeds, it means you are too busy to pee. If you double-dip a customer, he has tipped you twice. Not good, but sometimes they are too under the influence to be careful with their pocket change."

Hassan was tired. His speech began to slow, and if he paused too long, he yawned. No one else had come in that night. In fact, Missy couldn't remember seeing any headlights on the highway. She wondered how Hassan stayed in business.

"You should go to bed," she said.

"And I am very tired. The day has been long. And I am hungry as well."

Missy felt a jolt of energy shoot through her arms and legs. She'd forgotten how it was to be excited. She grinned at Hassan.

"The sleep I can't do a thing about. But I can do something about your stomach."

She left him sitting on his stool at the counter. She scurried to a position in front of the grill. With her back to him, she began to talk.

"My daddy used to make breakfast on Saturdays. He'd get us up early and make us whisper so we wouldn't wake up Mom. He'd make pancakes with fried eggs slipped between each one of them. Know what he taught me to do?" She paused. "Well, do you?" No answer. Missy turned. Hassan was asleep, his head flat on the counter, snoring into the linoleum. *He can sleep later,* she thought. *I'm auditioning.*

"Hassan!" she called.

He jerked his head up and tried to focus. "Yes?"

"Check this out."

She took an egg in each hand, cracked them at the same time on the side of the grill, and with double, single-handed motions, plopped two eggs on the hot grill. She turned around grinning, tossing the shells into a trash can under the counter.

Hassan smiled and shut his eyes. "And I had this feeling you would come. A miracle from the God of the Baptists," he whispered. "I felt it."

❖

Missy learned that when you worked at a Li'l Pancake House—even an ex-Li'l Pancake House—you ended up smelling like one. You carried around a pancake-syrup, greasy-sausage, burned-grits, cheeseburger perfume on your skin all day. She tried going straight back to her room and soaking in the rusty tub or standing under the hot, hot shower, feeling the water stampede on her head. She dried off, then rubbed on some smelly lotion from one of the tiny bottles Hassan provided. But no matter how much lotion she used, five minutes later, she smelled like an order of onion rings. The scent of Hassan's place climbed under her skin, where she couldn't get at it. And the smell invaded her nose too, made her snore and have dreams about the work she'd done all night long. She relived being a waitress while she slept. She could never get completely away from it. Not that she tried too hard. She was actually happy to have new problems, even the minor ones.

The first thing Wanda told her was, "Don't worry about the color. It grows on you." She was talking about the brown/yellow/orange decorating scheme in the Li'l Pancake House.

In their early days, the booths and walls were probably first cousins to neon, so bright you had to look at them from an angle. But the colors had faded to a tired, forgettable dimness. They didn't look dirty—they still shone when the light hit them just right, especially at night. But in the daylight, they showed their age. They matched the old Li'l Pancake House uniforms Wanda and Missy wore, official holdovers from the days when Li'l Pancake Houses dotted the highways around the South.

The grout in the floor seams was stained beyond cleaning, broken in a few dozen places, but Hassan kept the tiles scrubbed and waxed. One window, on the highway side, had spiderwebbed into a pattern of thin cracks, but all the other windows were washed to near invisibility. Every counter chair swiveled without squeaking. And the counter wasn't chipped. The jukebox played. The bathroom lock locked. The towel dispenser rolled. Nothing was new, but everything worked. And that, it seemed, was Hassan's theory of the universe. If it worked, it was good enough.

Wanda began to linger a few minutes when her shifts were over, long enough to sit at the counter and drink a Diet Coke and dispense free advice.

"Let me tell you something, girl, there are only three kinds of people who come by here. There's them you can't ever please. Them you can't help but please. And them that don't give a rat's ass one way or the other. You got to learn to pick folks out and put them in the right slot."

She rambled like a minister while Missy readied herself for the night. Made sure her pen worked. Checked the change in the drawer. Started fresh pots of decaf and high test. There would be no rush of customers, just a couple of regulars and maybe a lost soul or two that wandered away from the interstate, drawn by the strange, warm glow just beyond the tree line. She liked to feel prepared.

Without waiting for a response, Wanda moved on, expanding her knowledge.

"Them you can't please do funny stuff, like wipe out the booth with five or six napkins before they sit down. Or maybe check to see if the tops are tight on the salt and pepper before they shake them. If it's a couple, one'll always head for the bathroom and leave the other one sitting in the booth. There isn't any reason to use up a lot of energy on this type person, believe you me. They already know what they're going to tip you.

"Them you can't help but please just smile at you and nod at you when you walk up. You could give them a deck of greasy playing cards, and they'd slop on some ketchup and smile at you while they chewed it up and told you how tasty it was. And of course, they're the ones with the big tips. They're so scared they're going piss you off, they throw down twenty, twenty-five percent easy. If I had this kind of person blowing through here a few times a day, I'd eventually have the money to put my butt in the wind and move to Florida."

Wanda finished her soda and with two fingers started fishing around in the plastic cup for ice cubes. She put a piece in her mouth, but continued talking, working the ice like a piece of gum. Missy wondered if that was how she chipped her tooth.

"Now, them that don't care are usually drunk or stoned or depressed or a combination of them all, and the only reason they stop by is because eating is another habit they can't seem to shake. They scare me. Those folks who don't give a crap about anything scare me a lot."

Missy couldn't imagine Wanda scared. She was beginning to know her, starting to discover that Wanda was like some girls she knew in school, the ones who talked a big, loud game and were able to deliver. Wanda looked hard, like she had seen bad times and the shadows of those times flickered behind her eyes, even when she smiled. She had an open face, one that could wrap you inside its honesty or its curiosity. There were reminders of chicken pox or acne high on her cheeks, places she carefully camouflaged with thick makeup. And she had an abundance of hair she was proud of, usually twirled up in a bun on the top of her head. The rest of her fit nicely into her uniform. She never went outside without her sweater, the same thin, white sweater every day, top button buttoned.

Missy rarely said anything directly to Wanda. Mostly she listened, taking in what she thought was useful information and tossing the remainder of what Wanda told her into some sort of wastebasket in her brain. There was a good bit of trash already there, most of it tidbits Skyles had passed on to her, but Wanda was adding her share.

When Wanda finished her soda after her shift, she immediately headed for the door, leaving Missy alone until Hassan paid his nightly visit. She handled all the orders. Nothing overwhelmed her. In fact, Missy got to the point where she could cook without thinking about it. She could take an order, pour the waffle batter or crack the eggs, then time the delivery out, so everything went to the table at the right temperature.

Missy was getting so good and machine-like on the grill, she sometimes placed a full plate in front of the customer and suddenly wondered where all that food had come from. She certainly didn't remember fixing it. It scared her until she began to enjoy the mindlessness of the work, the wide-eyed strangers on a break from the real road, and the truck drivers who tried to make her blush with a dirty joke.

Hassan normally came in around midnight, freshly shaven, a new name tag stuck to his pocket. His stiff cologne did acrobatics with the usual coffee/grease odor in the air. She poured him a cup of decaf as he sat at the counter.

"You ever sleep, Hassan?" she asked once. She thought he might be one of those people who could live without rest. Or maybe he'd been without sleep for so long, going to bed was just a waste of time.

"And of course. I nap with regularity. Short tiny snoozes," he said, blowing ripples across the coffee.

"You know, it's been a month now." When she said it, she actually surprised herself. She didn't realize how many days she'd been free of Skyles. "You don't have to keep checking on me every night. I'm getting pretty comfortable with everything."

Not that Missy didn't enjoy his company, especially when it was slow. When there were customers, she didn't mind waiting on them while the boss looked over her shoulder. It was just that he worked the morning shift until Wanda clocked in around noon. Missy couldn't understand where he got the energy to visit her and run the restaurant. Not to mention the motel. He was always dashing from the diner across the parking lot toward the office when a car pulled in. As a rule, though, guests were so infrequent he could easily handle both places at once.

"And you don't want me here." His eyes were on his coffee.

"I didn't say that, now. I just don't want you to feel like you've got to show up. You should take a night off every once in a while. Do something fun."

Missy worked on the countertop while she talked, rubbing out a rhythm with her words.

Hassan put his coffee mug down gently, as though it were crystal.

"And I am," he said, "having fun, that is."

"Oh yeah, I'm such an entertaining person. If you think this is fun, you need to go watch some paint dry. You won't be able to stay in your seat."

Hassan's eyes clouded again. His face took on the blank, bottomless expression Missy had seen when people sleepwalked through Asa's funeral home. She had hurt his feelings, but didn't know how exactly.

"I'm sorry," she said.

"And you don't understand," he said. He still hadn't looked up from his coffee.

"Don't understand what?"

"Fun. For me, fun is seeing someone eat an omelet. Fun is watching you work the grill. I bought the Li'l Pancake House so if I desire, I walk in and drink a cup of coffee and no one tells me when I have to leave." Hassan paused to sip.

"I used to spend nights walking around the motel or through the parking lot. You are right, I can never sleep, you see. Now with you, I can at least talk to someone. Norris never talked to me at length. He was a man of many grunts. You? You are a woman who is never unhappy."

"Oh, I have been unhappy."

Hassan perked up. "When?"

Missy felt this was the opening Hassan had been fishing for. He'd yet to ask how she came to be on the road with a couple of Marines, where she'd come from or what sort of past she owned. She knew he was the curious kind. He had that look—a brow that furrowed too easily, sympathetic eyes that constantly shifted their gaze. But she wasn't ready to tell Hassan anything of importance. They weren't that far removed from being complete strangers. She dodged.

"C'mon, I don't want to talk about being unhappy. What a waste of time," Missy said, realizing it came out sharper than she had planned.

Hassan stood and reached into his pocket. He pulled out a dollar bill and laid it carefully on the counter. A slow blush rose from his neck, but with the darkness of his skin, it was more a cloud taking shape.

"And if we cannot be friends at late night," he said, "you shall be a waitress. Here is your tip, waitress." He walked through the doors and into the parking lot.

Missy's first thought was that she had been fired. She wasn't entirely sure. Before the door swung shut, she was around the counter and after him. Hassan had to know she was chasing him. She scuffed the pavement as she ran, loud enough, she thought, to be noticed. But he never turned, and she never yelled. She just caught him by the shoulder and pulled him to a stop.

"You are one stubborn little man."

He raised his chin. "And it is my heritage. To live in the desert takes a great deal of fortitude and stubbornness." She wondered when was the last time he'd seen a desert, other than the parking lot he owned.

"You see?" Missy almost yelled. "That's the problem."

"My heritage?"

"No. It's just that without even thinking about it, you tell me important things about yourself. Like living in the desert and all. I'm finding out a lot about you. But I can't just give out information like that. I'm not like that. I mean, there isn't that much to tell. But what there is, I tend to keep to myself. I'm sorry," she said. She felt as if she needed to catch her breath. The words had come out in such a rush.

Hassan looked up and Missy followed his gaze. Through the glow of the Li'l Pancake House, she saw a sky full of stars, too many to settle on watching just one. "And it was a man, wasn't it?" Hassan asked finally, still looking upward.

"A man what?"

"Who made you unhappy? You said you were unhappy once."

It sounded like a trick question. Missy began to twirl a section of long hair. She wished she had a place to sit down. Her feet ached, and she still had hours of standing left on her shift.

"I suppose," she said.

"Ah ha! And I knew it. Men who hurt women leave them with a certain look. A thin coating of bravery painted over something darker. The best way to wash the bravery off and deal with true colors is to have a good cry. Do you cry easily?"

"No," she answered, then rethought. "Maybe sometimes. Do you?" She meant it as a lighthearted comeback, but he took it seriously.

"And I cry at the drop of the hat! I cry during the commercials of Kodak, and when I get snapshots of my brothers and sisters, who, by the by, still live near the desert. Stubbornly." He flashed a smile at Missy, and she caught sight of it just as a big car, a Lincoln maybe, pulled into the lot and settled on one of the faintly lined parking spaces at the front of the ex-Li'l Pancake House. An older couple got out, both immediately stretching in unnatural poses, limbering themselves just so they could sit down again.

They're trying to pull an all-nighter, Missy thought. *I was starting to think only young people and crazy foreigners went without sleep.*

"I have to go," she said. She stuffed Hassan's dollar into the front pocket of his shirt, just below his name tag, and turned back toward the yellow glow, diffused and softened by the humid air.

She heard Hassan call to her. "And the person who made you unhappy is probably kicking himself today! Goodnight, Missy Belue." Hassan's voice echoed in her ears as she hit the door.

The older couple, dressed too warmly for this time of year, were busy with their preparations. The man plucked a handful of napkins from the dispenser and wiped the table clean, something Missy had done just minutes before. The woman made straightaway for the bathroom. Missy could tell by looking that they were coffee/soup/sandwich people. And they couldn't be pleased. Probably wouldn't tip well. But at least it was someone new to start a conversation with.

11.

Like some breed of cautious animal, Missy never ranged far from the Li'l Pancake House and the motel. There wasn't much to see. A few hundred yards from the parking lot, a small cluster of mobile homes bloomed off the shoulder of the road in a muddy dip in the land. During her first couple of weeks, one of the trailers burned and a man was killed in his bed. "If that fire don't get him, a tornado would have," one of her customers said that night, suggesting that life in a mobile home park relegated the inhabitants to particular types of demise.

In the other direction, a thick stand of tangled pines and scrub oak that had never been tended or thinned grew in irregular rows, held in its disarray by a maze of wisteria and honeysuckle vines. Missy knew a town was beyond that patch of woods, and so was the interstate. Sometimes, when she walked to her shift, she heard the rumble of the trucks on the interstate like thunder from a faraway storm. She imagined the drivers peering through their windshields, wondering what the faint yellow glow was just beyond the woods. They'd wonder, of course, but never stop, never know it was the warm, scrubbed, ex-Li'l Pancake House.

Town was a mystery. And she had no desire to see it. She'd heard Hassan talk about it. Wanda lived there, and she continuously filled Missy in on things that happened, like a flooded street after a sudden rain or the car that got away from a driver who mistook the gas for the brake and plowed through the front window of the Piggly Wiggly grocery store. But Missy was not interested in seeing the faces of the unfamiliar.

She'd found her solitary niche, a hideaway where she could live forever if she wanted to. Or live for only a short time. It was a compromise she struck with herself after miles and miles of Skyles's constant movement and the steady stream of sad strangers in the funeral home months before that. The Li'l Pancake House had a pace she never knew existed, and it felt good wrapped around her. Funny thing, though. For so long, she had been dying for motion and ever-increasing distance. Now, she'd found happiness as a body at rest. She sometimes worried if someone her age could be content without a constant buzz of energy surrounding her, without motion. But she told herself she'd always felt older than her birth certificate. And the work made her happy, though she was at the Li'l Pancake House seven nights a week. Once, Missy brought up the fact that she'd never been given a day off.

"So?" Wanda answered.

"So, are we allowed to take time off?"

Wanda launched into some lyrics of a song Missy didn't know. *"You don't work and you don't get paid."* When she quieted down, she turned to Missy and whispered. "He never takes time off. It never crosses his brain that somebody else might want to." But Wanda made sense. If you wanted money, you needed to work. So Missy did. Every day.

There was safety at the Li'l Pancake House, too. She felt like the world was somewhere else, somewhere around the curve or beyond those trees, and it couldn't get at her even if it wanted to. There was no *louise* scrawled on the windows. The yellow glow would protect her like some sort of force field, as long as she stayed in the light.

One night a thought struck Missy. *I have become like one of the monks at the abbey.* The brothers in their long robes had found a way to be happy and safe and stay in one place. They knew a rare secret of contentment. She was beginning to know the secret, too. Sometimes when she crossed the parking lot, she looked back toward the trees, expecting to see a pickup truck, with three or four monks sitting on the tailgate, watching her trudge from home to work and back again. Or maybe Skyles would be there, sipping from the canteen, wondering how she had managed to find a life without distractions. But the woods were always empty and quiet.

Missy settled in. If she needed something from town, Wanda picked it up for her. Hassan offered to run errands for her, but she turned him down gently. She couldn't imagine Hassan dropping by the drugstore to get her personal things. Clothes weren't a problem. She had a couple of uniforms that almost fit, and when she wasn't wearing one of them, she was usually asleep, under sheets that were changed every other day by a woman Hassan hired as a part-time motel housekeeper.

Wanda also offered to take her into town, to see a movie or go somewhere, as she put it, for "a liquid attitude adjustment." Missy declined. Her attitude was healthier than ever. She had a room, more food than she could eat. She was making friends. She was happy where she was, anchored somewhere just off the main highway.

Hassan kept a leftover box of official Li'l Pancake House stationery in his converted bathroom/office. Missy asked him if she could have a couple of sheets, so he brought her the whole box and laid it down at her feet.

"And you insult me," he said, winking. "Two sheets? Take them. Take them all."

In her room, she sat at the tiny desk, and using the same pen she took orders with, she wrote a letter to the Marines.

Dear Les and Oscar,

I do hope you all made it back to the Marines before they found out you were gone. I cannot say how much I thank you for giving me a lift that day. I am working now and getting by, which is the best any of us can do these days, right? I've made a couple friends too which is good for me after being on the road. How far did you say your Marine base was from here? Maybe someday you can come by for a visit. I can cook now and everything. I'm getting good on a grill.

When she got that far, she tore it up. It was boring to her, so she could only imagine how it would put Oscar and Les to sleep. She started again.

Dear Guys,

Well, here I am, thanks to you. Flipping pancakes and pouring juice for people I don't even know. Sometimes I feel like I'm in the Marines too. What with having to stay on my feet most of the time and stand over that grill that gets so hot you could fry an egg on it.

She wasn't sure if they would catch the joke about frying an egg. She rejected that letter too. Missy stared at the third sheet of paper. She just wanted to tell Oscar and Les that she was doing fine and feeling the same way. She wanted to tell them she appreciated the ride, and she was glad she met them. And she wanted to do it the quickest way she could without wasting anybody's time.

She ran across the parking lot and into the Li'l Pancake House. It was midmorning. Hassan was reading the paper behind the counter, scanning the headlines quickly as he turned the pages. Two of the booths were occupied, but nothing sizzled on the grill. Hassan dropped the paper.

"And it's a rare visit. You are not sleeping, Missy Belue?"

"I need something."

"Don't we all, sister," a man's voice cracked from one of the booths.

"And what is it? Anything. You tell me. You need a ride into town? We will close down immediately." The people eating looked up from their food, wondering if they could finish before the doors locked. "You need money? A raise? It is not my policy to give them so soon to a new employee, but for you? An exception. Because you are so exceptional."

Now the people in the booths forgot about their food. They wanted to see what *exceptional* looked like in this part of the country. What they saw was a long-legged, long-haired girl wearing a Li'l Pancake House uniform and no shoes, rocking impatiently from foot to foot, as though the tiles were hot.

Hassan glanced from Missy to his customers. He gathered himself, took a large breath, and spoke to them.

"And she came out of nowhere with the clothes on her back. Out of nowhere to work for me. I have thanked the Baptist God a dozen times for my fortune."

"She's a waitress," one of the men said through his grits.

"And she is more," Hassan answered.

"I just want a menu," Missy said in a near whisper to Hassan. She could feel the blood rising in her cheeks. She didn't want this to go on any longer or louder than it already had. "And an envelope big enough to mail it."

Hassan stopped. "Menu?"

"Well, yeah, it's for a friend. I could pay for it if we can't spare one."

"And spare? Spare. Of course, we can spare. How many do you want? A dozen? A box?" Hassan waved his arms like he was signaling an airplane.

"Just the one will do," Missy said, embarrassment rising in her voice.

"Take mine," said the same man from the nearest booth. "I ain't spilled nothing on it." But he was already wiping it with a napkin.

Missy couldn't tell if he was making fun of her or not. Still, she took the menu and turned to Hassan.

"I'm sending it to Les and Oscar. The guys who brought me here. It's sort of a souvenir."

The menus were laminated leftovers from the official Li'l Pancake House days. At one time, the tiny photos of the food—the burgers and breakfast plates—had been sharp and bright. Now, everything seemed a little dull, like it wouldn't taste very good. Half of the things on the menu they didn't have or plan on cooking again. Hassan had eliminated most of the items that required gravy. He told Missy gravy was "the sauce of infidels."

When Missy and Wanda waited on tables they never had a list of daily specials. They had a list of the lies on the menu. "If you want this or this or this," Wanda would say, pointing at the pictures, "you are in the wrong place." Missy had never heard of anyone getting up and walking out because of the spotty menu.

"And I am proud that you would send them something from here. Does this mean that this is your home now? Or is this like a postcard from your holiday spot?"

Even though he stared right in Missy's eyes, he was speaking to the customers, too, talking loud enough that they could be in on the proceedings.

"There's no place like home," said someone from the booth. "There's no place like home."

"Damn, I love the *Wizard of Oz*," answered the man who gave up his menu. "Except them flying monkeys."

"And you are home," Hassan said, the words hovering between a question and a conclusion. Missy knew the right answer, and she knew the one he wanted to hear.

"Yes," she said, trying to keep a smile from blossoming.

"Well, there you go," the man in the booth told her. Missy headed toward the door with the menu and a large envelope from Hassan's office. At once, the people began to form a line at the cash register, their wallets out, getting ready to pay Hassan.

"And see?" he said to all of them, dipping his fingers into the drawer for change. "Missy Belue arrives through the glass door and good things begin to happen."

One night, deep into her shift, Missy was in serious weeds. The booths weren't completely filled, but the ones that were occupied had complicated orders. Substitute this, extra that, put something on the side. Burgers and eggs and BLTs. She found herself sprinting from the booths to the grill to the register. Usually, she would have been glad for the crowd and the orders, glad she could burn up some energy. Missy was thankful Hassan was there, behind the counter, helping her out. Since business had picked up in the hot weather, the two of them sometimes overlapped a shift.

One of the customers, a long-hauler who came through every week or so, finished his burger and made his way to the register to pay. Missy rang in the order and calculated the change, digging for quarters in the drawer. Hassan squeezed behind her hoisting a large bag of frozen hash brown potatoes in one hand. He was on his way to the grill, but he had to get around Missy first. He didn't say a word, didn't say "excuse me," just pushed by, his little belly doing its own thing against the back of her uniform. She felt his hand cup the lowest curve of her rear end. Not a pat exactly or a pinch. Just a cuff with the palm. A little boost of the hand, like he was trying to lift her off of her feet by her ass. There—and then it was gone, so quickly she wondered if she had imagined it.

She considered turning around and glaring at him. It wasn't the kind of thing she ever expected from Hassan. Maybe it was a mistake, a slip. Whatever it was, it was over in a split second, and in that split second, she lost count of what she was doing with the trucker's check. A memory of Skyles's hands flickered through her mind. Missy froze.

"Hey, you. I need some change," the trucker said, spitting the words into her face. The sharpness of his tone snapped her back. She could remember exactly what he had to eat, but she couldn't recall what it had cost or why she had a dollar bill in one hand and her fingers in the quarters slot. She took the chance that the dollar was for him, so she handed it across the counter. "That ain't even close!" he said. "What? You think I'm some goddamn idiot?"

Missy said, "How much was your—"

"You tell me. You made out the damn ticket." He leaned toward her, and she smelled something alcoholic blow by on his breath. Slowly the events before Hassan copped a feel began to drift back to her. This guy yelling at her kept asking for a half a cup of coffee. "Just half full," he said, smiling. Missy would pour it, then a couple of seconds later, his cup would be about to overflow. He must have kept his bottle under his leg. Turbo coffee. High-octane trucker fuel.

"Little extra tip, huh? Is that what you're after? You want something extra, I got something for you," he backed away from the counter, grabbed his crotch, and yelled to the restaurant. The people in their booths couldn't decide whether to watch or ignore him. They tried to do both.

Hassan crossed behind Missy again, this time more quickly. She didn't even think about the hand. But there it was again, there and gone on the slope of her ass. Not a lift this time, but rather a reassuring pat. At a time like this.

"And we have a problem here?" he asked the trucker.

"You got the problem, Abdul. Bitch face here won't give me all my change." The trucker leaned forward, leering down at Hassan and Missy.

She could hear herself trying to clear this up. *Hassan, because you put your hand on my ass, you made me remember the things my cousin did to me in his pickup and while I was remembering this, I forgot about counting change for this guy. I'm not mad, Hassan, just a little tired of fingers and palms and remembering and forgetting.*

"And, sir," Hassan said, pointing to his name tag, "You must know this. My name is not Abdul. And women in my ex-Li'l Pancake House shall not be called bitch faces."

Then Hassan took that clever, quick hand of his—the same one he'd planted on her behind—reached inside a small, secret shelf beneath the cash register, a hiding place no one had told Missy about, and came up waving the tiniest gun she had ever seen, waving it right under the trucker's nose. It was the perfect gun for his little hand, the size of half a donut. Hassan's face changed color. It grew darker and angrier. And his breathing came fast and sort of thin, like he had just sprinted from the motel. He perched on his toes like a dancer.

The trucker sobered in a flash. He backed farther away from the counter. "Jesus, man, you crazy?" The other customers buried themselves in the booths.

Hassan animal panted. "Yes," he said between breaths. "Very much."

"I ain't gonna get shot for no two forty-seven," the trucker said, backing toward the door, bumping into tables.

That was it! Missy thought. She remembered. She reached into the slots in the register and grabbed the right amount of money. "Here," she told him, holding the money out in her open palm.

He took it, keeping an eye on Hassan and the perfect gun. Then, just as the trucker was about to pocket his change, Hassan said, "And the tip, sir?"

The trucker let one of the dollar bills flutter to the floor as he walked backward, toward his rig parked in the lot across the highway, facing them the entire way like he was playing some kind of kid's game. Hassan followed him through the door and part of the way to his truck, while the rest in the Li'l Pancake House, Missy and the patrons, pressed against the window, watching Hassan's gun shine in the light from the yellow sign.

The truck roared away and disappeared around the first curve in the highway. Hassan stood in the middle of the road, straddling the faded centerline, watched for a couple of extra minutes, stuffed the gun in his belt, and headed off in the direction of the motel, never once looking back at his restaurant.

The next morning, Wanda was in early, already talking before the door whisked closed behind her. "I hear Hassan put on his little Wild

West cowboy suit last night," she said as she unbuttoned her sweater. "He does that ever so often, you know, pulls out that little peashooter and waves it around like he's John Wayne or something."

"How did you know about that?" Missy asked. She was surprised to see Wanda at this time of the day.

"He called me while it was still dark. Said he wouldn't be making it in today and would I fill in his shift after you get off. He gets all upset when he plays cowboy. Has to stay in the bed a day or two."

Wanda stared at her reflection in the refrigerator glass and poked at the curls around her ears. There was a shimmer of sweat on her lip. Probably because she wore sweaters in the middle of summer.

"So he's done this thing before?" Missy was a little bit disappointed that she wasn't the first to benefit from Hassan's gunslinging.

"Oh yeah. Gets that desert blood boiling and sticks his face in somebody else's face. He reminds me of them little fyce dogs that don't have sense enough to know they're little."

A strange feeling swept over Missy. She felt like the two of them were having girl talk. The last time she'd gossiped had been with Angela. It was like a ghost had come and whispered in her ear, only now somebody new was on the other end of the conversation.

Wanda didn't appear to recognize the importance of the moment. She wanted to talk about the things that interested her.

"You know what they say about those kind of people? They are not afraid to die, that's what. They just don't care. They say that dying is the best thing they can hope for. Some kind of religious fever they get. Burns them up." Wanda took a pack of gum from the glass cabinet under the register. "No wonder he gets upset. His head's on fire."

"He seemed pretty brave," Missy said.

Wanda said, "Honey, he ain't brave. He's just one of them little fyce dogs."

12.

Missy walked across the parking lot to the motel after her shift, pulled through the sounds and smells that lingered from the night—the burned diesel, the vented grease, the trucks missing a gear on the interstate, the cicadas out looking for a place to lose their skins. The asphalt was beginning to warm up. She didn't make the turn toward her room. She walked in the direction of Hassan's. Maybe she wasn't so much drawn as she was pushed, prodded by a set of small, quick fingers that left a brand on her backside.

He answered the door in a T-shirt, a pair of jeans cut off at the knees and no name tag. He turned the knob quickly, after only a single knock, so he had probably watched Missy coming the length of the parking lot. He didn't say hello, only swung the door wide and motioned her to follow him in. Missy was expecting chitchat. Some of Hassan's far-flung banter. When he was silent, he upset her balance. She lost whatever slow-moving train of thought she was hitched to, and found herself walking into a life-sized travel brochure.

Hassan had thumbtacked huge posters to the wall, all of them showing perfect men and women enjoying themselves on beaches or in the mountains. Sailboats and skiers sliced through the photographs. Horseback riders and surfers. Everyone smiled. Every single one of the vacationers was beautiful, with beautiful teeth and beautiful bodies and beautiful lives. Cruise ships and honeymooners. All his furniture, the same exact furniture Missy had in her room, was covered with stacks of travel information: plane schedules, travel books, pamphlets about how to avoid parasites in a foreign country or spot pickpockets in a public square.

"And it is not what you expect, yes?" he said finally, sitting on the bed. His hairy legs were thin and spindly, like a kid's. That was exactly what he looked like. A hairy kid, but with a much older smile that he flashed like a business card.

"It's real interesting," she said, looking around again. She kept the open door in sight. Hassan jumped from the bed and flopped into the only chair not littered with papers and brochures.

"And I agree. You see, I like to travel. But I have never the chance to go anywhere, so I keep all of these ready. To give me ideas and information if opportunity ever arises. I am nothing if not ready." He waved his hand across the room.

"Well," Missy said, "maybe I should be going."

"And you've already accomplished what you came for?" he asked, smiling. "In only seconds?"

"I just came—well, I thought I'd—" She heard herself stammering, stopping and going like she was in the middle of a lie, when she was trying her best to tell the truth. She felt young, suddenly, young and stupid and unsure. She wanted to come by Hassan's room just to check on him after he'd waved his gun. She wanted to see if he was different now that he'd faced down a drunk trucker. She had to see if the whole thing had changed him in the space of a few hours. Some kind of new bond existed between them now, a common thread—a touch, a gun, adrenaline maybe—and she wanted to know what in the world it all meant.

And she wanted to tell him to keep his little hand to himself, that just because he backed down shitfaced customers, he couldn't go around squeezing her butt like it was a loaf of day-old bread. She wasn't going to get mad about it. Just firm.

"And let me help," he said, pulling himself up from the chair. He began to pace like a courtroom lawyer. "You are here because you want to thank me for saving you. Which is okay. It is really no big deal." He leaned toward her. "And I must tell you, the gun is not loaded. There is no need to thank me. It is my pleasure to be of service to you, Missy Belue." Hassan smiled broadly and bowed.

He pushed the door closed and motioned Missy toward a chair. Hassan flopped cross-legged on the bed, and for the next hour, he took Missy on his imaginary travels around the world. Hassan had it all mapped out. He had plans—real, thought-through strategies—to see every country he'd ever heard of, any country that had tweaked his interest. And for most of the ones he'd heard of, everything he knew came from a travel brochure.

He showed Missy pictures of marketplaces where he would buy the local fruit, and never once, he told her, would he get sick and have to "drink the pink." She assumed that meant Pepto-Bismol. He showed her beaches where he would sleep under an umbrella—"because even I can sunburn you know," he said—and read the books he'd never had the chance to read.

When he said this, he reached beneath the bed and pulled out a low, wide cardboard box. It was filled with cheap paperbacks, thrillers and sci-fi and romance novels, all of them with the front covers ripped off.

"And when I first moved to this country," he told her, "I worked near a bookstore. Sometime every month, near the end of the month, they would tear the covers from their unpopular paper books and dump them in the big green trash can in the back of the building. I took some of what they threw away. People throw away so much."

Hassan leaned over the edge of the bed and flipped the switch on his little hotplate and boiled some water. In a few minutes, he made them strong, black coffee. She was beginning to see how Hassan went without sleep. Drinking coffee and thinking about his future travels kept his eyes open most of night.

He waved his arms when he described all the places he would go.

He used the words he'd stolen from his brochures. He talked about luxurious days and fabulous nights. All of his times were "fun-filled" or "sun-kissed." All of his beaches were "ribbons of white" and the water was always "azure."

"What is azure?" Missy asked.

"The color of water when you are on holiday," he said.

He told her he would travel alone, because that was the only way to be open to the possibilities of a new place. "If you have someone else with you," he said, "there is always another opinion and another decision to make."

Hassan saw Missy yawn, and he immediately began to gather up the brochures.

She apologized. "I'm just tired from working. It's not that I'm bored or anything," she said.

"And I'm sure that you cannot share completely in my excitement. You are nice to listen to me about my plans." He cleared off the bed, and even though the pamphlets and brochures seemed to be scattered everywhere, he had a special place for each one. *His chaos is organized,* Missy thought.

"I like hearing about it, Hassan. I'm interested in traveling too. Not to the places like where you're going. Just moving. That's what I want to do, at least when I figure out where to go."

"And we hope you don't leave too soon. We like you at the pancake place," he said, smiling. The darkness of his skin sometimes made his teeth seem too white.

"Yeah, well, about the Li'l Pancake House. . ."

"And?" He sounded scared.

"Well, before the trucker gave me a hard time—" Missy stopped. She didn't want to actually repeat the entire ass-grabbing incident in front of the guy who did the grabbing.

"And?"

"Your hand?"

"Hand," he repeated, and it wasn't a question.

Missy talked quickly, filling in the awkwardness that was brewing. She heard the hot plate pop as it cycled off. "Maybe you don't need to do that kind of thing. Maybe you didn't mean anything by it. It's just that it kind of surprised me. Maybe, you know, we could do without that. The hand thing. On my butt."

Most men, when they were shut back or shot down, took it one of two ways. Either they became furious, like women had no right to tell them what they could and could not do. Or they simply denied everything they said or did and struck a posture that insinuated the woman must be insane for even thinking something like that. Missy had witnessed both reactions, but never in all of her life had she seen a man take a rejection like Hassan.

He began by beating his head against the bedpost. He wrapped his tiny hands around it and slammed his forehead against the post, simultaneously whining some kind of foreign-sounding chant.

"Hassan!" she yelled, and he just sang his song louder. "For God's sake, Hassan!"

She took two steps and was at the bed. Missy hooked her arms around his chest and pried him from the bedpost. He spun quickly and buried his face in her chest and sobbed, crying his eyes out, but still singing that song that no one from this part of the world could possibly be familiar with. He flapped his arms like a scared bird. When that stopped, he began to jerk on his hair, trying to pull it out by the handful. All the while his face was stuck right in the middle of her chest, right on the zipper of her uniform. She felt like a TV wrestler as she tried to put him in a hold.

Hassan, through all of this, said only one thing in English that Missy could make out. "And I should cut my hands off at the wrist," he said. "They are evil!"

Missy pulled his two hands to her cheeks, to show him she didn't hold them personally responsible. She made him give her a big hug. They eased back on the bed, side by side, and she still had a relatively good lock on Hassan's arms and legs, just in case he began to flail again.

Missy had grown used to lying with Skyles, who was a man without any middle ground. A one-way-or-the-other man. He was either snoring on his side of the pickup bed or he was maneuvering his way into her sleeping bag. But Hassan and Missy just lay there, in that middle ground that was so *comfortable* she couldn't believe she'd never discovered it before.

After what seemed only minutes, Hassan was asleep, his breathing rhythmic like a warm song into the folds on the front of her waitress uniform. She could see in the light from the night table that his forehead was sweating, and occasionally he moaned when he exhaled. Missy had never held a man so hairy. She felt like she was a little girl again, clutching a new stuffed animal that made real human noises when you squeezed it.

Directly above her, tacked to the ceiling was a poster Missy hadn't noticed before. She was wide-eyed from the coffee and used to the dim, almost dusky glow of the room. She could see a poster of a man and woman on horseback, galloping down a beach through the shallow, sudsy surf. They kicked up sand and foam. They were laughing.

The writing was big enough for Missy to read from the bed—*ADVENTURE! THE TIME OF YOUR LIFE!*—in big letters that spanned the azure water.

Dammit, Hassan, she thought, *you are not as helpless as you feel.*

It was like putting a cranky child to bed. Missy slid a pillow under Hassan's head, pulled the bedspread to his chin, made sure he was breathing, and left just as the sun broke free above the pines. Back in her own room, her bed was still made from the day before. Justine, the housekeeping woman, had pulled the corners hospital tight, and Missy eased between the sheets.

Her feet ached from the shift she'd finished earlier that morning. They pounded with her pulse as she lay in the fake darkness. A couple of shafts of light escaped from the sides of the window blinds, but for the most part, Missy was in the dark. Because she worked the late shift, she lived backwards, sleeping in broad daylight and destroying her feet at night.

Missy slept into the afternoon, and woke up around four thirty or five when the rumbling and gurgling in her stomach sat her bolt upright in bed. She threw up before she made it across the floor to the bathroom. For fifteen minutes, she knelt on the tile, her head on the toilet seat, waiting for the next wave to arrive. She tried to will it away, repeating out loud, "I will not puke, I will not puke, I will not . . ." It didn't work.

As suddenly as it struck her, the waves of nausea left. Her head was clear, her stomach calm. Her feet hurt, but that was normal. She began to catalog the day before—what she'd eaten, who she'd been in contact with. She wondered if she'd picked up something in Hassan's room. She hated being sick, and this time bothered her particularly; she'd been feeling so good since she'd arrived. The last time her stomach revolted was at that roadside place, the DeSoto.

She dressed in her own clothes—not her uniform—and made her way to the Li'l Pancake House. She expected to find Wanda there, pulling the back half of a double shift. Instead, Hassan was behind the counter, singing as he grilled a couple of steaks for the two men in the booth closest to the hallway and bathroom.

"And good afternoon, Missy Belue," Hassan yelled over his shoulder. "A moment, please."

He flipped the steaks, and they sizzled even louder when he flattened them with the spatula. He motioned for Missy to follow him to the office. She never quite made it that far. When she drew even with the men waiting on their steaks, one of them, the one facing her, spat out juice from the dip in his lower lip, right into a big plastic cup, already half full of thick, dark tobacco juice. It even had a tan head of bubbles on it, like a foreign beer. When Missy saw the cup and the hour's worth of tobacco spit, she headed for the bathroom, her stomach crawling up her throat again.

Hassan was waiting for her in the narrow hallway when she opened the bathroom door, dabbing her lips with a wet paper towel. "I've been sick today," she said. "Since I woke up. Throwing up."

"And my God!" Hassan screamed. "I've made you ill. The sight of me."

"I think it was more something to do with what I ate," she said, not wanting Hassan to start banging his head against the jukebox or try slitting his wrist with a butter knife.

"And you only eat here," he said. "If it is not me, it is the food I serve."

Missy turned toward the booths. "Hassan, it's probably just some bug that's going around. I'll be fine. I feel better when I throw up. Really. Just a bug." She kept her eyes straight ahead, knowing the spit cup was somewhere to her right.

"A bug, a bug? I will call an exterminator today. We will carry no bugs here."

The man looked up from his spit cup. "I got a cousin who's an exterminator. Cheap, too."

"And what is his name, please, sir?" Hassan asked, dashing toward the man as he pulled a pencil from his shirt pocket.

Missy decided that it wasn't worth the trouble to try and explain bugs to Hassan. She was beginning to understand that his excitement and passion directly affected his ability to listen to reason. If he wanted to get a bug guy out here, fine. The tobacco spitter wrote a name and number on the back of a napkin. "I'm surprised y'all don't spray for bugs in here already. Being a restaurant and all."

Hassan corrected him. "And no, this isn't for in here. It is for the rooms in the motel. Two rooms in particular."

"That motel yours, too?" He was impressed, honored perhaps that a motel/restaurant owner was frying his steak. His friend across the table played bumper cars with the salt and pepper shakers, fascinated by the glassy clink they made when they collided. Missy took a seat at the counter.

Hassan thanked him for the number and loaded their plates with the well-done steaks, home fries and soggy green beans. The smell of the food didn't bother Missy. The odor actually made her a little hungry, but she didn't chance looking at the plates. Hassan refilled their tea, gave them some Heinz 57, then turned his attention to Missy.

"And now," he said, "why are you here? I know you. You are usually not here in the afternoons."

"Neither are you."

"And true. Wanda filled in for me. But you know that. When I woke, you were not there, but you were there. I mean, I could tell you had been in my room. The smell, a good smell. And the empty cup. I felt so good. I thought I would feel bad after the man and the gun. But no. I felt so good when I woke up, I came over here and told Wanda to go take a hiking."

Hassan was not uncomfortable about what had happened. Of course, they hadn't really done anything. That's what Missy kept reminding herself. It was just one of those things that happened when people were tired and fuzzy-headed, and they'd talked long enough in Hassan's room to be better friends than they had been an hour before. It was just an event that had a beginning and an end.

"I'm glad you feel so good," Missy said, catching a reflection of herself in the window of the cooler. Her complexion appeared a little gray, but it could've been the light. "I'd better head back. I thought getting out would make me feel better. Could you hand me a pack of crackers?" Hassan dove behind the counter and came up with a small sack stuffed with Captain's Wafers. Missy sighed.

"And enough crackers, you will never have to ask again. Let me walk you back to your room. It is getting hot. Sick people should not be heated up."

"Hassan, I don't need you to—"

"And you are sick with the bugs. You don't know what you need." Hassan didn't bother walking the length of the counter. He pole-vaulted over the top and landed like a circus performer, his hands raised high, chest thrown out. He turned to the men who were chewing their steaks

"And you gentlemen, if you are through before I return, the steak is on me," he said, patting the closest one on the back. "Eat up, my friends." Hassan flashed them a huge smile as he held open the door for Missy and her sack of crackers.

13.

Hassan kept calling their trip to town a *date*.

For days, he'd stopped by during Missy's shift, in the middle of the night, stuck his slick head in the door, and reminded her about it.

"And don't forget," he would say as he entered, the bell on the door still clanging, "we have our date to see Mr. Doctor Wiley."

When the day arrived, Wanda showed up early at Hassan's request. Wanda wanted to know what was going on, why she had to fill in for Hassan again, but Missy could only thank her and smile. She was in no hurry. She wandered to her room, changed out of the brown-and-yellow uniform and found some comfortable clothes, things that were baggy and would catch any breeze.

She sat in the doorway of her room, in the wooden desk chair, and stared across the parking lot toward the highway. A carload of lost Northerners (a Pontiac with New Jersey plates) on their way to Florida pulled in for breakfast. They ate fast. While she watched them pay their checks and pull away, she felt a wave coming over her, and she headed for the bathroom, but it passed, pushed down by something else. By nerves, maybe. Or anxiety. Missy had been sick for days, and the intermittent nausea wasn't getting any better. And she wasn't looking forward to going to town, to leaving the simple safety of the restaurant and motel and her room.

Midmorning, Hassan finally stopped by her room, put her chair away for her, and the two of them walked toward the rear of the motel. He was excited about going to the doctor's office. Missy was mostly just tired and sick every afternoon when she woke up. That was why they were going to town, to find out what was going on with her system.

Hassan led her behind the motel to a small, low-roofed shed that was a different color than the rest of the buildings, but like the motel, the shed needed a fresh coat of paint. A serious padlock hung from a set of wide doors. When they got close enough, Missy could see that the lock wasn't clasped shut. "And the key is long missing," Hassan said. Like a game show host revealing the grand prize of the day, he swung both doors open and stepped back, waving into the dark opening. Missy couldn't see what he was hiding in the shed, until he reached inside the door and threw a switch, and behind the light that suddenly poured from the opening, she saw the chrome grill of a bone-white Cadillac shining out at her like a stupid grin.

Five minutes later she was riding toward town inside the most beautiful car she'd ever seen. Not a speck of dirt on it. Clarence would have been envious of the cleanliness. Everything that could gleam, gleamed. The wood on the dashboard had a wet, rained-on look. The engine rumbled as though it would power them right off the edge of the world. The Cadillac was a convertible, the late-model kind, with a pair of fish-like fins that rose up in the back, but the car didn't show its age. From the way it stuck to the asphalt on the curves, Missy could tell it was a heavy machine. *Let off the gas, and this Cadillac will take a couple of miles to roll to a dead stop,* Missy thought.

Hassan was a man in love with his car. Missy could tell when he started it, the way he let it run for a few minutes before they got going, the way he stroked his tiny hands over the steering wheel. He talked to it every couple of seconds, warning it of potholes. But the car floated right over uneven spots in the road like they were skating on thick ice.

After a minute, Hassan pulled to the side of the road. He pushed a button and the top began to curl back slowly. Suddenly, they were in the sun. Now the dash looked like it was sweating. Hassan leaned toward the middle of the seat.

"And now," he grinned, "we are on our date."

It was Missy's first time away from the motel and the restaurant, the first time she'd been on the road since she came to the ex-Li'l Pancake House with the Marines. Nothing official on the shoulder of the highway told her they crossed the town limits or what the population was, no cheery welcome sign. Just a rusted, round Kiwanis Club marker that said meetings were held the second Tuesday of the month. There was a speed limit sign full of bullet holes to make sure they didn't go too fast. No such worries with Hassan.

He crept along like they were in a parade, like they *were* the parade. Missy thought how easy it would be to imagine herself as a beauty queen at that speed. She could move to the back and sit on the folded-down top and wave at the imaginary people lining the sidewalks.

"And there is where I get my gas," Hassan said, pointing to the left. "You, Claude! Hello!" he yelled at the man sitting in the shade of an awning. Claude nodded and rose from his chair, heading for the door. Missy imagined he was calling ahead, warning the townspeople that the great white Cadillac was making its way up the street, take cover.

"And there, that is where they have maps from all over the world all in a single book," he said and shut his eyes for a second, easing off the gas as they rolled past the county library. Hassan recovered from his momentary travel fantasy and turned back into a tour guide as they approached the center of town. He identified every building they passed, and he seemed to know the name of every person they cruised by. And not just names; he knew how everybody was related. He told Missy who was the uncle of whom, who was divorced, who was new to town.

"New just like you, Missy Belue!" he said.

They drove by the biggest house in town, then the oldest, then the only stone house in the county. They saw a diner that sold "the feet of pigs in a jar" and the "house of a thousand flowers." Hassan's eyes glassed over from excitement, and he bounced up and down in the driver's seat. He was a man in love with the place where he almost lived.

Near the far end of the town, which was only a dozen or so blocks long, they pulled up to an elementary school that was closed for the summer. In the sticky, black parking lot, four boys perched atop the empty bicycle rack like birds on a wire. Their shoes lay tangled in piles across the blacktop. Hassan drove through the gate, and the big Caddy lumbered up to the boys. Hassan slid into a parking space marked *Principal* and cut the engine. He grinned up at the boys, the same grin he flashed at Missy every day.

"Man," one of the boys yelled at them, "you know this ain't fair."

They were all the same age, twelve or so, probably too old to go to this particular school, yet they seemed comfortable and familiar with the parking lot.

"Ain't fair," the boy said again.

"And how are you boys today? So good to see you again. And it is so fair because I am the champion, and until I am unthroned, it is fair for me to come here," Hassan said, reaching down toward the gas pedal and the brake where Missy couldn't see.

Another boy, a smaller one, spit through his front teeth on the pavement. "I believe you go off somewhere and practice, that's what I think."

"And no sir," said Hassan. "It is just in my blood. My ancestors in the desert walked for miles and miles across the burning sands without so much as a snort or blister. You were going to walk without me this day? That is a sign of disrespect."

The leftover exhaust from the Caddy billowed over the car and floated into the seats, filling Missy's nose and head. She was afraid if she opened her mouth, she would lose her breakfast. But she was totally lost in the conversation, so she took a chance.

"What?" she said. "What's going on?"

"Contest," answered another of the boys.

"One that ain't fair for him to be in," the smaller one, the spitter, said, pointing at Hassan.

He hopped off the bike rack onto the grass strip that ran the length of the parking lot. The others followed him, and Hassan opened the door. In a couple of quick steps he was on the grass, trailing right behind the group. Missy saw he was barefoot, just like the boys.

He called out to her. "And watch good, Missy Belue. At this, I am the best."

They walked fifty yards or so to the far end of the lot. From where she sat, they looked to be dancing, but it was only the early heat waves rising from the asphalt that shimmered their bodies.

She couldn't tell which one was Hassan because her eyes started to water, and so did her mouth, the hot spit seeping out from beneath her tongue. She smelled the hot, sour tar. Tasted it, too. The burned-gas smell of the hot Caddy still floated around in her head. *Whatever you do,* she said to herself, *don't throw up in his Cadillac.*

A thick wave of sweat slipped out of her scalp and flowed like oil down her forehead. The last thing she remembered was Hassan, walking like a ghost out of the heat waves and across the parking lot, screaming, "And I am the hot-pavement walking champion of the world!"

Behind him, the boys picked up their feet like long-legged birds, running on their toes toward the safety of the strip of grass in front of the school. She never saw Hassan break stride as he calmly strolled across the scalding pavement. Then, she toppled over, passed out across the Caddy's big, soft front seat.

Hassan thought Missy was dead. And he thought he had killed her. When he got back to the car, after showing off and walking farther than he ever had before on the hot, black tar, he looked down in the seat, and her eyes were wide open, like she'd been surprised, and her face was a cadaver gray. He moaned, standing outside the car, the tar burning the soles of his feet.

"The pain on my feet, it was my punishment. I thought I had killed you. I wanted to die there also," he later told her.

He also told her the rest of the story, how the boys put on their shoes and sprinted to the Caddy. How they grabbed Hassan and shoved him into the back seat of the car. For a second they stood looking at the bottoms of Hassan's feet, which by this time were blistered raw and bleeding from the hot asphalt. They decided that foot pain was the reason he was screaming. Then one of them noticed Missy's condition, and they took a second or two to decide if she had passed away. At that precise moment, Missy made some sort of noise, a gargle or a cough. Hassan heard it, too, and fueled by a quick burst of adrenaline, sprang into action. He dove for the steering wheel and the ignition. The boys ran for cover as Hassan slammed the car into reverse, then into drive, the transmission groaning, and headed for the doctor's office, which, Missy came to find out later, was on the other end of town. So the two of them screamed down the main drag again, mocking the speed limit, the Caddy eating up the road as they backtracked.

Hassan told her this from a swivel chair in the examining room. His feet were propped up now and wrapped with thick, white bandages. Missy lay on a bed, a cool cloth plastered to her forehead and sheets that smelled brand new tugged to her chin. Hassan machine-gunned words at her, talking so fast she only picked up a few things at a time. There was something about a police car chasing them. He said all of the people who'd seen them in the Caddy were now crowded outside of the window, a few feet away, trying to peer through narrow slits in the blinds, wondering why this odd couple ended up at the doctor's office. When he said this, Missy noticed the buzz of voices outside the window.

"And," he went on, "the way it all turns out is very funny."

"This doesn't feel funny."

"Well, we were coming to see this doctor anyway," he said. "But what is funny is that I thought you were dead. I thought that I had killed you in the heat. But this whole thing is not about death." He grinned. "It is just the opposite of death."

"Yes, I'm alive," Missy said. "The opposite."

"And I can't say more. Only to say that you are very much alive and I am happy. Opposite of death. Very opposite. It is a miracle!"

He shut his eyes and leaned back in the chair, smiling at the ceiling. They sat in a small office, but bigger perhaps than the usual examining room. Still, it felt crowded. The bed Missy lay on sagged toward the worn middle and creaked when she moved. The blinds were louvered shut and the window was down, but she felt lukewarm air flowing from somewhere. Next to her, she saw a wooden cabinet with a lock on it and a little table where Hassan put the key to the Caddy, along with his name tag.

"Hassan," she started to say, but the doorknob rattled a warning. In walked the doctor, a young man with hair just beginning to gray at the temples. In a town like this, Missy expected an elderly man of medicine, a slow-moving, old-school physician who could stare at you from a distance and tell you what was wrong. The man in front of her was more like a made-for-TV medicine man.

He didn't say hello, probably because everyone had made introductions while Missy was passed out. He launched into an interrogation.

"Sick at work, especially when you see certain foods?" Missy nodded. "Going to the bathroom more than usual?" She thought for a second, then nodded again. Missy had just assumed since it was such a hot summer, she was drinking more water and iced tea. No big deal.

The doctor turned to Hassan, who had tipped his chair back down and was grinning at the doctor now. Missy did not understand the joke.

"Well, I think it's just what I thought. Be sure in a bit. But it looks pretty clear cut to me." A phone rang in another room, and the doctor cocked his ear at the door. "Lucy's gone to lunch, so I have to answer. Hold on." He left the door open after he made his exit.

"You need to tell me what's going on," Missy said.

"And I already told you. The opposite of what I thought." There was the grin again.

"Dammit, will you stop smiling and tell me why I'm here?" She'd rarely cussed around Hassan, and the minute she let it slide between her teeth, she wanted it back. Knowing how he acted at times, she wondered if he would burst into tears.

Instead, he said, "Ah, and your nerves are a little on edge? This is not to be unexpected at such a time as this."

"Why?"

"Think, Missy Belue. Opposite of what I thought. I thought you were dead."

"Right, right. Nobody died."

"And you are close to the truth. But you are wrong really. The opposite of death is, Missy Belue, birth." He grinned again, this time even clapped his hands quietly, like he was watching golf.

When Hassan said *birth*, Missy's head filled with a picture of Skyles Huffman. There, in that doctor's sterile office, she could smell him and feel his breath close to her mouth. She remembered a night, *it had to be that night,* when he lay on top of her and she told him that she hadn't been able to find a drugstore, so he'd better wait a day or so. And he told her he didn't like waiting on anything, and he moved on her more and finally in her, shaking the both of them until the pickup squeaked on its struts, Missy staring at the roof of the camper top, trying to see the pattern in the rivets. She remembered Skyles checking the truck the next morning, pushing down on the back fenders and letting them spring up, trying to recreate the sound of the bad struts, and she wanted to cry, knowing if she heard that sound again, she might die a little bit. It wasn't but a couple days after that she left on her own, walked right out the back door of that restaurant, and before too long, she was too busy to worry, so busy she didn't notice her period disappeared.

Now, she wanted to cry again. She wanted to run out the door. Or maybe just lie on this clean-smelling bed for days and days, with the rest of the world curious about her, but safely on the other side of the shuttered window. The only reaction she could muster was to say his name, out loud, maybe too loud.

"Skyles," she offered up to the room.

"And a fine American name for a child!" Hassan leaped to his feet, landed on his bandages, then screamed as he dropped to his knees, reaching behind him toward the pain. When he caught his breath, he said, "Skyles is a name to think about." He climbed back into his chair. "This is the best day of my whole life," he whispered.

The doctor appeared in the doorway. "OK, well, the problem here is that I don't think you've been eating too well. Just because you work around food all day doesn't mean you eat the right kinds of things."

"So I'm pregnant," she said. It wasn't a question. She just hadn't heard the real word yet.

"Well, yes, of course. I thought Mr. Kamir would have told you." It was the first time Missy had heard Hassan's last name.

She looked up at the doctor. "I just want to hear you say it."

"I'm ninety-nine percent sure you are. I have to wait for the test to come back. We don't have a lab here. But I think you can count on having a baby in seven months or so. I'm guessing mid-March, somewhere around then. When was your last period? Oh, and I have this information sheet that tells you the kinds of things you should eat, what you should be getting, vitamins and things."

Hassan piped up. "And I will make sure she gets the food and the very best of vitamins. And no more work. No more up on the feet all night. I will help take care of this miracle."

"Fine by me," the doctor said. "Come and see me in a week, and we'll check your weight and check some other things. Get a real due date. You probably don't feel like going through all of that right now."

The doctor walked toward the window. He was grinning again, just like Hassan, like they had taken lessons from the same smile teacher. "Next time you come, don't worry about the police escort. You won't attract so much attention," he said and pulled on a cord, raising the blinds. Outside, a half dozen faces filled the window, a couple of them pressed close to the glass. The only one Missy recognized was the attendant from the gas station, Claude. Claude saw the three of them staring out from the little office, and he yelled, "Hey, Hassan! Nice work there, chief!" The voice sounded like it came from somewhere too far away to worry about.

Back in the Caddy, Hassan glowed like a low-watt light bulb. He could hardly keep his hands on the wheel, could barely keep the car between the yellow lines and the ditch. He talked fast, waving at his words with his hands. Making plans. Yammering about miracles and the beginning of life and the opposite of death. The top was snapped down tight, and the air conditioner blew so hard Missy's hair whipped out of control and a piece blew into her mouth. She all but gagged when she sucked it down her throat. *Wait a minute,* she thought. *It isn't the time of day to be sick.* Missy had become accustomed to the clockwork of her nausea. *When you work the late shift, morning sickness comes in the middle of the afternoon,* she told herself.

"And you are too cold?" Hassan asked her. "Not cool enough, perhaps?"

Missy didn't answer. She'd only been pregnant officially for half an hour, but she already realized what it did to people. Made them think, made them talk. Hassan chattered on about miracles, and Missy just let her thoughts find their own path. And she was not thinking about miracles.

Instead, she thought about anchors:

Now I got a miracle-anchor growing inside of me, weighing me down even now in the big, soft seat of the Caddy. I will never be able to run again, much less run away. I know of people who live their whole lives like they are tied to the dock. But once I left home, I never had a rope on me. But now. Now.

Missy wasn't stupid. She knew what was happening inside of her. She'd seen pictures in books of the little bug-eyed-looking thing that was going to turn into a baby. That thing hooked up to her with the cord that resembled old, twisted ski rope. *Who's tied to who?* she wondered. *Who's got the strings on them now?*

Then she got scared like a girl who was eighteen and living in a faded motel next to an ex-Li'l Pancake House should act when she found out news like this. Missy, for the first time in a long time, felt young, too young to be where she was, too young to be away from home. She began to cry. Like an eighteen-year-old was supposed to cry. Hassan was smart enough to keep driving, to keep his hands on the wheel, his eyes forward and his mouth shut. He let Missy Belue feel the way she wanted to.

A pregnant woman changes the way the world spins around her. Hassan was more watchful than ever for bumps on the way home, easing into the wrong lane to dodge winter potholes that nobody bothered to patch that summer. At the edge of town, he pulled into the parking lot of the grocery store and wheeled into a handicapped space. It was an old-style Piggly Wiggly, square and red-bricked. The sign had dulled decades ago and was missing a few important letters. *PIGGL WIGG*, it said near the nearly-invisible drawing of a jolly hog. He eased the shifter into park and turned toward Missy.

"And while I am inside, you will sit here, in the conditioned air," Hassan said, trying to decide how to walk on his tender feet. "Much better for you to stay in the car than to waste energy up and down the aisles."

"An hour ago you would have wanted me to come," she said.

"And within this hour, everything has changed." Hassan smiled.

"Come to a screeching halt, more like it," she answered him under her breath, but he wasn't listening.

"And the world is whirling at a new speed." Hassan eased one foot out of the door and gently placed it on the asphalt.

"Go away," she said.

"And?" He was a little surprised.

"Just go buy the stuff." She tried to mimic one of his smiles. She knew it was a sickly effort. "I'm a little tired. Sorry. I'll be here."

"And fruits. Vegetables. All the colors of the farmer's rainbow!"

Hassan stuck his other foot out, then light-footed across the parking spaces, trying hard not to make contact with the asphalt. "All the foods of life! Every one!" he yelled as he neared the door.

The Caddy shuddered beneath her a bit, hissing and wheezing, working hard to keep things cool while it idled. The cold air felt good and dry. Missy stared across the Piggly Wiggly parking lot. All she saw were babies, babies she would have never noticed before. She thought, *It's like when you buy something new—and, you think, unusual—but suddenly, like magic, you start seeing that thing everywhere you look.*

Today, it seemed every child in the county under the age of five had journeyed to the Piggl Wigg. A heavy woman, her hair bundled up with a bandanna, moved slowly through the door, from the cool of the store into the wavy heat of the parking lot. She juggled two full bags and a new baby. Missy saw her start to shine from fresh sweat. Her baby, a girl Missy guessed, wasn't misbehaving. She was just heavy in her momma's arm, not unlike another sack of groceries.

A second woman, this one older, but faster, arrived with her three children. They stair-stepped in size, all of them too young to go to school. She must have spent years' worth of months being pregnant. Missy wondered what her husband looked like. Her babies, the two that could walk on their own, scattered in opposite directions when they hit the pavement, one toward the road and one toward the door of the Piggl Wigg. She didn't bat an eye, just yelled at the one going the wrong way. "YOU GET HIT BY A TRUCK YOU WON'T GET NO ICE CREAM SANDWICH!" He skidded to a stop and made a quick U-turn back toward the store. *I like that woman,* Missy thought. *I could probably learn a thing or two from her.*

A muddy man in work boots and a thin T-shirt stepped out of the store reading a newspaper while he walked, a little boy following him like a duckling. The boy tried to keep up, but he didn't have his daddy's gait down yet. But like his father, he didn't watch where he was going either. Finally, they both stopped and gazed around for their car like a couple of lost kids.

While Missy watched, she didn't notice the signs of the Caddy slowly dying. Its last groan and shudder pulled her attention away from the babies scattered around the parking lot. She saw a puff of white smoke or steam billow from beneath the hood, and clouds of the same stuff suddenly flowed out of the AC vents. Skyles would know what happened and what to do, but Missy just sat, waiting for a fire or an explosion. She couldn't bring herself to run. The smoke through the vents quit as she reached for the key to kill the engine, even though it had already shut down. The Caddy gave off no confident, big-throated rumble—now only the leftover metallic clinks of a heavy, hot car mercifully cooling down.

Missy looked around for someone to be mad at. *It better not be broken down for good,* she thought, *or Hassan will need a doctor for more than his sore feet. He'll go into mourning.* The electric windows wouldn't open. In just a few seconds, the air inside the Caddy began to thicken and heat up, and as much as she wanted to sit and watch parents with their babies, Missy knew sweating to death in the Piggl Wigg parking lot would not be a good way to die. Not today anyway.

Missy walked through the automatic sliding door of the Piggl Wigg, and the smell stopped her stock-still on the threshold. It was a sour, aged scent, like the inside of a refrigerator about to go bad. There was no sign of Hassan or any customers for that matter, just a bag boy working a toothpick between his lips, one side of his mouth to the other, and a hard-looking girl leaning against her cash register, admiring the bag boy's singular talent.

Missy began searching for Hassan at one end, near the vegetables, and worked her way to the other side of the store, toward the frozen foods. Halfway there, she found him, pushing one loaded cart and pulling a second. Hassan limped on the outside of his thickly gauzed feet while he pulled and pushed. Missy wanted to feel sorry for him, especially when she remembered she would have to tell him his Caddy lay dead in the parking lot.

But, Missy thought, *we've all got our problems, and he didn't have to buy everything on the doctor's food list right off the bat.* That list hung from his mouth, freeing up both of his hands for the carts. The way the piece of paper dangled from his teeth, it looked as though Hassan were foaming at the mouth. A mad dog in the spice section.

He spat the paper into a cart when he saw her. "And what is this?"

"I had to come in," she told him.

"I'm taking care of everything. I told you! I am taking care of you now! Just me! I can do this!" He leaned against the front cart, set it in motion, and started to limp behind it. He didn't seem mad, just belligerent and confused. He was trying to figure out, on the fly, how to take care of a pregnant woman, a woman who sprouted miracles. And that was the last thing in the world Missy wanted. She'd never had it in her plans to be somebody's summer project.

"And please, go back to the car," he stammered. "Let me do my job."

"I can't," Missy said.

"Please. I beg," he said.

Missy didn't hesitate. "The Caddy quit. Something is wrong. There was some smoke, I think, then it just quit. You better come."

Hassan's eyes widened, and he shifted into a new level of energy. He took his hands off the carts and tap-danced down the aisle on his bad feet. Even bandaged, he moved fast, so fast that the automatic door wasn't automatic enough. He nailed it nose first. It opened on the impact, and he kept right on, bloody nose and all, into the heat. From where Missy stood, peering through the glass, things seemed normal at the Caddy, except for the thin funnel of smoke rising between the headlights. Hassan reached the car, opened the hood, and a giant smoke signal puffed into the sky.

Hassan collapsed to his knees and started his head-banging routine on the bumper. Missy wanted to rush out and snatch him and say, "You're going to burn your kneecaps, too." He stopped banging and rested his head on the Caddy's bumper.

All the children Missy'd been watching—and all of their parents—quickly gathered around Hassan, parting only to let Missy pass. She heard a woman ask no one in particular if they should get a doctor.

She never got an answer. Hassan fell off his kneecaps and curled up on the hot asphalt on his side, fetal style.

The children who were old enough to put together sentences wanted to know what was wrong with the man. Why were his feet bandaged? One boy was a little more advanced than the others his age. He looked at his daddy and said, "How come he's crying about a car?"

Another question that no one seemed to have an answer for.

In the tow truck, they didn't speak. Hassan knew the driver and Missy thought she recognized him from a late night at the restaurant. According to his shirt, his name was Lloyd, and he was nice enough to let Hassan pile his grocery bags in the space behind the seat. Missy thought the Caddy looked weak and humiliated chained to the muddy truck, like a sad, defeated white whale hooked in the lip, being ferried to a dock somewhere. Lloyd tried to make some conversation, but it fell flat after a couple of single-word answers to his questions about the heat and the year the Cadillac was made and the part of the world Hassan was from.

He dropped the two of them in front of the Li'l Pancake House, promising to take the Caddy to a mechanics' place just off the interstate, a shop Hassan used for regular maintenance. "They know her," Hassan said. "They will recognize her."

Without another word, Hassan limped toward the Li'l Pancake House like a wounded veteran, his shoes in one hand, bandages unfurling behind him like kite tails. From inside the restaurant, Missy saw Wanda watching them, a hand on her cocked hip. They were hours longer getting back than they should have been. Missy thought, *I would be mad, too. Hassan can handle her.* All Missy wanted was to lie in her bed and try to figure out how not to worry herself to death in the next seven months.

Back in her room, she stared at her ceiling for minutes or hours—she wasn't sure about time passing—until she noticed that the sun had dipped low enough to turn her room a smoky gray color. She thought she heard a careful shuffling outside. Then, someone knocked and she didn't answer at first, but she knew Hassan wouldn't go away. When she opened the door, he limped right in without looking at her.

"And I'm sorry for the way I have acted. I'm not sure I'm ready for all of this."

His attitude, the way the world seemed to have done him a disservice, made Missy's heart leap in her throat.

"You don't have to do anything with *this.*" She gave a little snarl, and it hurt him. She could see his reaction, even in the dim light. Missy suddenly possessed a newer, sharp-edged attitude. She just didn't know where it came from. *Maybe*, she thought, *this is what being pregnant does. Makes you care a little less about the rest of the world.*

"And I do not have to do anything I do not want to do. But I will. And I am not ready for the changes that you are bringing to this place, I guess."

She wanted to tell him that he was getting way ahead of himself. Instead, she said, "I can be out of here tomorrow." That hurt him worse.

"No! I mean to say that this miracle will take getting accustomed to. Miracles are that way."

We're back to that, she thought. "Hassan, understand, this is no miracle. It isn't that hard to figure out how it happened. I mean, I know that much."

He walked through the room, picking his way cautiously around the pieces of furniture, the wrapping on his feet now a dirty mixture of red and gray and brown. He hesitated before he spoke, which was something that Missy had rarely seen—Hassan thinking before he opened his mouth.

"And *you* must understand," he began slowly. "All the days I'm here, I think that I must someday make a move to somewhere else. Run to another place and then another. I dream about travel. I read all about it. But I never go anywhere. And you come to this place, and now I see that I can escape without moving a foot in any direction. You are what people like me wait for."

Hassan didn't pause to see how Missy would react to his explanation. He just kept talking, telling her how he solved all his problems. He talked about the man who would repair the Cadillac. "And he only has four of his fingers on one hand," Hassan added. "One was eaten by an angry fan belt." He told her how all of her food was stacked perfectly inside the large walk-in cooler in the Li'l Pancake House, and she was supposed to eat all of her meals there, so Hassan could keep an eye on how she was doing.

"And if you want to work . . . I do not know. The doctor says that some work is good and healthy. But only half a shift, two or three days a week, middle of the day. No more whistling in graveyards for you."

Then he was done, satisfied. A couple of limps, a wave, and he was out the door. They weren't any closer to the whole truth. Or at least, he wasn't. He thought some kind of heavenly body got inside of Missy—when heaven didn't have anything to do with it. It was just Skyles.

She didn't want to think about Skyles, didn't want to be mad or sad or anything in between. She pulled the *National Enquirer* from underneath her bedspread. She'd lifted the magazine from the checkout line when the girl and toothpick guy ran out to see Hassan banging his head on the bumper of the Caddy. One of the headlines caught her eye, and she couldn't resist the temptation. She tore the whole article out. It was about this boy and girl—brother and sister—who were Siamese twins, and they were never separated. After living side by side, so to speak, for years, they decided, what the hell, let's get married, but they couldn't find a preacher anywhere who would marry a brother and a sister who were *separated*, much less connected for eternity. No matter where the two of them went, marriage between siblings was always illegal or a sin or a sideshow. In the black-and-white picture, they smiled at each other. The headline read,

JOINED AT THE HIP, BUT UNMARRIED.
A TRAGEDY OF LOVE.

Missy didn't have tape, so she slid the edge of the article between the glass and the frame of the full-length mirror on the back of the bathroom door. None of the words were covered up. She could see it every time she looked at herself.

Missy took all of her clothes off. She was mostly white, not even the hints of tan lines, odd for her at this time of year. She couldn't recall the last time she'd worn a bathing suit. Everything about her was long. She filled up the mirror, top to bottom. Long hair. Long legs. Long feet. Long, bony fingers. From the side, she saw the little pooch of a belly beginning. At least she thought she saw it. Somewhere, she'd heard they would shave her when she had this baby. It would make her feel younger, like an elementary school girl, she believed, not to have hair down there. She suddenly remembered a lot about elementary school, mostly things about her and other girls, even the ones who didn't like her and steered clear of her on the playground. It was nice to have an old, familiar memory surface, if only for a moment.

14.

Missy knew the safest way to phone home was to call collect. Collect gave the person on the other end the chance to say no. The long-distance operator had to play matchmaker, fixing up two people, miles apart from each other.

Missy dialed, thinking, *What in the world do I really want to say?*

The nasal monotone of the operator: "Collect from Missy Belue, will you accept the charges?"

Missy heard Asa scream. "Mona! Missy is on the line. What do you want to do?" Missy thought she heard a touch of excitement in his voice, which surprised her. Then, the click of another phone being picked up, probably the extension in the kitchen.

"Hello? Missy?" Missy tried to answer, but the operator was going through her protocols, making sure that someone agreed to pay for the call.

Missy felt tears welling. She wasn't sure why she wanted to cry. Maybe out of longing or fear or loneliness. She felt six years old again and her mother had forgotten to pick her up from school.

"Is someone accepting charges, ma'am?"

"Oh, for God's sake, yes," Mona said. The operator faded off.

"Momma," Missy said, croaking the word out a bit.

"I got it, Asa. Hang up." A click from his extension.

"Missy? Bless you, I'm glad you called. How are you? Where are you?"

Missy recognized something different in her mother's voice, genuine worry perhaps. And there was another quality, too. Mona seemed anxious. The fact was, for the first time in months and months, the voice on the other end of the line sounded like a mother.

"Momma?" she repeated, this time turning it into a question.

"I've been so worried." Mona took a breath in the phone. "Skyles is back and you weren't with him."

So Skyles was back. Well, not all of him, she wanted to say to her mother. *A little part of him is floating around in my belly right now.*

Mona kept talking. "And when you weren't with him, I automatically began praying that you were okay wherever you were. Praise God. Don't you think it's about time you stopped all of this and came on home? I'm sorry about everything. About anything you can think of. Asa and I miss you, and now that Skyles is back, there isn't any reason why you can't come back too, right?"

Missy wasn't overcome by any waves of sadness or fear or longing. Now, she just wanted some information. "Did you talk to him?"

"I haven't had the chance. I just saw his truck go by a couple of hours ago. But I didn't flag him down, for God's sake."

Missy had more questions. "What did he look like?"

"It was from a distance. And he was going fast. Going too fast."

"Did he have the camper top on?"

Mona started to cry. Missy could hear that tiny crack in her mother's voice open up when she tried to say something and her next words just evaporated into empty space.

"The camper top. Was it on?" Missy repeated.

Mona sobbed now, sucking up the air around her. Asa picked up a phone from somewhere, probably the one in Mona's hand. He had to be in the same room with Mona now. Missy pictured him snatching it from her, taking over, becoming the man who directed grief.

"See what've you done? I think you do this to torment us on purpose. Your poor mother."

All of the sudden, Mona had the phone back, talking right through her tears, her voice thick with crying.

"Oh, poor nothing! I try. Lord, I try. I'm not mad anymore about you running away. There are no grudges here, Missy. I just want you to come home. Is that too much to ask?"

She heard Asa in the background, like a bad echo. "Too much to ask of her, I imagine."

You see, Momma, I want to come home too.

The sound of the words bounced around her head, never making it as far as her lips.

I'm lying here and I call and I want to come home while I'm dialing the numbers. I want to come home the whole time the phone rings. I want to come home the first time I hear your voice, when you say hello. Then something happens like a balloon breaking. You say something. Always the wrong something. Like "Skyles is back." If you would only say the right thing right off the bat, I would come home. Now, all you're doing is getting mad again.

Mona stepped into the gap of silence. "Why do you do this to me? What have I ever done to you? We were all doing the best we could. Lord, help us," she said.

Asa in the background again. "Wasn't good enough for her."

Mona told Asa to shut up. This was her fight now. She sounded like she was through crying and something new and determined was coming out. Missy was busy counting the references to God. Suddenly, she knew exactly what had happened back home. Mona had found religion again, which meant she may have stopped worshipping a Smirnoff bottle. Her mother constantly shuffled the objects of her devotion.

"Run off with someone in the family, and you just a little girl. Stay away for months and months. Every day, I alternate between being so mad I could kill, to being so sad I could just melt away into a little puddle. Well, it isn't my fault that I'm your mother, and I can't help loving you the way I do, but you can just go to hell. And may God have mercy on your poor, runaway, horrible soul."

"To hell in a goddamn handbag," Asa said behind her. "Sorry, sweetheart . . . In a *damn* handbag."

"Shut your mouth, Asa. That's my daughter."

There was another pause of silence. They were waiting for her now, waiting to see what kind of answer she could come up with. Finally, Missy said, "Momma, if you talk to Skyles tell him I got a job."

"If I get close enough to him to talk, I'm going to kill him. Lord, forgive me."

"Momma, it isn't his fault."

"Right, right. Takes two to tango. Anyway, it's your daddy's fault, God rest his soul." Missy didn't quite understand this new logic, blaming what happened on her father. *It's a trick,* she thought. *A new way to get back at me.*

"Momma."

"Wait a minute! Where are you? Tell me! Tell me!" Mona sounded like she was on the verge of losing control of herself, like hysteria loomed just on the other end of the line.

"I want you to tell Skyles."

"I heard you. You got a job."

"No, Momma, tell Skyles something else. Tell him I'm pregnant."

The silence stretched out like a long, straight road, extending into the distance. Then, after what seemed like minutes—but was probably only a few tormented seconds—she heard Asa faintly in the background: "Well, what is she saying now? What now?"

Mona whispered into the phone. "God almighty, Missy. God almighty." The two of them hung up at the same exact second, a single click, and everyone was disconnected again.

So, her mother had uncovered religion again. Missy heard it in her voice. Her mother had done this a few times when Missy was a kid. She found religion the same way people found out they were carrying a disease. One day the whole world changed, and everything was because of and due to the Lord. Religion had been there all along, floating in Mona's blood, and finally one day, it just started coming out of her like a slow sweat. God was responsible for everything, from a hurricane to a crack in the plaster. Then, right before Missy's father died, she went into religious remission. Missy expected her to have a flare-up of the spirit during the funeral or right after, but she'd seen no sign of it. Until today.

If Mona were standing in front of her, she'd probably tell Missy all the throwing up and the passing out in the Caddy and whatnot was punishment from God for having a child outside of wedlock. Not only outside of wedlock, but *inside* the family.

Punishment. That's what Mona thought God did in his spare time. Strike people down with a nod of His head. Missy didn't really have an argument for that.

15.

The time soon came when Hassan wouldn't let Missy work. He insisted, commanded. He said she had a big enough job ushering a baby into life. That was his word—*ushering*. By the time fall arrived and left, he and Wanda handled all the shifts. He enjoyed being in his restaurant, mingling with the after-midnight people who came through the door. He'd stroll up, they'd see that name tag of his, and before long, it was like they were all long-lost pals who mysteriously rediscovered each other in a little hideaway just off the highway.

Missy usually walked to the Li'l Pancake House around ten in the morning, no matter the weather, and slid into the last booth, the one near the bathroom. She was peeing now every half hour and needed a direct path to the toilet. And she was getting bigger by the day. Her stomach rubbed against the edge of the table when she eased into a booth. By that time in the morning, Wanda was there, and she would bring Missy big plastic cups of apple juice. If she kept that down, she'd give her some toast and fruit. She was long past throwing up, but she hated the memory of it so much, they took precautions.

Wanda would sit and talk with Missy for a couple of minutes. Always the same type of conversation. Something like "God, Missy, you all but glowing."

"Glowing?" Missy would say.

"Like you're in love or something," she'd say. "So, are you?" And she would grin at Missy, waiting for her to confess the whole story about Hassan, even though Wanda figured she already knew it. Missy had told her nothing, had told no one. She didn't tell her about those nights when she walked over to Hassan's room and lay there staring up at his travel posters, with him just curled up like a kitten next to her. She never told Wanda that was as far as their touching ever went.

But Wanda was one of those women who caught rumors like a bad cold. She found things out without meaning to, spread what she heard as soon as she could, and somewhere in the process, the information got all screwed up.

"I'm not in love," Missy told her. "I'm pregnant. I just don't feel well."

"Sweet cheeks, you don't have the baby glow. You have the love glow. And by the way, being in love and feeling like you're going to lose your lunch go together in the end."

"I suppose you know all about it, Wanda." She wasn't trying to be combative. She just wanted some information too. Missy didn't mind a bit of gossip herself.

"Oh, I've been in love a time or two. I'm about to do it again, with this fellow who works for the county. But sure as I'm standing here, I'll be sick about it sooner or later," Wanda said. "Most times, it's worth it."

Missy's glow had nothing to do with love. Maybe it was the location or the air or the humidity—but not love. She surely didn't love Hassan, not any more than she had been in love with Skyles. But sometimes she felt sorry for Hassan. Sometimes she wanted to carry him home to Kingstree, plant him on a front porch, and let him grow old there. But she sure as hell didn't love him. She was beginning to wonder about love, about it being an idea as old and worn out as an old motel near the interstate. She was too young to think about love that way.

"How you going to know what to do with a baby?" Wanda asked once.

"I'll just do what feels right at the time," Missy answered.

Wanda snorted behind her hand and said, "That's what got you in trouble in the first place, honey."

Wanda didn't know half the trouble. All she knew was that there was a pregnant waitress at the Li'l Pancake House. She and everybody who came through the door on a regular basis knew about it. Hassan made sure of that. He told people eating at the counter. He reminded the customers who waited at the cash register to pay their bill. "And the miracle baby," he said, holding his hands close together as if he were describing the fish that got away, "is growing stronger with every passing day." Then he pointed to the booth where Missy sat, surrounded by her empty juice cups and banana peels, and the whole place turned toward her, doing a half-spin on their squeaky Naugahyde seats. It sounded like the entire Li'l Pancake House broke wind at once.

Missy never looked up when she heard the sound of people watching her. She kept her eyes glued on the letters she wrote, like,

November 17

Dear Les the Marine—I figure we are even now. I have written you enough to pay back the money you gave me so these are free letters now, or if anything, you owe me. First off, I have forgotten what you look like. If we passed each other on the street, I don't think I could pick you out of the crowd. Oscar either. The two of you don't seem really real anymore, which isn't a reflection on you, just on me. How are the Marines? I don't mean to ask how is every person who is one, but how is it being on that island being a Marine yourself? Do you people practice how you will act if you kill somebody? Lord. You remember how I told you I was working here and the place had no regulars, just strangers who want food? That's different now. Been here enough to know the truckers who stop in on this end of their runs. I see faces over and over and they see me, smiling like always. Please give Oscar a hello.

Your friend,
Missy Belue

PS. Is there any particular reason you don't write me back? It's OK, but I'd enjoy a letter every now and again.

Missy learned something crucial about writing—the most important part was what she didn't put down on paper. She did not tell Les she was pregnant and had stopped working. Why would she tell him? She knew the two of them on paper, mostly. And things hadn't changed since they pulled away in that ugly car. Missy assumed she still looked the same in their mind's eye. She wasn't puffed up like a cartoon. For Oscar and Les, she was still the girl she was months ago, still needing a shower and smelling of the road, and that's the way she wanted to keep it between the three of them.

One afternoon Hassan snarled about an errand he needed to run. Missy and Wanda only caught bits and pieces of his bad mood—something about a part for a refrigerator or a bank mistake on a deposit or a prescription at the drugstore. It could have been all three. Missy didn't really care. Hassan's absence was an opportunity to do an errand of her own, something she needed to do without him watching over her shoulder.

Missy caught a ride into town with one of her regular customers. She had a half dozen options for rides to town—she knew this—because men loved to help a pregnant woman. Even the crustiest man went soft around a woman with a round, large belly and a glow. Missy asked Sammy the bread-truck driver to drop her off at the county library in town. She told him she'd figure out another way home, maybe a taxi.

Missy had never set foot in the library. She'd only passed it in the Caddy. Wanda, who actually possessed a current and well-used library card, had to remind her where the building was located. Missy could tell the library had been something else in a previous life. Perhaps a bank or a restaurant. It was a small building. On one side, a grown-over strip of pavement ran by a long-shuttered drive-thru window. The façade featured two wide and long windows more suited for a clothing store than a library. Inside, however, the building was definitely a place for books.

The smell of musty pages surrounded Missy as she entered. She didn't mind the smell, just this side of moldy, because it suggested permanence and respect. Only something important could make a perfume that solid. Missy wandered for a minute, taking in the smell, noticing how perfect the books were aligned on the shelves, shelves separated by a narrow maze of aisles. She stood scanning the titles, unaware of the young woman who snuck softly up to her and asked if she needed help. Behind the librarian's glasses, her blue, magnified eyes cut down to Missy's belly, then quickly back up again.

"I need a medical book," Missy said. "Something with definitions. A dictionary, sort of, I guess."

She told Missy in a rehearsed, practiced whisper that this was a small library and the only things they had were novels, self-help books, celebrity biographies, encyclopedias, and some current magazines. She said that someone at the doctor's office would probably have any kind of medical reference book she might need. "A doctor might definitely be of some help," she said, her eyes again twitching in the direction of Missy's stomach.

Missy thought she detected sweat breaking out on the upper lip of the librarian. Maybe the need for medical information and her belly pushing the seams of her Li'l Pancake House uniform made the librarian uncomfortable inside the artificial cool of her library. She had noticed how differently people reacted to pregnancy. Some assumed so much from only the clues that struck them head-on—big belly, restaurant uniform, the need for medical information. The librarian was imagining the worst. *Maybe she heard about the scene at the Piggl Wigg,* Missy thought. Maybe she was even in the parking lot that day. The librarian wrung one hand on the other, washing herself clean of Missy, it seemed.

"Thanks, I'll try the doctor," she said. "I have some other stuff to look at, but I can find it by myself."

Missy sat at a small table near the front window and thumbed through a dictionary that was almost too heavy for her to carry. She turned to the *I* section, trying to appear nonchalant. There was the word, nestled comfortably on the page, just after *incessant.* It wasn't printed in red, didn't have a little flag beside it, no alarms sounded off in the library when Missy put her finger beneath the type. *Incest* was not bad by definition, at least from what Missy read. There was no warning in the words. *Sex between relatives who can't legally marry.* But buried under the definition was another word. In fine print. *Taboo.* She had done something taboo. She looked that word up, too. She felt smart, like she did in high school when she would occasionally dig and dig for answers to questions she actually cared about. Taboo meant untouchable. Something primitive. It was a word designed to bring out a little voice that whispered in your ear, "Whatever it is, don't do it." She looked up *primitive.* There was a long list of definitions. The one that caught her eye told her she was unsophisticated, crude. She turned back to the *T*s. At least taboo made a better sound than the other words.

Missy's father always told her not to worry until she had something to worry about. "Don't fret ahead of time," he said. "It's a waste of energy." But maybe the time had come to worry. *Taboo. Primitive.*

Missy felt the flutter of a wing under her side, beneath her ribs, and it was the first time she was sure the baby moved, rather than something she ate disagreeing with her. *I am primitive for touching what I shouldn't have touched, and I will have a baby to remind me of it the rest of my life.* She'd heard stories about taboo babies, how they cried when they were old enough to look in a mirror and see what kind of surreal picture incest sketched on their faces. *Taboo.* The word pulsed in her head like a drumbeat.

Missy placed her head on the table, one ear pressed to the wood, and she could hear the heating system strumming somewhere in the building. In the direction Missy looked, she saw a wrinkled-looking man in a dirty T-shirt, asleep, his mouth wide open and pointed at the ceiling. Another man read a newspaper in a chair. He looked over the top of the page at her like a school teacher. He seemed dying to tattle on her for trying to nap in a library. Missy's eyes closed, and she felt the drift of sleep coming on fast. She was seconds from an escape into dreams when she felt a sharp poke on her shoulder. She jumped like she'd been touched with a match. *The librarian has come to throw me out of the building.* That was the first thought that ran through her head.

"And you thought you could get away from me the whole day?" Hassan slid into the other chair at the table. "You have come here to find a quiet place to sleep?"

Missy blinked and stared. "No . . . nope," she said, not surprised he found her, just surprised at being jolted from near sleep. "I came to read. To look for something."

Hassan spotted the dictionary she still had open to the *T*s. "And what are you trying to discover?"

"Just things."

"Things?"

"This," she whispered loudly, patting her belly. The man behind the paper rustled through a new section. Missy was afraid he could hear every word they said. The rustling caught Hassan's attention too, and he glanced toward the man. They knew each other. Hassan waved, and the man gave them a grin over the top of the paper.

"And that," Hassan whispered back, nodding toward her stomach, "is something that you will never understand. It is a miracle and miracles happen for no reason we can ever know. That is why they are called miracles."

"You don't know the difference between a miracle and a mistake," Missy said.

"And you don't see, do you? I have prayed for this. I have touched the ground with my head again and again, asking for this. I have prayed to the God of the Baptists. It is no mistake. There were prayers to be answered." Hassan sighed and cocked his head to look at the ceiling. "You, Missy Belue, are a Madonna. You are sent to us."

Madonna. M. *One* d. *Two* n*'s.* She had to be sure, and Hassan didn't stop her from running her finger up and down the column of words until she found the one she was searching for. *Madonna. Mary, mother of Jesus. Holy shit,* she thought.

Once he was sure she'd finished reading, Hassan continued. "And you see, the two of us never had—and you know what I am saying. Each never had the other. And yet you carry this child. You came to us from nowhere. From the air. A *virgin,*" Hassan said too loud. Behind the paper, the man peeked at them. "A virgin birth," he whispered.

Missy had never been called a Madonna. Here was someone who actually thought Missy was part of an intricate religious plan and was going to give birth to a baby that grew from some rarified holy seed planted in the middle of the night by God knows who. Or rather, by *only* God knows who. And even if it was completely untrue, even if Hassan was the one who came up with the idea, it took her breath away for a second.

Missy thought she was going to faint until she remembered what happened the last time she passed out in town. For a second, when her breath returned, she was an important person. Madonna. She was primitive, okay, fine, but not taboo anymore. Maybe she was part of something big, at least to Hassan. She felt the bird's wing wiggle under her ribs again.

"Have you told anyone about this?" Missy asked, leaning in for the answer. "This Madonna thing?"

"Oh no, no. I would never tell. This isn't the time . . . not yet," he said.

The baby stopped moving. "Hassan, you know as well as I do, this isn't the way things happen. You have to have sex to have a baby. That kind of miracle just doesn't happen. I mean, it happens in the Bible, but that's, I mean, that's the Bible. Weird things happen there. The dead get out of bed. Seas part. Babies show up when nobody's had sex. But most babies don't happen this way."

"And most babies. Not this baby," he said.

"You're not making sense."

"And can you name a miracle that has ever made sense?"

Hassan, she thought, *I can blow your miracle right out of the water.* This was the moment she should tell him about Skyles, about how this baby was not a miracle, but an accident of geography and timing, just her and Skyles. In a pickup, in the dark, somewhere in a campground. Hassan, she could say, my belly is growing because I lost count somewhere and I ran out of pills just off Interstate 10.

"Nothing makes sense to me," she said instead. "Can we go back to the motel now?"

"Whatever you would like," he said.

Missy closed the big dictionary quietly. "How did you know I was here?" she said.

"And I always know where you are, Missy Belue. I can always find you," he said. "That may be another miracle. That may be something else you cannot explain." He guided her through the stacks of books, past the sneer of the librarian and into the chill of the morning.

The annoying details of pregnancy. Missy thought about these at night while she tossed and turned, searching for the position that was the least uncomfortable. Comfort was a memory. Nothing was completely painless or completely at ease, day or night. Now, there was only compromise, compromise with her body.

She stared at the walls or the ceiling and thought about the word *impending.* Someone had used it in the Li'l Pancake House earlier that morning.

"How is the impending event coming?" this older couple with leathery, tanned skin asked her. What a strange, almost-foreign word to use about the baby that somersaulted and hiccupped under the tight skin of her belly. For Missy, *impending* sounded too far off. Time had ground to a snail-paced crawl. Minutes stretched like pieces of cold taffy, inching apart from each other, but never completely separating.

There was no mistaking it. The baby was a real thing. It was going to happen, was beyond the point of stopping. Sometimes Missy wondered why *that* thought—stopping the baby—never crossed her mind in the early days. Perhaps because she had so quickly been dubbed the carrier of a miracle. Now, ceasing things was no longer a choice. Still, the date was in the distance, due actually in those weird days at the end of winter, when you could close your eyes and almost catch a taste spring, but usually ended up catching a cold wind right in your teeth.

Young Doctor Wiley had penciled in March 17 as the day for Hassan's miracle baby. Yes, Hassan had confided in the doctor that Missy had been impregnated by the simple, miraculous acts of simply wishing and hoping. And Wiley had, like Missy, assured Hassan that sperm do not travel well when fueled only by telepathic, fanatical energy. Hassan remained unconvinced. He knew a good miracle when he thought it up.

For Hassan, the birth took on hereditary concerns, in addition to the miraculous. He confessed to Missy that on late nights during the early winter, he had started sitting in a rusty pool chaise beneath the awning of his pale motel, wrapped in a blanket. Sometimes he tracked a thumbnail slice of moon through the pine trees and listened to the bee-hum of trucks and cars, settling into their grooves on the distant interstate. When Missy asked him why he sat in the cold, he told her he was worried how everything he had—the Thoroughbred Motel, the Li'l Pancake House, the travel brochures, etc.—would all fall away one day into different shades of sand and dust, once he and his name tag had departed for the great check-in desk in the sky.

But, he told her, a son changed everything. That was something to leave behind in the world, something that would last, like a handprint in a slab of concrete.

Son. Missy watched as Hassan let the word slide through his teeth like cigarette smoke. Hassan had a theory. A son, he said to her, is a gift that could be given twice. First, God gives a son to the man, he told her. Then the man, upon leaving this life, leaves his son to the world with a note pinned on his back that reads, *Don't forget! There's some of me peeking out from this boy!*

Even though Missy was the one who asked the question, Hassan acted like he'd heard a voice that spoke to him from the trees.

"What if it's a girl, Hassan? You think about that?"

Hassan blew the question away with a puff from his cheeks. "Never to happen," he said to no one in particular, especially not Missy. "I was born to be the father of men."

The sharp angles of Missy's body gave way and turned to softer flesh. Her hair thickened and seemed to grow hourly. Her skin shined as if it were covered with a thin wax coating. And her eyes were now a deeper brown, set behind eyebrows that had been left to grow wild and directionless for weeks. She enjoyed wearing the maternity clothes Wanda borrowed from her friends in town. Missy began to enjoy the adventure of looking at herself in the mirror in the mornings. If she stared long enough, she would discover changes that had slipped onto her overnight.

These days, Hassan only saw her in the Li'l Pancake House during her morning and evening visits, or when he took her to town in the Caddy for doctor's checkups or to get some air. At most he saw her an hour a day. At night, they were always apart. She didn't knock on his door, nor him on hers. But when he did see her, he treated her like the Madonna he'd dubbed her. When they weren't together, he talked about Missy—to customers, to vendors, to anyone who would listen. Some of these ramblings echoed back to Missy. And they were always about how beautiful she was, about miracles, about baby boys. And Hassan still dreamed and talked of travel, of seeing new places. Meanwhile, Missy felt anchored by the sheer weight of a new human life, and any discussion of travel left her exhausted and depressed and longing for the days when a compass was important to her.

Though she wasn't up to moving much, Missy's mind wandered, her brain turning traitor at times, especially during the hours she spent by herself. For example, she was almost beginning to believe in Hassan's miracle mumbo jumbo, like maybe there was the slimmest thread of possibility that Hassan himself could have been responsible for the melon shape beneath her belly button, with a healthy dose of divine intervention mixed in. It made her afraid of him, a little wary of his attempts at affection, such as they were. In her mind, if this man could actually *wish* her pregnant, who knows what else he might do? And Hassan, he was content to be alone because that was how he spent most of his evenings anyway, staring at the stars or in bed, where he'd tune his portable radio to an AM station a thousand miles away. Missy could hear the music through the door if she happened to walk by his room.

In the early days of pregnancy, they still got together and talked and drank tea and lay on Hassan's bed in the cool of the air-conditioning, staring at the travel poster on the ceiling. But once Missy's belly took on its new shape, that was when they began to spend evenings alone. But still, Missy felt safe. To have Hassan a few doors down, to have friends as close as the parking lot, to have a baby feeding off her every move—it might have been something she had always desired without really knowing it. It was a new and unfamiliar peace of mind.

There was no burning itch to put miles behind her, no urge in her belly to find out what people acted like in the next time zone. Her belly was too full now for mere urges. Life was going on there. Safety. With Skyles, she'd felt that the sense of motion was going to be her saving grace. She'd thought he was the perfect savior, a messiah with a pickup, someone who could make sure she would be the newest stranger in town at the end of each day. But traveling with him became as dull as sitting in one place.

Missy knew that her fear of death-by-routine was one of the things that drove her to leave home. It was also the same thing that sent her through the back door of that restaurant and into the emergency lane of that highway. Doing the same thing over and over. Drive, eat, let Skyles crawl on top, sleep. With a little bit of the mysterious Louise mixed in.

The Li'l Pancake House saved her. New people through the doors every day. New stories. Wanda and her men. Hassan and talks about trips he'd never taken. And suddenly, a baby stretching its arms in her stomach. It felt like the middle ground—a safe compromise—between a speed limit and an easy chair. Missy decided it was what she'd needed all along.

She also wanted a nest to feather. She woke up one day with the urge to prepare for the child, but the more she looked around at her motel room, she began to have third-world visions of her hungry baby, its mouth pleading with her dry breast, the two of them surrendering to the heat and humidity and flies in Room 107. Of course, that was an overreaction, a hormone melodrama. There were no flies and the air-conditioning worked fine. But her room was pretty bland and certainly no place for a fresh baby to catch its first glimpse of a new world.

One afternoon, she went to Hassan during his shift and slid into a booth. The Li'l Pancake House wasn't busy.

"There's something I need to talk about," she said, resting a forearm on her belly. "I need a new place to live. Now, before you go and say something, I like it here. But," she continued, "I just don't feel right about bringing a baby from the hospital to a motel room that hasn't been painted in years."

Before she could lay out her rationale for relocating, Hassan interrupted her.

"And I will paint. Tonight!" he yelled. "THIS is where you should live." He punched a key on the register. "I will buy it all, the paint, brushes and turpentine," he said. "I will make it new!"

"Wait, it isn't just the paint," Missy said. "I need a place I can fix up on my own. You know, with little baby things." Hassan looked at her across the counter. She saw the fear in his eyes, fear that she was on the verge of running away. And taking his miracle boy with her.

Missy made a sound that combined a whine and hiss. "Dammit, Hassan, I think I'm feeling motherly. I'm not used to it, you know."

Missy should have known better. Conflict tended to unravel Hassan's thought process. He dipped into the cash drawer, glaring at

Missy. He snatched a fistful of bills and was through the glass door before Missy could spin herself and her belly around.

"Now you did it," Wanda sang out as she walked in the door. "He's got that look in his eyes. Don't get in his way."

"He took money," Missy said.

"Probably buy you something you don't need," Wanda replied and headed toward the bathroom to adjust her uniform. "Men do that all the time."

Missy didn't see Hassan that night or any of the next day. No one seemed to know where he was. The Caddy sat in the shed, and the shade was pulled tight over the window of his room. If he was inside, he never came to the door when someone knocked. Wanda was a little irritated that he'd just disappeared.

"Probably off blowing something up or whatever it is those camel jockeys do when they get mad," she said loud enough for most of the customers to hear. Missy actually helped out with Wanda's tables.

She was surprised at the way she reacted. Without Hassan, she was bobbing a little, drifting away from anchor. She'd found a safe place to spend days and nights, there at the Li'l Pancake House and the motel, but without Hassan's presence, she felt a little like a freeloader. He always made her feel wanted inside the walls he owned.

The following evening, Missy sat in her room, listening to one of those talk shows on a little desktop radio she'd bought in town, one of those shows where someone strips themselves naked in front of God knows how many thousands of strangers. Missy didn't mind eavesdropping on other peoples' troubles.

Right in the middle of a woman's story about losing her house to the IRS, there was a knock at Missy's door. Through a crack in the curtain, Missy spied Hassan, and he looked awful. His hair was greasy and matted and speckled with what looked like three or four different colors of paint. Brown, moon-shaped sweat stains hung under his armpits, and his shirt was unbuttoned to his belly. Despite the chill, Hassan was without shoes. He knocked again and called out.

"And I have come to show you something. You have to come with me." His words slurred around each other.

Missy opened the door. "I was just making sure who it was. Where have you been?"

"And it is good to be so careful. There are men in this world who carry craziness in their blood."

"Where are your shoes?" Missy asked.

"And my ancestors could walk the desert at noon with nothing between them and the burning sands but the soles of their feet. You have seen evidence of this. I have been busy in a desert of my own."

"You're confusing me. It's late," Missy said. She started to shut the door.

He put out a hand to stop her. "For a day and a half, I have been acting like a man I have never known. I was changed. Come," he said and walked down the row of motel doors. Missy grabbed a bedspread and wrapped it around her shoulders. It wasn't cold out, but she had this definite feeling she would want something warm before the night was over.

Hassan walked like a stiff robot. He stopped at the door to his room. When Missy caught up to him, he said, "And I have stopped my traveling," then swung the door open for her.

From inside, the smell of newness cascaded over Missy. The paint was so fresh, she could taste it on her tongue. She smelled new wood and the sharp odor of newly installed carpet, or maybe a rug. There was noise, too. A children's song, a melody that tinkled from somewhere low in a corner. The light was bright, like it had bounced back and forth between the new, yellow walls, gaining intensity until it exploded out the door and onto Missy's face. What Hassan had done, in a day and a half, was create the only nursery in America next door to a motel lobby.

"Your room," Missy murmured like she was talking underwater. "This was your room."

"And no. A room for the two of you. I will just switch with you. This is where you stay now."

"But all of your posters. All of the books. Where?"

Hassan waved his arm. "Away," he said. "It was only the stuff of my pipe dreams. Now I have real ones." Hassan was too tired to be happy with his work. He slumped into the middle of the floor, then fell on his side, grabbed his knees and shut his eyes.

She circled the room in the light. Hassan had bought a white crib and stuck it in one corner. It was filled with a single stuffed animal, a huge, smiling, droopy-eyed dog of some kind. A long, narrow changing table stocked with diapers and boxes of wipes bordered one wall. More boxes lined the other, items Hassan had bought, but hadn't had the time or energy to put up. A mobile of an airplane squadron. A tiny table with the ABCs painted on and scattered in no particular order on the top. A framed announcement of some kind that would eventually go on the wall, telling the baby's size and length and time of birth.

Hassan had stocked the bathroom with books, not children's books, but books for her. A volume of Spock, of course. And a larger one, one with pictures and drawings. Missy was fascinated. She sat on the toilet and read. Hassan snored softly in the other room. There were pictures of actual births, of the mother stretched beyond imagination, a slick, dark head squeezing between her hips. In the pictures, a man always stood there beside the woman. He usually bent to her ear, holding her hand, wiping sweat from her forehead. The picture began to swim in front of Missy's eyes. She suddenly imagined herself lying on a table, heard a scream build in her chest, then explode from her mouth. In this bad daydream Skyles was beside her, but he wasn't whispering encouragement in her ears. He was calling her a cold-hearted bitch for bringing a baby into the world that no one could bear looking at.

Missy leaned forward and laid her cheek on the cool porcelain of the toilet tank. She felt nausea rising in her throat, somewhat like the scream, but she fought it back. The coolness felt good, helped bring her back under control.

"And you are not well?"

Missy's head snapped up. Hassan stood in the doorway. He came closer. "Are you happy with things I've done?" he asked.

Just as the words left his mouth, a whiff of his body floated into Missy's nose. It was a sour, burned smell, like something old and made of wet wool that was on fire. She was too far along to be sick again, but she felt it coming, and she knew that there was no stopping it, even if she clamped her teeth shut. She leaped off the toilet seat and pushed past Hassan, leading with her belly. She knew if she could make it outside and to the parking lot, there would be no mess. It would only be a bad spot that would eventually wash away, and if someone happened to see her, she might pass, in the dark, for a drunk who lost control of his stomach. An image of the DeSoto Diner flashed in her mind.

Every breath she sucked in on her way toward the door sent the smell of Hassan farther toward her stomach. She never made it. She threw up against the wall, splattering onto the yellow paint. She paused and looked back at Hassan, who was already reaching for towels. She started to apologize, then retched again, this time in the direction of the toys and gifts still in their boxes. When she made the door and pushed it open, the cold air opened her eyes like a nightmare, and her stomach seemed to fall back into place. She didn't turn back. She just headed for the other yellow—the glow of the Li'l Pancake House.

16.

Missy fled the new room and headed across the lot. The Li'l Pancake House shone at this time of night, like a glowing Oz. It was warm in there. Safe. She could wash her mouth out, and nobody would ask her why. She was the pregnant woman. She was granted some latitude.

The hotel was no longer safe. Hassan had seen to that. She knew he meant well, but he had taken too many of these matters into his own hands and out of hers. She wanted to make a place for her baby. She wanted to get ready for the world to change, and she wanted to do it in her own way. But he did it for her, with a few gallons of yellow paint and a bunch of spinning planes hanging over a crib.

Dammit, she thought, *I already have a room. I don't want his. No wonder I am sick to my stomach.* She'd had this feeling before, this idea that someone was taking over. At the funeral home with Asa. On the road with Skyles. That suffocating feeling that men tossed over women like a heavy blanket.

As she made her way, she sensed Skyles at her shoulder, breathing in her ear. He followed her—or rather, his sensation followed her—across the pitted asphalt and wouldn't let her go, the sound of his voice and the memory of his face.

She needed the warm feel of an orange Li'l Pancake House booth wrapping around her. Needed to hear the sound of money falling into the jukebox and Wanda calling out to the customers that she'd be right with them.

Outside, a couple of semis parked side by side in the back of the lot. One still idled, its diesel rumbling in a low register. A county sheriff's cruiser sat near the door. Missy ran her hand down the side of his fender. It was slick, just washed.

Inside, everyone was eating and happy. A couple of guys glanced up when she walked in. They waved and winked. Wanda would be surprised to see her at this time of night. She was usually back in her room, counting the number of kicks in her tummy. Missy felt better immediately.

Music from the jukebox, country music, filled the room, probably at too loud of a volume, but it didn't matter. Wanda was nowhere to be seen, not behind the counter or in the small storage room. She wasn't in the back bagging up garbage. But she hadn't gone far. Her sweater dangled from a hook near the door.

Missy had to pee, and there was the aftertaste of vomit in her mouth. It felt as though the baby were trampolining on her bladder. She almost ran to the bathroom door, which was shut, but unlocked like usual. Missy knocked and swung the door open, already unbuttoning her pants, and there, cramped into the narrow bathroom, was Wanda and the new man she'd mentioned, the one who worked for the county, the sheriff's deputy.

He sat on the edge of the sink, his pants bunched down around his ankles. One of his hands was behind him somewhere, near the faucets. The other was on Wanda's head. She leaned forward, her hands on his knees, her head bobbing between his legs. She didn't stop moving when Missy walked in, but the deputy threw up one hand and sighted it between Missy's eyes and his, like he was trying to keep the two of them from looking directly at each other. Missy smelled the blue cake of cleanser Hassan put in the toilet tanks.

Missy stood there only a couple of seconds—long, long seconds—then fell back into the tiny hall and pushed the door shut. At the table nearest the bathroom door, two men in a booth were working hard to keep giggles behind their hands. One of them leered up at her as she walked backwards down the aisle between the booth and the jukebox.

"Sorry, sweetheart. Shoulda told you. Sam's working undercover this evening." He slapped the tabletop and his friend across from him said, "Now, that's damn funny." Missy rushed for the door. It clanged shut on their laughter.

She tried to trot back to her room, but it hurt and pulled too much on her belly, so she walked as fast as she and the baby could take and tried to make a plan. She needed that. A definite plan.

She thought, *If I was any good at making plans, I wouldn't be here. Wouldn't be pregnant. Wouldn't walk in on Wanda and Barney Fife.*

Missy opened her door, half expecting to find Hassan already moved into 107, but he was nowhere to be seen. A quarter hour later, she'd thrown what she owned into Asa's old duffel bag. She left her Li'l Pancake House uniforms on the hangers. When she passed the yellow nursery, she saw Hassan curled up in the middle of the floor, just like before. He hadn't even bothered to clean up Missy's mess. His eyes were closed. He was sleeping or praying, maybe alternating between the two.

Missy felt dumb for the first time in months. Dumb and too young. She told herself she had some nerve, thinking she was safe in a place like this. Some crazy short order cook wannabe makes her out to be the mother of a miracle, tries to put her in his roadside nursery. The Li'l Pancake House, the same one that glowed like a church from a distance, was full of men who couldn't keep the personal parts of their lives in their pants and a snaggle-toothed woman who didn't mind meeting them face-to-face.

Safe, my ass, she thought. *This is just a little tiny world all to itself, a tiny little orange world that drags its belly in the mud like every other place on the map.* She hated feeling stupid. Missy angled toward the back of the motel, in the direction of the shed.

Her plan was to get moving. A moving target was harder to hit, especially when the world was slinging its crap. In the dark, just around the corner of the shed, she felt for the nail and found where Hassan hung his spare car key. The lock was unclasped as usual. The Caddy started easily, like it had been waiting for her. The idle settled down to an even hum. It wouldn't even wake Hassan. He'd be out cold for hours, she guessed, the hours she needed to put some miles on the road. Missy let the Caddy idle for a couple of seconds while she checked the glove box for the gas cards. They were there. She slid the car into drive and eased out into the evening.

The radio was on when the car started, and when Missy swung out of the parking lot and pulled away from the Li'l Pancake House, the deejay said it was eleven o'clock and he had a treat for his listeners—an hour of nonstop music. From now to midnight all she had to hear was music. She wouldn't have to hear anybody talking. The traffic was light on the highway, and the bright lights on the Caddy lit up every dip in front of her. It was good to be on the road again.

Missy Belue floated down the highway, the Caddy wrapped around her like a fine-fitting shoe. It was trickery, she decided. Trickery made her leave. She had been tricked at the Li'l Pancake House, tricked into thinking she was something she wasn't. She hadn't been in motion for months, other than a ride into town. Standing still had given her a false sense of security. Now, all of the right senses kicked in.

Hassan would find the empty shed soon. He could do one of a few things, Missy supposed. He could call the police. *Not likely.* He could wait for Missy to return. *Possibly.* Or he could bang his head against the side of the shed until he saw stars. *No doubt.*

Missy couldn't worry about Hassan just yet. Right now, she had no idea where she was going. But it was none of the usual north-south-east-west complications. She only knew she was going away from something. *Away from.* It was a solid direction. But if she could just decide where she wanted to end up, she could relax a little.

She pulled the Caddy over to the shoulder, and the wheels crunched in the gravel. Missy pushed buttons on the console at random until the right one clicked, and the top began to lift off the Caddy, folding into itself like a closing accordion. Once the top was in its place behind the seat, Missy arched her neck and looked up into the cool sky for a sign—maybe the path of a shooting star or a moon waxing toward full, but she saw nothing but clouds. It was approaching midnight. She sat on a stretch of highway so straight you could see cars a mile in either direction. In the grass just off the gravel, Missy squatted and used the bathroom. The baby rolled inside her, almost flopping.

"Clumsy thing," she said to it and patted her belly with both hands. She thought about *Clumsy Belue* as a name, shook her head and said out loud, "I'll know what you are when I see you." *Maybe Taboo Belue. Right,* she thought.

Standing in the middle of the empty highway, Missy suddenly recalled her daddy and a trip home so many years ago. She and her parents were driving home from a beach somewhere in North Carolina. They were late on the road, because they had stayed at the campground as long as they could, playing on the beach until the sun set, and the tide and the moon rose. They didn't even change clothes, just climbed in, sandy and sweaty. Missy was probably seven or so.

She hung over the front seat between parents. Her father had a Braves game on the radio. The team was out west somewhere. The greenish lights from the radio dial shined a strange glow on the dashboard compass that bobbed back and forth, hunting for directions on the highways that led back toward Kingstree.

"Missy," her daddy said, "why don't you lie down? We have a good ways to go. Close your eyes."

"I ain't sleepy."

"I'm not sleepy," her mother corrected. Mona's eyes were already shut, her head on the door against a makeshift pillow of beach towels.

"Well, I'm not."

Her father laughed, then cut it short when something happened in the game. By the sound of the announcer, Missy could tell it was good, but she didn't understand baseball enough to pay attention.

Her daddy said, "Stay up. Suit yourself. Tell you what, though—"

"What?"

"You stay up until we get home, and I'll give you a silver dollar."

"A whole one?"

"A whole dollar."

Mona said, "Don't give the child money for staying awake. She'll be out of control tomorrow without enough sleep."

"No, I won't. I promise I won't get out of control. And I'm not even sleepy anyway. How far are we from home?" Missy said.

Her father checked the compass, then his watch. He peered through the windshield, searching the dark for a landmark. "We're probably an hour and forty-five minutes away," he said and reached over to pat Missy on the head. "Pretty long time to keep your eyes open."

"No problem," she said.

Missy tried concentrating on the ball game. A man named Milo was the announcer. She began listing all of the words that rhymed with Milo. She could hear the umpire yelling balls and strikes.

Missy rolled her window down just a crack, thinking the night air rushing through the car would help take her mind off of her eyes, which suddenly felt too large for her head and too scratchy. She had the entire back seat to herself and decided if she just lay down, she could concentrate on the miles rolling beneath her. When her daddy slowed down for a curve, the air through the window carried the blasts from frogs and crickets hidden along the roadside.

Missy woke up at one of the stoplights in Kingstree, confused about whether she'd been asleep or just daydreaming. The first thing she said was, "Where's my silver dollar?" Her father laughed, then put his finger to his lips to keep his daughter quiet.

"Your mom's still asleep. And you've been sawing logs for the last fifty miles, Missy."

"I have not! I was awake the whole time."

"Missy."

"I was just real quiet."

"Okay, then," Daddy said, "who won the ball game?"

She thought about guessing, since she would have a fifty-fifty chance of getting it right. Instead, she said, "I don't like baseball."

The light changed, and they began to roll toward home.

"The Dodgers by four," Mona said, her eyes still squeezed shut.

Missy smiled down at her belly. She was not a sleepy child anymore. She was in charge of the miles now. In the distance, she spotted the pinpricks of approaching headlights on the road she'd just come down. She cranked the Caddy up and took off, spraying gravel behind her. She didn't want anyone to catch her. She was lost. She hadn't noticed a road sign in hours. She had a couple hundred dollars in her pocket. The air rushing around her was cold enough to bring tears to her eyes. She patted the baby.

"Away from, sweetie," she said to her belly. "That's where we're headed."

17.

Missy knew driving at night made you a foreigner when the sun finally rose. In the dark, you drove and drove and never saw what you passed. You nearly fell asleep watching the car suck up the dotted lines like bits of candy, so you checked into a motel, and when it was light enough to see, you were in another country. You hoped you spoke the language.

Missy had no compass in the Caddy, so when she opened her eyes the next morning, she had no idea where she'd landed, only that she was at a motel called the Sea Breeze. She recalled the rheumy-eyed night clerk, his hair flattened from sleep, who gave her a key and pointed her in the direction of her room. She remembered a paper strip across a clean toilet in the dark. Now, in the honest light of morning, she opened her eyes and saw the ceiling above her, almost expecting to see a travel poster thumbtacked there.

She lifted herself carefully, grunting from the effort, and felt the baby buck. The no-name baby was already different. He or she slept when Missy slept and moved when she moved. Missy had read that most babies were on opposite schedules from their mothers, fighting them during the night and sleeping during the day. Not this one. Missy and her baby were already good traveling companions.

She showered, then lay on the soft mattress, so worn and shapeless she could rest directly on her stomach without shoving the baby into her ribs. She took a pamphlet from the nightstand titled *Where To Go, What To Do.* It told her the best places to eat and where all the historical houses were located. She found out the town was known for its fleet of shrimp boats, which were actually blessed in a huge, public ceremony every spring when the season opened.

So, she thought, *we are near the ocean. South in the dark. That was the direction we came.*

If she desired, the pamphlet said, she could cross a bridge over the marsh near the southwest edge of town and in mere minutes be at the gates of one of the nation's finest Marine training facilities, "where the Few and the Proud learn to be fighting men and women."

This cannot be an accident, she thought. Something pulled her and the Caddy toward the Few and the Proud. Who needed a compass? Near the phone stood a little tent card that screamed at her: *NO CHARGE FOR LOCAL CALLS.* She grabbed the phone book from the drawer and thumbed the pages looking for Marines under the *M*s. She ran her finger down the columns, reciting the ABCs under her breath, when her finger relaxed on a listing for Madame Lowey, Indian Reader and Advisor.

"This," she said out loud, "isn't any accident either." She wondered for a few seconds why she had suddenly become a big fan of fate, of the rare combination of time and place, and she was still considering this as she dialed Madame Lowey's number. A man with an old voice answered after several rings. He didn't even say hello.

"The Madame don't do readings 'til after lunch," he told Missy.

"That's fine," she answered.

"Forty dollars for a whole life reading. Twenty-five for a half-life."

"I'm not sure I understand the difference," Missy said.

"Whole life gives you pretty much all the future events. Half-life just gives you highlights. It's like a movie preview. Most people go with whole life. They seem happier that way," he said. With the man's directions, Missy drove through the strange, new land after she had some lunch, a twenty and a five folded and tucked inside her pocket.

Madame Lowey's place of business was a blue mobile home with a beautiful, intricate hand-painted sign of an Indian staring wide-eyed into an oversized, open palm. *Indian Reader and Advisor,* it said.

Madame Lowey's trailer perched on high cement-block stilts, and after Missy climbed the half dozen steps to the porch, she paused to catch her breath. She caught the strong, rotted funk of low tide on the breeze. *Of course her trailer's up in the air,* thought Missy. *Madame Lowey isn't that far from where the tide hits.*

Before she could even knock, a voice came from the other side of the trailer door. "You are pregnant and you are worried." Missy didn't flinch.

"You saw me through the window. And every pregnant woman worries," Missy said back.

"So, what do you want for free?" The door swung open, and there was Madame Lowey, waving Missy in. She didn't look anything like an Indian.

"That was just a little sample. I give you a little peek of how good I am, next thing you know, you want to see everything. You want to hear everything. You want to know every in and out of your own life. You're staring. What? You've never seen a psychic Jew? All Jews are psychic. It's a curse of my people. Nice car. Is it yours?"

Missy sucked in a breath. She'd almost forgotten she was driving a stolen Cadillac. She still didn't think Hassan would report it yet, but it made her uncomfortable. Madame Lowey spun smartly like a soldier. She was a short woman. Solid and tilted forward a bit on her heels as though she were bucking a stiff wind. Her hair was a reflective shade of fake black, and it fell straight from her head—no curls or waves—just to the edge of her dark, round eyes. *That,* Missy thought, *is why she is a reader. I'll bet she can see right into you with those eyes.* Madame Lowey smelled like a holiday, but Missy couldn't place which one.

"The car, it belongs to a man. I feel it. A seat. Take one. He is after you . . . no, wait. He is after something else first. ALVIN!" A thin man in an oversized T-shirt lumbered from the other end of the trailer. Madame Lowey bent toward Missy to confess something.

"The talent I have, and I fall in love with a man who rarely has thoughts worth reading." Then, in a louder voice, "A favor, Alvin, sweetheart. Draw the shades, then give us time. I have miracles to perform."

Missy flinched at the word *miracles,* rubbed her belly, then scanned the room to take in the details before Alvin doused the sunlight. A Star of David hung above the hallway door, but other than that, nothing stuck out. No crystal ball. No art on the walls. The room was actually boring, and suddenly, it was dim. The Madame noticed Missy studying her surroundings.

"Not to worry. We are harmless people, my Alvin and me. The dark helps us concentrate. Now, you are here for what?"

"Advice," Missy said.

"Advice, I have in abundance. How much advice? That's the question of the hour. You want all the details or just your high points?"

"I spoke with Alvin about a half-life on the phone." Missy felt for the bills.

"A business manager he's not. You realize, a half a life reading satisfies only half your curiosity."

"I only brought twenty dollars. That's all," Missy lied, hoping to save five dollars. She pulled the right bill from her pocket. Madame Lowey gathered her hair behind her head with both hands and curled it into a tight bun that stayed in shape without rubber bands or clips. Missy wondered how she did that. Even in the dark, Missy saw stray light from somewhere flicker on the Madame's fingernails.

"Ready or not," she said. "Now, take your money and hold it against your forehead. I'll see what I can do for twenty dollars. Close your eyes."

Madame Lowey closed hers as well, and the two of them squinted at each other, each cheating, looking through eyelashes. "Your aura and your baby's aura . . . they are banging against each other like a couple of bumper cars, which, by the way, I love to do with Alvin at the state fair every fall. But I digress. I sense you want to know why."

"Why what?" Missy pressed the bill into her forehead.

"Why you are lugging a baby around, of course."

Missy sighed. "I know why."

"Okay, so whom. You want to know whom."

"I know who."

"I knew that you know." Madame Lowey paused, squeezing more time out of the twenty dollars. "Okay, enough already with the colliding auras. You want to know if it's a boy or a girl. Where was this child conceived?"

"In a pickup truck."

"Oh, so you're having a little redneck. Just kidding, just a joke. A boy. Definitely a boy," the Madame said.

"That doesn't matter," Missy said. "Here's what I want to know. I want you to tell me if I'm going in the right direction. I stopped moving for a while. Now, I'm on the move again. I just want to know."

Without waiting for a signal from the Madame, Missy launched into an abbreviated rendering of her story. She told Madame about Skyles and the driving, about the ride with the Marines that took her to Hassan's, about stealing away in the middle of the night. What she left out was important, but not to the Madame. *Besides,* thought Missy, *if she's so good, she can fill in the gaps herself.* "I don't know what I want to do," she said finally. "I think I'm near the Marines, their base or whatever. That's kind of like fate, you know."

"Well, of course I know," Madame Lowey said.

"So maybe I should just do nothing. But I just can't seem to figure it out."

"You already know what to do. But since you're paying me the twenty dollars, I will make it easy for you. You should call the man who can make the biggest change in your life. For example, if I had to call someone, if someone put a gun to my head and said, 'Hannah, dial the number of a man who can change your life,' I wouldn't call Alvin, for goodness sakes. It would be my lover from college with whom I haven't shared so much as a cup of coffee in thirty-five years. But—and you know what I mean—he could change my life. With you? The same. Call the one who can shake things up. I can tell you don't understand. Am I going too fast? All of these men, they have already given you a sign of what they can do. You have three choices. One gives you a ride. One takes care of you. And one has left you with a baby who has an aura that glows like a volcano. They are men, these people. You know men. They are only capable of acting when something either scares them or makes them mad. They are waiting for you to scare them or, dare I say, piss them off. But you have to do this soon. Today, I would say."

She stopped talking and, as if on cue, Alvin returned and opened the door, letting in a wide slant of sunlight. "Of course, none of this applies to Alvin. He's far beyond the clutches of fear and anger."

"Huh?" Alvin grunted.

Missy jumped from her chair when a cat she hadn't noticed wrapped its tail softly around her shins. On her way up, she kicked the cat by accident, sending it yelping toward the open door.

"Golda, the cat," Madame Lowey said. "All the animals in the kingdom, and I have a cat with the brain of an earthworm. You're already standing. We're through, of course."

Missy handed over the twenty and Madame Lowey saw her to the porch. "By the way, dear," she called down to her. "Your baby, it is healthy. You have no worries there. So stop already with these dreams of children with no arms."

Missy stopped, stunned. She felt her bladder begin to give way. She'd had a recurring dream for weeks that the doctor in the delivery room handed her a child that would never be able to hug back. An armless baby. A taboo baby. Taboo Belue. She never mentioned any dreams to the Madame.

"Thank you," Missy whispered just under her breath. That piece of information was worth twenty dollars.

Madame Lowey yelled down. "Enough already with the thanks. It's a job."

A tight fit inside the phone booth. No fast turns here, Missy thought, *not with this stomach.* It was one of those phone booths stuck on the side of a lonely road, flanked by a couple of dusty parking spaces. Madame Lowey told Missy she had three choices for her call. Madame Lowey was wrong. Missy knew the man who could make the biggest difference was behind door number four. She shoved a little stack of quarters into the phone.

First ring.

It's Saturday. I know he's there, she thought, *planning some new kind of funeral service.* Maybe he was at a funeral. Maybe in front of the television, clicking through the channels, looking for one of those putt-putt tournaments he loved to watch.

Second ring.

Missy imagined the smell of tuna fish in the kitchen, his favorite thing for Saturday lunch. He probably had a smear of mayonnaise at the corner of his mouth. *What if Mona answers?* Missy wondered. She tried not to think about it.

Third ring.

Missy was about to give up when she heard the click of an answer.

"Floyd here."

"Asa?" Missy blurted into the phone.

There was a pause, then he answered her. "I'll get your momma—"

Missy hurried to stop him. "No, wait! I want to talk to you first, and I don't want Momma to know I called."

"Good lord, are you in more trouble?" She heard a mumble far in the background. Her mother's voice. Asa leaned away from the receiver and answered her, "Somebody selling aluminum siding." A pause. "Because I like talking about siding, that's why." Asa dropped his voice. "She wants to know who it was. I told her you were a salesman." He snickered, then remembered that he didn't particularly like who he was talking to. "What do you want?

"I want to know what you'd do if I came home."

As soon as the words left her mouth, a county deputy wearing dark glasses cruised by and eyed the Caddy for what seemed much too long. Missy stopped breathing, but he drove on after an official-looking wave.

"Well, let me say this about that. Do you realize that if you come back here, things will take on a different feel? I will not, *will not*, let you break your momma's poor heart again. I know the minute she sees you and that pregnant belly of yours, she'll fall off the edge. I can't let that happen. Different is what I want."

"I'm different, alright." She rubbed her belly unconsciously.

Asa sighed. "You know what I mean. And Skyles," he said. "I don't know what he's going to think. You know, he comes by here for a cup of coffee once, twice a week. With your momma."

Missy felt herself wanting to scream. She caught the sound in her throat and just said, "That so?"

"Sure enough. How are you paying for this call?"

"I have some money. I'm paying for this, so you don't have to worry about that, at least," she said, taking a breath. "So Skyles and Momma are friends?"

"Oh, yes ma'am. He convinced your mother that you broke his heart, too. Grief tends to bond people, you know. I've learned that over the years. They have something in common now. Plus, they still like you, which in my mind is the sickest thought of all. I think you're just about evil enough to sprout horns," Asa said, his voice dropping into a hiss.

"Does he know about the baby?"

"I'm not sure. I wouldn't be surprised. But I don't believe your momma told him anything about it."

Missy sighed deeply. The phone booth was beginning to smell like her. "I want to come home, Asa. It's your house. That's why I'm asking. I just want to lay down in my own bed."

"Beats the hell out of a pickup truck. Or have you advanced to a motor home by now?"

"I'm not fighting with you, Asa. I'm driving a Cadillac. I'm all by myself."

"Break another heart, did you? Somebody who owns a nice car?" Asa wanted to needle her. She could hear it in his voice. He wanted to win this conversation.

"No. I just left a place," she said meekly.

"I'll bet somebody else is mad at you now. Excellent work. If you keep it up, you'll be lonely forever. And by the way, I am not raising someone else's baby."

Missy was listening carefully, but she couldn't help her mind from wandering. She had a vision at that very second of Hassan behind the counter in his Li'l Pancake House, grease spots dotting the front of his shirt, flipping pancakes. He hadn't slept. He was telling the whole place about how the miracle mother stole his car *and* went south. He kept telling them that she'd be back, and the car would be fine.

Missy said, "I can be there pretty quickly. I think I'm close. I haven't seen a map. It shouldn't take too long."

"So you don't even know where you are? Typical." Another mumble in the background. "No, hon," Asa said, his voice distant, like he'd covered the receiver. "We aren't getting any siding for the funeral home."

He hung up without saying goodbye or go away forever, which Missy took as a good sign.

18.

Missy wandered after she called Asa. She drove slowly through the streets of the coastal town, watching the shrimp boats bob in their slips. The air near the docks was thick with the odor of fish parts going bad. She rode and listened to the radio, ordered fast food at a couple of drive-ins and ate on the move. She found a dirt road that led to a low spot between a pair of sand dunes. She could see the ocean from the car, and she put the top down and sang to the radio. It was a mild day for the time of winter, no breeze to blow away any of the smells or sounds of the beach. Missy even napped in the sun for a few minutes.

She only saw one policeman. She wondered if he'd received a call about a pregnant woman in a Cadillac. But he appeared completely disinterested, almost bored with her, and turned the other direction.

Only once did she get out of the car. There was a shop for pregnant women on the main street that divided the town from the beach. After she used their bathroom, she tried on clothes for almost an hour, then bought a big green dress that flowed around her like a robe. It was so big, it captured air and ran it up her legs. She also bought some maternity underwear and a bathing suit that was on sale. She noticed her money was getting low.

"You know, this really isn't bathing suit season, honey." The woman at the store held up the suit. "We had to mark it down. It will look wonderful on you in the summer. My goodness, but you won't be pregnant this summer. Maybe with the next baby, you'll be able to use this suit."

Missy left the store wearing the big dress.

Near dark, she pulled into her hotel. The clerk, one Missy hadn't seen, waved at her from the lobby. She handed Missy a message: *Got me a two day pass. Les*

Missy's breath stopped short. She wondered how Les had found her, then she remembered. Before she left for Madame Lowey's, she called the Marine base and left a straight-to-the-point message with Les's company clerk. She may have even suggested it was almost an emergency. She let Les know she was at the Sea Breeze, near the interstate, but only for a day or so. Missy even confessed to Madame Lowey about trying to get in touch with Les, so it didn't count as her who-could-make-the-biggest-change call.

Les's message didn't tell Missy a lot. She parked the Caddy at the rear of the motel to keep it out of plain sight. It was a long walk to the other side of the building, and when she rounded the corner closest to her room, she saw the green Bel Air, lurking in the parking lot like some kind of giant trash can on wheels. All of its windows were down, and Les sat in the front seat, trying his best to blow smoke rings. The radio was playing just loud enough to keep him occupied.

"Hey, Marine." Missy leaned in the door, and Les launched out of his seat like he'd been stuck with a needle. The Bel Air looked worse than she remembered. Inside, the headliner hung like a dirty hammock, dipping nearly to the back seat. The red carpet was pulled up in most places, faded and worn where it was still attached. The dash peeled like a sunburned back. There was a smell inside—like sweat and salt. When Les's eyes relaxed, they looked tired.

He hopped out of the car and stood beside the fender, soldier-style, at attention beside the open door, but he was dressed like a tourist.

Skinny white legs sticking out of a pair of bright, billowy shorts. A windbreaker over a T-shirt. "Damn, girl, you having a kid?" She'd forgotten: he had no idea about the baby. "You could have wrote us and said so. Where's the daddy?"

"Where's Oscar?" she answered back.

Les collapsed back into his seat. "I could have sent you the letter about that, too, I suppose." Instead of Oscar, Les had a huge Styrofoam cooler in the seat beside him. He reached inside of it and fished out a beer floating in the dingy water. He nodded at Missy and held up the beer.

"No thanks," she said, pointing at her belly.

He pulled the tab, tossed the ring in the parking lot, and took a quick swallow, sucking in the foam. He turned the radio off, then on again. He fingered all of the knobs still left on the Bel Air, flicked the lights on and off. He flipped on the heater and clicked the blinkers both directions. He ran his finger around the speedometer and wiped the dust on the wet beer can. He finally ran out of ways to stall. "Oscar," Les said, "he died."

Missy put her hand to her belly, as though Death had hitched a ride in the Bel Air, and the mere mention of its name would bring it out in the open, too close to her stomach. She didn't know what to say. She could tell he was serious, that this wasn't a joke of any kind. It was her turn to talk, to say something appropriate. But Les wasn't worried about social convention.

"I don't like thinking about it much," he said and took another swallow.

"You can't just tell me Oscar's dead and not tell me anything else. I've got to have more than that." The second she said it, she knew the tone was too harsh.

"Hey, he wasn't your fucking friend. It won't mean that much to you anyway."

She walked around the car and opened the passenger door. The cooler had leaked all over the seat, and when she squeezed in beside it, she felt the cold seep through her big dress. Les wouldn't look at her, even when he moved the cooler out of the way.

"I haven't known many people who died," Missy said. "Just my daddy." It was true. She'd seen plenty of bodies at Asa's, but without names and without any particular memory to associate with them, she hadn't paid much attention.

Les had a point. Missy wasn't weak-kneed with grief because Oscar was dead. She just wanted to know what happened. It was the worst type of curiosity.

"You're right. You don't have to tell me if you don't feel like it. Let's go inside where it's warmer," she said.

"I'm going to take a shower. I could use a fucking shower. I got a room," he said, hugging his cooler. He walked up to the door next to Missy's, slipped a key in the lock and walked in. Missy followed as far as the entrance.

"How'd you know where my room was?" she asked.

"Just asked. I look honest, I guess. Or too dumb to be trouble. The lady gave me your number. Gave me a room right next door." Les grinned. "I'll see you in a bit."

Through the wall in her room, Missy heard water whooshing in the pipes, and it crossed her mind to take a shower herself. She'd been out all day, alternately perspiring and drying to the point that her skin was stretched tightly across her face. In fact, her skin was stretched everywhere, drawn for the most part by her belly. She thought if things got much bigger, if her skin got much tighter, she wouldn't be able to blink.

Instead of the shower, she decided to get organized, to put her new clothes on motel hangers, to count the cash she had left. For a frantic couple of minutes, she couldn't find her pocketbook. She checked the bathroom and the drawers. She eased herself heavily down to her knees and peered under both beds. What looked to be an empty pizza box hid under one, and she couldn't bring herself to touch it, but there was no pocketbook anywhere. She finally remembered she'd left it in the Bel Air, when she'd slid into Oscar's old seat.

The window was partially open, and the pocketbook sat on the seat, but Missy couldn't reach far enough through the opening. She would have to actually get inside the unlocked car. Once she sank in the seat, she decided to stay for a minute and rest. Lately, by this time of the day, Missy was breathing hard and moving slow, letting her belly lead the way. The afternoons weighed more than mornings.

The Bel Air made noises even when it stood still. An afternoon breeze off the water flowed through the windows, fluttering the drooping headliner like a thin drapery. Each time Missy moved in the seat, the car squeaked on its worn suspension. Sometimes it just creaked of its own volition, like an old house shifting on the foundation.

The Bel Air was a museum for road trash. The floorboards, rear and front, were filled with a variety of French fry containers. An empty can of motor oil had lodged under the seat. She could see a dirty shoe with no match in sight. Maps and a couple of different phone books layered the dashboard, along with several superhero comics. Here and there, you could find money, matchbooks, and receipts from fast-food joints that had been crumpled and scattered like ugly confetti.

Compared to the Caddy, the Bel Air was a rolling dumpster, but it fascinated Missy in a way the Cadillac never would. She never had the desire to explore the nooks and crannies of Hassan's car. She had only wanted to ride in it. Yet the Bel Air poked at her curiosity. She opened the ashtray and saw only the sticky remains of a piece of old gum. The cigarette lighter still worked. Tucked under the sun visor, she found a picture of a group of Marines, standing at attention at the edge of a marsh or a swamp. Missy could pick out Les and Oscar. Nobody in the picture smiled; they had an official, unhappy look pasted on their faces.

Inside the glove box, there was an empty aspirin bottle and a bundle of postcards and letters held together with a thick rubber band. She recognized the letter on top of the bundle. She'd sent it from the ex-Li'l Pancake House.

The rubber band slid off easily. She told herself if it was hard to remove, if it put up a struggle or broke, that would be a sign to leave the letters alone, to put them back into the glove box and forget about spying on Les. But, she added in her head, these were her letters anyway. She was violating absolutely nothing. She already knew what they said. One of the letters was postmarked just after she started work. Another, when she told them about Hassan pulling the gun on the trucker. In one of the letters, she said she was feeling sick—but didn't mention she was suffering from morning sickness that showed up in the afternoons. Most of the letters, she remembered, were filled with the usual pen-pal chitchat, how-are-you-doing, I'm-doing-fine sort of thing. The only thing she didn't see was the big Li'l Pancake House menu she had mailed early on.

But beneath her letters, the bottom half of the stack were envelopes addressed to Missy at Hassan's motel. Each was carefully stamped and sealed, but never mailed. Missy turned them over in her fingers, then counted. A dozen envelopes. Missy glanced again toward Les's room, then down at the letters. She guessed they would probably be in order, just like hers had been. She only took two, the top one and the bottom one, then bundled up the rest and shut them away again. She wanted to read where it was cool and she could think.

Inside her room, she heard water still running on the other side of the wall. Les was obviously enjoying his shower. Missy opened one of the letters.

Dear Missy Belue,

Me and Les are in trouble.

Oscar wrote it. Missy shuddered, like a ghost just whispered in her ear.

We got back late not AWOL just late. We will probably not be able to get a pass forever. They gon to give us trouble anyway. They call me nigger when nobodys looking and watching what they say. And they call Les faggit because he rides around with a nigger. Les is not a faggit but he says the only way to prove he is not is to go do something dangerous and probably end up in prison and he says he'd end up being a faggit anyway if he goes to prison so he says he may as well just let them talk and one day he will get back at them. If we ever get a pass again we will come see you. Thank you for the letter you sent it was nice to hear from you. Here all we do is sweat. They have figured out how much water we have to drink exactly so they give us the same amount of water every day, that's how much we got to drink. We drink all that water and sweat so much of it out we never pee. If you go pee they say you aint working hard enough at being a marine so they make you sweat some more. One time I had to pee so bad I went in my uniform but nobody ever new because I was soaking wet anyway. I saw a flipper fish pop out of the water today and the mosskitoes are getting worse. If we ever get a pass we will find you again. I remember where the waffle place is. Les says I couldn't find it if I tried, we hope you are doing ok and we appreceate you writing us letters. Les tells people they are from his girlfriend. He hopes that is ok.

Your friends,
Oscar and Les

Missy could tell that Oscar had signed for the both of them. She started to read it again when the shower next door turned off. She quickly tore open the second letter. This one was from Les.

Dear Missy,

Oscar is dead of heat stroke. That's what they are telling everybody and it could very well be true.

They found him in the middle of the marsh and he was a different color than he had ever been. I have to go meet his momma when she comes to the base today and I can tell you I'm not looking forward to seeing her face. Sorry to have such news. I hope all is well with you and you are over your sickness.

Les

Missy rolled onto her back and stared at the ceiling. The baby pushed on something important, so Missy shifted until she could lie comfortably. There was no pattern in the ceiling, nothing to count. She looked until she decided to close her eyes. She heard the click of the door between the bedrooms and realized she'd forgotten to lock the pass-through. She kept her eyes shut though, feigning sleep. She sensed Les in the room.

"That's a fucking violation," he said flatly.

Missy didn't have to see him to know what he meant. She didn't move. "They were addressed to me. They were already mine. In a way."

"Where are the rest of them?"

"Still in the car," she said.

"Open your eyes." Les sat on the bed next to Missy's.

"I'm resting," she said.

"Oscar wrote most of them letters to you. I was the one supposed to mail them. I guess I'm sorry. It just seemed like a waste of time to send letters to you, being so far away and all. I don't know why I didn't mail them. I do things like that sometime and I can't explain them later on," he said quietly.

The baby rolled, and Missy caught her breath.

"I don't care that you didn't mail them. That's not what bothers me. What bothers me is when important things happen to people, and I don't find out about it until later. That bothers me." Her eyes were still shut. She wasn't ready to face anything.

"You mean like dying?" Les asked.

"Yes, like dying. Important stuff happens, and it changes everything and everybody, and if you aren't there to see it and feel it, then you're just confused. Like you." Missy finally opened her eyes and kept them trained on the ceiling. Les continued to stare at her, then flopped on his back, giving his attention to the ceiling as well.

"What the hell you mean, like me?"

Missy took a deep breath. "You're different now."

"My friend died."

She let the air out. "That's exactly what I mean. Oscar died, and now you're different, you say. You aren't the same person I met on the highway. And I don't know how to act because you aren't what I expected, this time around."

"Jesus, we was only with you for a little while. You act like we was fucking married. We aren't even friends. I mean, like the ones who see each other and talk and stuff." Les sounded angry, but he kept his gaze locked on the ceiling.

"But you and Oscar did something for me. You gave me a ride and started me into something else . . ." Missy trailed off, hearing Madame Lowey's instructions ringing in her ears. *Did she say to call the man who "made" a difference, or call the man who could "make" a difference?* Missy couldn't remember, and the distinction seemed important.

"Well, you're pretty damn different, too, you know," Les said.

Missy felt her feelings bruise suddenly. "Yeah?"

"There's two of you now. And you sure didn't tell us anything about that."

They lay there, on the separate beds, while the light faded lower and lower. When Missy turned her head, she could barely make out the line of Les's nose. It was minutes maybe before Missy said, "I'm sorry about that. I think I need to go home, Les." She sounded like a high school girl who'd been taken to a motel room after the prom, who thought it would be fun to play grown-up, but stopped short of peeling off her fancy dress.

Les didn't answer. She heard his deep and slow breathing. The baby was playing now, spinning inside her, exercising. For the first time in months, Missy felt her age. *I am too young, Too young to be here with a baby floating inside of me. Too young to hitch rides with people who die from the heat of the sun. Too young to have a sad Marine sleeping in the room.*

Missy rubbed her round belly lightly beneath her dress until the baby was still, and the rest of the evening dropped darkly into the room. The heavy, breathless feeling that she needed to cry a good cry passed. She got up and used the bathroom without turning on a light and thought about finding something to eat, but decided that sleep was more important, so she lay down again and closed her eyes.

The following morning, still like the prom queen protecting what was left of her virtue, Missy repeated that she had to go home. She told Les she felt it somewhere inside, in her bones, in her heart. She assumed it was the beginning of a goodbye. She didn't expect he would ask to go with her.

"I don't mean to your house, exactly, but maybe to your town. I have to get outta here anyway." He sounded a little desperate. "It's your turn to give me a ride."

"What about the Marines?"

"Fuck the Marines. I don't really have a pass anyway. I lied about that. I'm already AWOL. If I was them, I wouldn't waste time trying to get me back. But I gotta sell the Bel Air first. That car's famous in certain places."

"Well, mine's stolen." Les's eyes popped wide awake, and she continued. "I took it from Hassan, the guy at the Li'l Pancake House. He owns the motel, too."

"See, I said you were different now. Damn grand fucking theft auto!" He laughed at her, and within a half hour, they had concocted a plan. They would sell the Bel Air for whatever they could get. The Caddy would be their transportation. They both felt they would be safer in a hot car, rather than a notorious one owned by an AWOL Marine. Missy was banking Hassan wouldn't tell the police a Madonna stole his Cadillac. In fact, in his own twisted way, Hassan was probably relishing the thought that the miracle baby was being ferried around in his car. She knew he would be mad, but his anger usually stayed close to home.

They drove the Bel Air and Caddy to the first used-car dealer they spotted. A man wearing a clip-on tie gave them 200 dollars and a big grin for it, knowing he would resell it by end of the day and double his money. All he needed was some sticky spray to fix the headliner. Les took the letters and cooler, but left the trash in the car. The dealer wanted to deduct a clean-up fee from the two hundred, but he backed down when Les threatened to walk. "You and your wife enjoy that Cadillac now," he said. "You ever want to do business on that particular piece of machinery, you come see me."

They went through the drive-in window at Hardee's and ate in the parking lot with the top down, enjoying the sun despite the chill. Les tossed his biscuit wrappers in the back seat, but Missy made him pick them up and carry them to the trash can.

They put the top back up and drove toward the center of town, Les behind the wheel.

"You know, you don't even have to steer this thing," he said, his voice high with excitement. "You just gotta think where you want to go and it reads your mind." Which reminded Missy, she had no idea which direction to take. So far, she'd been guided by instinct and dead reckoning, pulled toward the coast by some Marine Corps homing device.

Les braked at a stop light and asked her which way to head. "Let me think," Missy told him.

"You never have told me where you're from, you know," he said. "I mean, if you're going home."

"Kingstree," she said. "It's in this state somewhere, I think. I just don't know where, exactly. I'm not very good on directions." She wished for a compass on the dash of the Caddy. "You had some maps in the Bel Air. We should've grabbed one."

"Don't need it. We ain't taking much of a trip. Kingstree's only a couple hours or so away, give or take. We'll be there by lunch. You know, I had this idea that you and me were going to be together for a long time, lots of miles. At this rate, you could almost walk home."

"I didn't know I was this close. I didn't even feel it," Missy said, doubting herself a bit.

"I wouldn't worry. When you start seeing familiar things, you'll get all excited and start wiggling in your seat." Les laughed, and Missy could feel him coming back, turning into the person he was when he and Oscar picked her up on the highway months ago. *Some people change when bad things happen,* Missy thought, staring at his face. *And some people just think their life is different forever.* The longer they drove, the more she realized Les was the same old Marine. She had been wrong to think he was a new, changed man. She was happy she'd been mistaken.

They left the coast, and after a few miles, the smell of the marsh and low tide no longer rushed through the vents in the car. The air turned sticky and a little heavier when the morning started to burn off. The marsh land gave way to swamps that crept up to the shoulders of I-95. It had been a fairly wet winter so far, and all of the potholes were full, the watermarks high on the trunks of the cypress trees. When they left the interstate, the narrow highway was littered with dead possums who'd come out the night before, drawn by the lights on the pavement.

Les stopped once for gas. While the tank filled, he bought beer and ice and loaded his cooler. Missy used the bathroom every twenty miles or so, at gas stations and rest stops. Les didn't mind. He enjoyed waiting on her in the parking lots, leaning against the hood of the Cadillac so everyone passing would think the big car belonged to him.

Toward the middle of the morning, they angled a little more north. Missy felt herself growing drowsy. She tried to fight it off, but gave up. She leaned against the door, the sound of the road rumbling in her ear.

"What's it like to be pregnant?" Les asked just as she was about to doze off.

Missy's eyes were closed. "What part are you talking about?"

"I mean, what does it feel like to be pregnant?" Les glanced over at her. "Jesus, I'm sorry," he said, "I didn't know you were sleeping."

"It's all right. You want to know what it's like?"

"Yeah."

"It's like somebody played the worst joke in the world on you. It's like they snuck in one night and put this baby inside of you and tell you this thing is going to grow and grow until you can't hold it anymore, and once it's time to get rid of it, you've got to hurt a lot." She stopped for a second. "Other than that, it's just about the greatest thing that can happen."

"Can't be both." Les shook his head.

"Wanna bet?" Missy said. "It's the greatest thing when the baby moves or get hiccups."

"No, now. What? Hiccups?"

"Yes, you can feel it get hiccups. That's one of the good things. You know, when the baby does things to let you know it's there, that's one of the good times." Missy changed her position in the seat. "Here. Give me your hand."

Les reached across the long seat of the car. Missy took him by the palm and placed his hand on her belly. As if on cue, the baby made a lazy roll across Missy's stomach. Les snatched his hand away as if he'd touched something hot.

"Son of a bitch!" he yelled. "That's the real fucking thing, ain't it?"

"It sure is," Missy said, and leaned against the door again. Just as she was about to drop off, she felt Les's hand return to her belly. He patted her lightly a couple of times, then rested the hand flat. Missy smiled and went to sleep and stayed that way until she felt the rumble quit and the car roll to a stop.

They were at the crossroads. In front of her sat Kozma's store, with the drawing of the red pig on the swinging sign. The Kozma girl's house—a big farmhouse with a porch that wrapped all the way around it—loomed on the other side of the road. Missy knew exactly where she was. She'd been to that house as a kid. Missy pointed right. "That way."

"How far are we?" Les asked.

"There should've been a road sign," she answered. "Maybe we already passed it. It's just a few miles from here. We have to go past the turnoff to the abbey, then through the swamp, and I'm home." As Missy and Les pulled away, Mr. Kozma came to the front stoop of his store and spit across the rail and stared for a few seconds. Then he waved like they were long-lost friends.

19.

As Les maneuvered the Caddy around the last right turn before Floyd Funeral Home, he pulled over for a slow-moving procession coming the other way, heading for one of the cemeteries near the town limits. Two black limos led the line of cars, every one of them with their headlights burning. Asa sat in the passenger's side of the first car, staring straight ahead, a look of absolute detachment plastered across his big, blank face.

Missy ducked down in the seat and peered over the dash. From the look on Asa's face, she knew he was somewhere else at that moment. In his head, he was lying on the beach down at Pawleys Island or chasing a golf ball at the country club. Anywhere but leading the way to a graveyard. Missy was sure he couldn't spot her in the front seat of the idling Caddy. He would never associate her with a car that nice.

"I think it's really great, the way people in a small town pull over for funerals. People in cities, they could care less when somebody dies. Death just isn't enough of an excuse to stop a car in the city," Les said.

"This is a big one," Missy answered, counting off cars in her head. She was up to twenty-seven when Skyles's pickup crawled by. Like Asa, Skyles's eyes were fixed on something out of sight, not on the taillights of the car ahead of him. The camper body was in place, and the truck actually shone a bit. He'd probably gone by the funeral home while Clarence was cleaning up the limos and talked himself into another free wash.

Missy surprised herself. She didn't lose her breath or begin to pull her hair out the first time she saw Skyles's face. She'd had these visions that she would instantaneously lose her mind when he came into sight. Instead, she studied his face through the windshield. *He has nice cheekbones,* she thought. *I hope the baby gets his cheekbones.* His hair was pulled back into a tight ponytail. He had on a tie. Maybe even a suit. He looked his age.

"You reckon your stepdaddy's in that bunch of cars?" Les asked.

"Could be. I don't really care. I didn't see him." It felt good to lie about Asa.

"You still going by the place, aren't you?" Les asked her.

"That's it, right there on the corner. I don't see why you can't at least stay for a while. Spend a couple of days here. Asa might even have some work, if that's what you're looking for." Missy said the words, but even she could hear their hollow echo. She didn't mean what she was saying. She needn't have worried. Les had other ideas.

"I've got a couple of places I need to be. One of them is out of sight. I'm still a runaway Marine, you know. Which way is the train station in this town?" He glanced around as though they were parked right beside it.

Missy pointed behind them. "It's all the way across town. The funeral people are going that direction. They'll drive right past it."

Les squinted at her. "I don't know any of these people. I'd never get a ride."

"No, no, I mean, why don't you take the Cadillac? Just leave it at the station, and I'll pick it up later. Put the keys on top of the front tire."

"Really? You mean it? I sure do appreciate it. I swear I won't steal it." Les sounded like a kid at Christmas.

"You don't look like much of a car thief, Les." He seemed hurt by her characterization.

"Well, neither do you, Missy Belue, and look what you're driving up in."

Missy eased herself out of the car and reached back in for her duffel bag. Les took her by the wrist. "I'm going to save a little postage here, okay?" He put the bundle of letters in her hand. "If I could think of a better thing to do with these, I'd say it. But right now, this seems like a damn good idea. You probably need to read the rest of them. Oscar, he could put a spin on a fucking phrase when he was real relaxed or real drunk."

"You sure you don't want them? There's a lot of Oscar in here."

"Oscar's dead. There's other things going on. Like getting lost if I don't catch up with this funeral," Les said. He put the Caddy in gear just about the time the last car in the procession eased by. "Take care, Missy. Let me know what kind of baby you end up having. I'll let you know where I land." He waved as he pulled off and swung a U-turn. He flipped on the headlights. The last thing Missy saw was Hassan's Cadillac, bringing up the rear of a funeral procession, the top easing down despite the chilly weather.

Though it was only a half block to the funeral home, Missy was wheezing when she walked through the front door. Lately, there was no good time for a stroll. She felt every step, and every step just made her more tired. The funeral home was full of sad strangers, the next group who would make the slow drive to the cemetery. No one noticed the pregnant girl with the army duffel, a mustache of sweat on her upper lip. They weren't bothered with who was coming at that moment, only with the ones who'd left for good.

Missy started to drop her bag just inside the front door, but decided against it when she looked at the strangers around her. She hugged it to her stomach and made her way down the hall. She turned a corner and leaned against a door that looked like all the others.

She was in the hallway again, *that* hallway, the one she'd been taken to when she fainted at her mother's wedding, the one she'd almost forgotten. She leaned harder, and the door opened, and inside the room, under a circle of bright fluorescent lights, Mona bent over a body, adding color to the white cheeks. The only thing that moved was her wrist, as she dabbed the face.

Missy took another step toward the light and stopped when her mother spoke. "Clarence, I'll give you a ride in a minute. I'm busy with Mrs. Fairey. I'll be through as soon as I match the color on these cheeks."

When there was no response, Mona turned and squinted under the lights. Missy could see that her eyes were clear and shining. *Of course,* she thought, *she's working. She's always sober when she works, especially when she's found religion.*

Mona recognized her daughter standing in the shadows and light that spilled in from the hall. She did her best to stay seated and bit down hard on her back teeth to keep from smiling.

"Well," she said. "My God. This is a sight."

"I decided I needed to come home."

"Asa said you might be on your way. But nobody knew how far away you were," Mona said.

"Not as far as I thought," Missy said. She felt her legs going weak, quivering the same way they did the afternoon Mona and Asa were married. She and her mother were talking like they were old classmates from college who never really liked each other in the first place. Missy wanted to grab her mother, cup her face and let Mona feel, through some sort of magic touch, how her daughter had changed, how she was different than the daughter who left, maybe not better or wiser, but different. Missy was someone Mona would have to get to know again. But instead of reaching for her mother, Missy relaxed her hug on the bag and let it swing to her side. When she did, Mona dropped the brush she was working with and stood up from her chair.

Missy waited for the first word. She wanted to remember the first thing out of her mother's mouth when Mona really saw her belly. She looked at her mother's eyes again. They were still clear. Mona crossed her arms in front of her.

"When?" she whispered. It seemed as though the word had to fight its way from behind her teeth.

"I'm not sure. Exactly. Sometime in Florida," Missy answered.

"No, no, Lord. *When.* When are you due?" Mona's voice caught in her throat. Her eyes filled to the point that any blink would free the tears.

"Momma—"

Missy no longer knew when the baby was due. She had lost count of the days and weeks, but it really didn't matter. It would happen with or without a calendar.

"Momma," she said again and felt her knees giving way to a tiredness she'd been lugging around almost as long as she'd carried this baby.

Missy slumped on top of her bag, burying her face in the crook of her arm. It wasn't an out-and-out faint, just a small surrender to the intimidating feeling that her head needed to be at the same level as her feet, if only for a couple of minutes.

She waited for the soft hand on her head, for the feathery stroke that would let her know she was truly home, and it was the right place to be. She waited for the sound of Mona's slippers padding across the tile floor, waited for another question, another whisper about who or when or where. But nothing came. When Missy finally looked up, she saw Mona hunched over her work again, putting a new face on the dead.

Clarence was the one who finally scooped up Missy and helped her to her old room upstairs. He put one arm around her waist as they climbed, the duffel in his other hand. Missy wanted to cry, but she was dry, emptied of water like Oscar and the sun-parched Marines.

"You're carrying low, Missy. I think that means you'll have a boy. I always get these old wives' tales mixed up. Anyway, you're carrying low," Clarence said as they walked.

"Thank you," she said.

"Don't thank me. It's nice to see you back. I'm sure your momma is glad you're here, too. Maybe you just caught her by surprise. Some folks don't take surprises well. The things she's doing now, with the bodies . . . I mean, you don't get surprises from dead folks. Only the living do that. Maybe she's gotten a little spoiled dealing with only dead folks."

Her room had been shut up tight. The air inside was thick, like it hadn't been disturbed in years. Clarence laid the suitcase on the bed and cracked the windows. "I'll let you unpack. You don't have a doctor, do you? In Kingstree, I mean."

Missy shook her head.

"I'll find out who should take care of you and that baby. Only two to choose from, anyway. Be sure and shut those windows as soon as it airs out in here." He started toward the door.

"Clarence?" she asked, stopping him just before the hallway. "She isn't my mother anymore, is she?"

Clarence turned and took a breath. "I'm no expert on mommas, Miss Missy, but it seems to me when a daughter is about to become a mother herself, things change, no matter what, like the two of you share something new, but you're even more apart than ever before. Maybe you're just farther apart than you figured on, right now." He shrugged as if to say he'd given his best effort for advice. He headed for the stairs.

"If you see Skyles—"

"I'll be sure and tell him you're here," he answered without looking back.

Missy collapsed on the bed and lifted her swollen feet onto the duffel. It felt good to have them elevated. She fell asleep without trying and dreamed a new dream this time.

She and the doctor are looking at her new baby, still covered with film just moments after the birth, still attached by the umbilical. He holds the child up and counts toes. He always comes up with the right number. Then, he passes the baby to Missy, and she counts. She always comes up with something different. Nine or eleven. They spend what seems to be hours handing the baby back and forth like a package, counting different body parts. Fingers, eyes, nipples. Missy never gets the correct number. She begs the doctor to cut the cord, knowing that once it is disconnected from her, most of the mystery will end.

Missy woke slowly, the dream lingering like an echo. Evening was straining to get started, the light in her room a thin drapery of gray. Her feet had fallen off the bag; now they straddled it, and the smell of the funeral home had found its way back to her room. It was heavy in her nose now, the embalming fluid odor biting the back of her throat.

She was scared to fall asleep again, scared even more of the dark that was coming, now that she was in a stranger's house. She'd gotten used to that feeling—to this house—once before. She realized she may not have the energy to do it again.

20.

The next morning, Missy met Asa in the hallway, on his way to breakfast. "You just don't think sometimes, do you?" he said. "You just don't think what it will do to someone, for you to just come strolling up, like you've been away on a holiday?"

"Where's Momma?' Missy said, ignoring his questions.

"She's where she always is this time of the morning. Sleeping. She works late, she sleeps late. You see, we have activities we've settled into here while you were gone. We have a routine. She knows what I do. I know what she does. I know where Clarence is. I also can tell you what Skyles is up to because he's around here all the time. He'll probably show up today, about the time your momma wakes up. If you just stay quiet and keep your eyes open, you'll see how we live now. You may not like the way it is. But it's none of your business. None of it."

Asa was right. When he left, Missy sat near her window and watched the day begin to unfold. She saw routines through the glass. Clarence washed cars most of the morning, drying them with a chamois he wrung out after every half dozen passes. Asa met with a family—each member possessing a similar blank, wide-eyed face, a product of genetics and the shock of death.

For a couple of hours that morning, when she gathered some energy, Missy began nesting with a vengeance. She cleaned her walls with the same kind of disinfectant that they used in the rooms downstairs. She snatched down the curtains and stuffed them in a dirty pillowcase so she could run them to the dry cleaners. On the hardwood floor, she used some Murphy's Oil Soap she found in a kitchen cabinet and a couple of old towels. When she was finished, the pine boards shone like they were covered with a sheet of ice. She was on her knees and up on her toes. She walked around the room, a rag in her hand like a gun, so when the sun changed its position during the morning and sliced into her room at a different angle exposing new pockets of dust, she was ready to wipe them away.

Near lunchtime, Missy stopped at her mother's door and listened to the deep, half-snore on the other side. She wanted to knock, but thought better of interrupting. Instead, she wandered down to ask Clarence for a ride to the train station. She had convinced herself that the Caddy would still be there, that Les hadn't experienced a change of heart and headed farther away from the coast in the car he drooled over.

Two blocks from the station, Missy saw the Cadillac in the parking lot, a splash of glare blasting off the chrome window strips. Les had put the top up and left the keys right where they'd agreed. The car was so spotless, it seemed like it wasn't real, more like a magazine ad, rather than a car that had been stolen and driven hard for a couple of days.

Missy shook the keys at Clarence, and he drove off, leaving her by herself. Inside, Missy expected the air to smell of Les, or maybe even her. Instead, the interior was the odor of a deep forest, as if a few hundred pine trees ripe with sap had been cut and left to turn to fat lighter. Dirt was a stranger inside the car. So was dust. The leather seats were slippery-clean, and when Missy tried to relax, she slid forward, her belly lodging against the steering wheel. She smiled, wondering how long it took Les to find a carwash in Kingstree. She didn't even know if there was a carwash in town. *Probably hired some guy off the street,* she thought.

She wanted the top down, even though it wasn't warm out. She hit the button and the roof began to peel back. Sunlight flooded the car, and that was when Missy saw the envelope gleaming white on the dash. All it said across the front was *M. Belue.*

"Maybe Les finally did write me a good letter," she said out loud.

She started the car, tapped the accelerator to calm down the engine, and let it idle. It wouldn't take the engine long to warm up on a day like this one. She found a radio station she liked and tore open the envelope. Inside was a short note, with handwriting as familiar as a relative's.

> *And you should use special wax for wood part of dash. Tires look better when you use armor spray fluid but not use on other things inside. And top should last for 2 years more. Wash every week. Tires good for thousands if you go that far. We all miss you. And I already have a new car.*

Hassan had scrawled his signature across the bottom. Folded together with the note was the title to the Caddy, with a little yellow sticky note telling her how to get it transferred to her name at the motor vehicles office.

She spun frantically in her seat and squinted in every direction, but there was no sign of Hassan. But he had to be watching. He couldn't pass up the chance to see her reaction. There was no way in the world he could leave her the title to the Caddy and just drive off. He wanted something from her now, something he could store in his mind's eye and examine whenever he wanted.

Missy's mind whirled. How had he found her? She remembered only one time she'd mentioned where she lived, during one of those late evenings beneath those same posters. Could he have possibly filed that away? Had she mentioned the funeral home? Maybe. Kingstree was small enough, it wouldn't take long to find a big Cadillac convertible sitting alone in a parking lot. Had he tailed them from the coast somehow? Hassan always bragged about how his ancestors could find a tiny oasis in an ocean of sand. She remembered something he said that day in the library. *I always know where you are, Missy Belue.*

She had some options about what to let Hassan see, if indeed he was watching. She could squeal out of the parking lot, leaving the bitter smell of burned rubber and the sight of a fishtailing Cadillac behind her. She could get out of the car, kick the fender, fling the keys into the nearest dumpster and walk home. That would be a statement. She could yell "*Thank you!*" and just drive away. She slumped behind the wheel while she decided. She watched the sun glint on the white hood.

That was when her water broke on the Caddy's slick leather seat.

Missy kept glancing at the speedometer. For weeks, things moved so slow, she noticed every little change because there was time. She watched a blue vein on her leg grow and divide until it looked like a tiny roadmap. She watched her belly button pop out and go flat as an old scar. She felt her hair grow thicker. Her walk changed a little every day.

I never use my toes anymore, my feet are flat as boards. Time was moving so slow. Now, I'm supposed to go as fast as I can. Just like that.

Missy knew from her trips to Dr. Wiley that if or when her water broke, she was to call him, and he'd meet her at the hospital. Now, she had no one to call, but she had a hospital to go to. Kingstree only had the one, Williamsburg County Hospital, a place that served every ailment in a thirty-mile radius. It was on the other side of town from the train station, which in a place the size of Kingstree only meant a three- or four-minute drive.

For some reason March 17 stuck out in Missy's mind, but she couldn't be sure. *I will be a terrible mother. I can't even remember what day this baby was supposed to be born.* Dr. Wiley had given her a due date, then said, "Not a doctor in the world who believes in due dates. It's a crapshoot. But it sure makes mothers feel better."

If his date was anywhere near accurate, Missy was almost a month early, but she knew it wasn't anything to panic over. Plenty of babies came early.

No pain. Something is wrong. I'm supposed to be in pain. No wonder the baby hasn't moved in a day and a half. It's been resting up for the trip.

She remembered a picture she'd seen. A baby upside down like an acrobat, headfirst, diving into the world. *If I had just a little pain, I'd know this wasn't some kind of trick, that it was the real thing.*

The first labor pain struck her as she pulled into the hospital parking lot, rolled over her like a wave, so strong and intense she couldn't localize it, couldn't put a finger on it if she tried. It was a pure, unadulterated sensation that rode beneath her skin like dull electricity, almost paralyzing her. Missy snatched the wheel and gripped it like a life ring and misjudged her turn. The Caddy banged over a curb and through a bed of scrawny evergreens, then back onto the blacktop.

She negotiated the car into a parking space, and the pain peaked and subsided as quickly as it had come. She rested her head against the wheel, catching her breath. She knew her feet wouldn't work yet, so she sat, the engine idling, the clammy wetness still spreading on her skirt and across the seat.

Missy decided to forget about a calm, assured walk to the hospital door. She swung the Caddy around and made a quick U-turn toward the Emergency Room. Once under the covered entrance, she leaned on the brake and the horn at the same time. The sound echoed beneath the roof. An orderly fast-walked out, a scowl creasing his face, as though he'd been interrupted by someone with a hangnail who wanted a stretcher. Within a few steps of the car, he saw Missy's expression and the size of her belly as it pressed against the steering wheel. His scowl gave way to surprise as he turned and ran for a wheelchair.

"Don't you worry, now," he told her seconds later, as he slid her into the chair. The Caddy was still idling. At least she'd remembered to put it in park.

"My keys," she said, just as a second pain snatched her breath away. "I need them."

"I'll get somebody to park it and bring you the keys later. You doing okay? Where's daddy?" He made a spin with the chair and wheeled it through the automatic doors, into the antiseptic light of the ER lobby. He made a beeline for the elevator.

"My daddy's dead."

"Not yours, hon, the baby's. Where's daddy?"

"The father is working," Missy said through her clenched teeth. "I'm gonna push! I really need to push!"

He brought the chair to a halt and placed a huge hand on Missy's shoulder. His voice was calm and metered like a song, like a lullaby.

"Lady, don't you dare push. You ain't having a baby in the hall. The hall ain't no place to have a baby. You wouldn't want that, I promise you. So, don't you push until somebody who knows what's what tells you to."

To Missy's right, a man in a bathrobe stuck his head from his room. "Who's having a baby in the hall? Can we watch?"

"Mister Tisdale, I'm gonna let her have it in your room if you don't shut up!" He punched the number on the elevator again. "Dammit!" Then, calmer, "How many kids you got?"

"This is the first."

"How long you been in labor?" he asked quickly.

"Since the train station."

"What?"

"I don't know. Five minutes or so," Missy said.

He thought for a second, punching the button again. "Coming this fast, it ought to be your fourth."

Missy had bitten the inside of her cheek during the contraction, and she tasted blood. "I'm better now," she said.

"That's what they all tell me, lady. It's bad but it always goes away."

The elevator doors spread, and he backed her in. Inside, it was quiet, only the gentle hum of the motor straining on the cables as the car rose. Missy shut her eyes and let her head fall back.

"I don't know how to do this," she whispered. "I got no idea."

"Neither do I," he laughed. "But my grandmomma had seven children, and she was dumb as a bag of hammers. She always said, 'The way they got women behaving these days with all this reading and meeting and huffing and puffing before the baby comes, it's a wonder any of us old folks ever had children.' She says really the only thing you got to know about a baby is to touch them soft and love them hard."

Missy smiled. "She sounds like a really smart person . . . I'm scared something's wrong with my baby." She didn't know why she was confiding in an orderly, in an elevator, but it felt natural and cleansing, almost like those breaths she was supposed to be taking. The elevator dinged to a stop and the doors slid open. A nurse met them.

He leaned to her ear. "If you didn't think something was gonna be wrong, we'd have to take you up to the fourth floor and put you in a crazy room. You about to be a momma. You supposed to worry. That's your job now. For the rest of your life." Without a word, the nurse took the chair from him, and Missy saw him wave as she headed for the room where her baby would come to life.

Expect the worst. Expect it and if the worst doesn't happen, then you'll feel like you got a good deal. Expect the worst. Expect it.

Missy kept repeating her homemade mantra over and over silently. During the pains, she chanted it just under her breath, in a whisper that came from deep inside. She said it again, when the nurse, a woman she'd never laid eyes on, snapped open a rubber glove and stuck a couple of her fingers so far up Missy, she thought the woman was trying to snatch out her tonsils.

"Excuse me?" the nurse snipped when she heard Missy whispering.

"Nothing," Missy told her, teetering on the edge of another wave of labor.

"You'll want something for pain, I imagine," the nurse said. It wasn't a question.

Not from you, lady, Missy thought while she shook her head. "I'm okay," she said.

The doctor on call showed up smiling. He was tall and dark-haired and had the biggest hands Missy'd ever seen, the size of dinner plates. *He'll never drop a baby, no matter how slick it is,* she thought.

"Missy, isn't it?" he said and smiled even wider.

She tried to answer but nothing came out of her mouth. Missy just nodded.

"I'm Dr. Montgomery. Let me ask you, did you have any prenatal care?" He probed her stomach while he talked. Then, he searched for a clean glove.

"Yes, but I haven't seen him in a couple of weeks, I guess. Yes, a couple of weeks ago."

Montgomery was gentler than the nurse as he searched inside of her. "No problem. Everything's great. Head is down and on the way. Actually, it's more than just on the way. This baby is arriving real soon."

Missy winced. "Breathe through it," Montgomery told her. He showed her how, and she mocked his puffing. The pain peaked, and Montgomery made her take a deep breath. "Do you have a partner? A coach?" he said.

Faces flashed through her mind like cartoons. *Skyles, Les, Hassan, Asa.* "No," she said. "Just me."

"Me and you," he corrected her and left the room, leaving the door cracked. He called back to her. "I'll be right back. Hang on for a minute." It was the safest Missy'd felt in days.

She closed her eyes and listened to the hospital buzz outside her half-open door. She was surprised at how quiet she'd been to this point. She'd seen births on television, when the woman sweated and screamed during hard labor. So far, the loudest thing Missy had done was a little whine each time a contraction neared its peak. It wasn't as though the pain was any less. It's just that she wasn't surprised when it arrived. It made her think that a person could handle anything if she could just see it coming.

The noise from the hallway grew louder. *A nurse or Montgomery must be about to poke their head in,* she thought. She kept her eyes shut tight, waiting for the pain to return. Someone was there, watching her; she could sense it. She was about to glance up when the smell of the funeral home reached her nose and lodged somewhere at the back of her throat. Her eyes popped open.

Mona was two steps inside the door, her eyes bright with tears. She tried to smile, and Missy tried to decide how to act. The impending pain made her hesitate, made her mix up all the other sensations she could possibly have at that second, like fear or forgiveness or anger. She couldn't sort them all out. Mona took another step toward her as the contraction began to build.

"A little foreign man. He said his name was Hassan and he was a friend of yours. He came by the funeral home. He told me where you were," Mona said.

Missy's only answer was a wail at the top of her lungs. She grabbed the mattress edges at her side, tried to curl them up and around her baby, around the pain, trying to smother it. She screamed again.

Mona was next to her. She squeezed her hand, then talked into her face, calmly, in a sing-song voice. "Go ahead. Make your baby, sweetheart. It's time." Next she turned from Missy and yelled toward the door. "Where the hell is that doctor?!"

Missy knew it was on the way, the one, the single pain she wouldn't be able to stand. She felt it lurking in the next minute. She yelled for painkiller. Montgomery, now sitting on a low stool between her knees, told her she was too late for drugs, probably too late when she came through the door of the ER.

"Just push when I tell you," he said, holding out his big hands. It arrived with an almost electric jolt, the one, the pain that made her feel like her body would explode, like her bones would disintegrate into clouds of white dust. Missy was convinced she was going to break apart.

A final push, followed by a rush of warm, even calmness, the pain disappearing like smoke in front of a fan. *Expect the worst,* she thought, *expect the worst.*

The next thing she saw was Montgomery holding up a baby slick with life, gathering its energy for a loud announcement to the world. He tilted the baby forward. There was no sound in the room for Missy, just a stream of white noise in her ear, shattered only when the baby cleared its lungs of new air.

"Baby girl," Montgomery said, as the baby gulped air and let out another cry. Montgomery laughed. "With an attitude."

He cut her cord, and the nurse cleaned the new child off with a few strokes of a soft cloth, swaddled her up in a blue towel and brought her toward Missy. She couldn't bring herself to look. She whispered the mantra again, just under her breath. *Expect the worst.* Mona hovered in the background, behind Montgomery and the circle of light from the bright overhead bulbs. Now, the baby rested on Missy's chest, squirming a little inside its blanket, happy to be close and confined again.

Missy looked down. The baby stared back at her and opened one bright-blue eye, searching for something to focus on. Missy couldn't see a speck of fear anywhere in that eye. It was a curious eye. A beautiful eye. A perfect one. Mona came quickly into the light, and the three of them began to cry while they all touched each other.

21.

Weeks later, the day finally came when Missy could drive again. She didn't understand why she had to wait so long to get behind the wheel. Sure, for ten or twelve days, she couldn't even sit without using one of those little whoopee cushions. But she kept staring at the Caddy parked under the long carport with all the hearses, begging to get out.

Skyles was gone. When she got back from the hospital, she half expected him to show up to see the baby he knew was his. But a couple of days after her return, she got an envelope with an Alabama postmark and her name on it. Inside was a newspaper clipping from the *Birmingham News,* cut roughly with his pocketknife. It was a short article explaining how babies that slept on their backs were less likely to die of crib death, according to some new study. That was all. No note. Just information from a local paper.

Missy didn't mourn the loss. She'd left Skyles and all his baggage behind, at some roadside café months ago. Anyway, she had too much to be happy about now. Mona was smiling. Asa was keeping his distance. Even Angela had come to see her, whining about being married and having to live under the same roof as her parents. All

Missy could do was smile at her. Angela seemed more like her little sister now. In fact, everybody had changed, mostly for the better.

She bundled the baby up like a cocooned bug and grabbed the keys to the Caddy. The infant seat was already in the car, strapped down according to directions. Missy and Clarence had taken care of that days ago. The engine fired to life on the first try, rattling the baby from her sleep. She whimpered until Missy rubbed her cheek gently with a knuckle. The baby wrenched her mouth toward the finger, trying to suck it in.

"Now, I know you can't be hungry. You just ate," Missy said.

They pulled away from the funeral home and turned toward the river. Missy drove slowly, wishing she possessed the power to clear every road in the county of all traffic until her daughter was at least six or seven years old. The rumble of the Caddy's engine beneath the seats lulled the baby back to sleep, and Missy drove toward the swamp, turning onto the two-lane that led away from town.

She never even approached the speed limit, preferring to go casually, for safety's sake, sure, but also to notice the trees and the bridges and the men spitting tobacco juice off of them. She quietly pointed all of this out to her baby girl, who was fast asleep and drooling onto her chin.

Missy swung down a narrow road, then into a familiar stand of pines with its perfect rows. The Caddy was almost too wide to fit between the trees in a couple of places, but Missy inched it by. She parked on the little rise above the abbey. It was midmorning and activity buzzed around the buildings. The brothers scurried in the not-quite-spring chill, their legs whipping their long robes, as they carried baskets and buckets and even chickens from building to building and back again.

The sun couldn't pierce the thick canopy of trees, but Missy still put the top down. She wanted fresh air. Her baby would be warm enough. On the slightest of breezes, Missy heard the distant sound of voices, the noise of the brothers at work. She'd never heard them speaking before. In fact, Skyles had told her time and again that the brothers kept a vow of silence and could never talk except to chant their prayers. Another thing he'd been wrong about. Today they sounded like regular people.

Missy unlatched the buckles on the baby's seat and plucked her up and out. She stirred inside her blankets. Missy watched her tiny fists opening and closing, all ten fingers working the air. Her baby had the perfect number of everything, in all the right places. Missy unzipped her own jacket and unbuttoned the middle buttons of her shirt and worked her breast out through the opening.

The baby squirmed a bit. Her face twitched as she detected food somewhere close by. She began to burrow toward the nipple, her eyes squeezed shut. Missy gave it to her, and she sucked immediately. Missy's milk let down, burning for a second as it hit the baby's mouth, and she began her rhythmic suck-suck-breathe, suck-suck-breathe.

"Well now, Miss Rose, you were hungry after all, weren't you?"

Missy watched her drink for a few seconds, watched tiny beads of sweat pop out near her temple, then she glanced again toward the abbey. Missy shut her eyes, too, while Rose tugged gently on her.

She knew if she wasn't careful, they would both fall asleep, happy in the clear air beneath the pines, within a whisper of the holy men.

ACKNOWLEDGMENTS

This novel had its beginnings in a short story, "Sort of a Prophet," that first appeared in *Black Warrior Review* and later in the anthology *New Southern Harmonies* (Hub City Press). That was a long time ago, when my daughters were young and went to sleep early, and I wrote at the kitchen table until after midnight. I wanted to make a story for them about a girl who was strong and independent and wandering and finally happy with the path she chose. So thanks to them and to Jack, a constant supporter. Thanks to readers through the years, especially John Lane and Deno Trakas during those Friday afternoons at WoCo. Thanks to Rowe at The Book Concierge. Many thanks to the good folks at Koehler Books, especially Joe and John. (Joe hates parentheses, so this is for him.) And thanks to Lyle Lovett, whose song "Closing Time" was the last thing I listened to each night when I put the manuscript down and went to bed. Finally, immeasurable thanks to Shannon, who always has my back.

Scott Gould is the author of the story collection *Strangers to Temptation* (Hub City Press). His work has appeared in *Kenyon Review, Black Warrior Review, New Ohio Review, Crazyhorse, Carolina Quarterly, New Stories from the South* and others. He is a multiple-time winner of the Individual Artist Fellowship in Prose from the South Carolina Arts Commission, as well as the Fiction Fellowship from the South Carolina Academy of Authors. He lives in Sans Souci, South Carolina.

www.scottgouldwriter.com
Instagram: scottgould
Twitter: @scott_gould
Facebook: @authorscottgould

CPSIA information can be obtained
at www.ICGtesting.com
Printed in the USA
FSHW010040071020
74473FS